DEATH WARMED UP

Jack Scott and Sian Laidlaw are forced to remain in Gibraltar with Jack's mother after she breaks her ankle. When a chance meeting with a young photographer, Pru Wise, leads them into the path of trouble and up against a ruthless diamond robber, it becomes clear that there are some dangerous forces at work. Then the dead body of Pru turns up in the boot of a car registered to Sian . . . In order to unravel a web of intrigue, the duo must face a violent climax in the house of an ex-diplomat, and survive a fight to the death on the rocks of Gibraltar's most southerly shore.

JOHN PAXTON SHERIFF

◆

DEATH WARMED UP

Complete and Unabridged

ULVERSCROFT
Leicester

First published in Great Britain in 2013 by
Robert Hale Limited
London

First Large Print Edition
published 2014
by arrangement with
Robert Hale Limited
London

A catalogue record for this book is available
from the British Library.

ISBN 978–1–4448–1932–8

Published by
F. A. Thorpe (Publishing)
Anstey, Leicestershire

Set by Words & Graphics Ltd.
Anstey, Leicestershire
Printed and bound in Great Britain by
T. J. International Ltd., Padstow, Cornwall

This book is printed on acid-free paper

Author's note

The Kusuma Promenade — opened at the end of May 2012 — is just one impressive section of all the wonderful work done at Gibraltar's Europa Point over the past few years.

However, at that most southerly of locations I have again tinkered with geography, ignoring all improvements made by the Kusuma Trust Gibraltar and Her Majesty's Government of Gibraltar except for the flights of wooden steps leading down to the rocky shore. That's where some of this story's vital action takes place, so at least two of my characters were pleased to see those steps. It's more than forty-five years since I lived in Gibraltar; I remember a much trickier clamber down to that shore, on the many warm evenings when I used to fish off the rocks.

My thanks to Tyrone Gomez and his son, Warren, for the help they provided with the many excellent photographs they took at Europa Point. And, as always, I'd like to stress that this is a work of fiction, and all characters spring fully formed from my imagination, and nowhere else.

Part One

1

'If Eleanor hadn't fallen down the steps and broken her ankle we wouldn't be here,' I said reflectively. 'We'd be back in North Wales breathing that bracing mountain air. Listening to the waters of Afon Ogwen gurgling merrily over those shiny black rocks under the bridge — '

'Oh yes?' Sian cut in, 'And what about the wind howling across the high peaks of the Glyders, the cold rain lashing the windows? Your crisp mountain air probably reeks of dead sheep lying putrefying amid wet brown bracken. And we'd be holding mugs of hot chocolate to keep our blue hands warm, not tall glasses of ice-cold gin and tonic misted with condensation.'

I widened my eyes. 'Can this really be the same determined woman who wore me to a frazzle arguing that a return to the UK was the right thing to do?'

'It was, and still is. The difference is that the change of plan caused by your mother's inelegant stumble means we're now on holiday; we're enjoying ourselves.'

I sighed. 'Dammit, yes, it does make a

change from working for a living. Or fighting crooks. And I must admit sleeping on board Tim's yacht in Marina Bay gives the old ego a bit of a boost.'

'Bloody right it does, because living on board any yacht in any location is an absolute first for both of us and puts us on a par — sort of — with all those millionaires in their floating gin palaces . . . and anyway, getting back to what started this, your mother didn't deliberately put herself in hospital.'

'Her memory's not at all clear about what did happen. She told the doctors she tripped and fell, but she does vaguely recall somebody rushing up behind her from the vicinity of the American War Memorial.'

'But didn't mention it?'

'Not to the doctors. She told Reg, and he told me.'

'Yes, and we'll look into that. If she was pushed we'll sort it, but one thing leads to another and whatever the cause, we're now sitting in the Eliott Hotel's excellent bar in the centre of Gibraltar Town on a warm Mediterranean evening enjoying a postprandial drink and listening to a modern jazz trio that plays here every Thursday, and if you think that's so terrible — '

'Take a breath.'

'I did.'

'Which was probably painful. After our recent violent encounter with Ronnie Skaill[1] and his son your cheekbone's still sore, I'm getting over nursing a broken nose — '

'How do you do that, I wonder?' Sian said. 'Nurse a nose, I mean? Anyway, stop moaning. There's a stunning brunette behind you. She's alone at a table over by the rail — balustrade? When she's not looking at her laptop she keeps casting surreptitious glances in your direction.'

We were leaning close across the table the better to hear each other above the scintillating solo being played by a young Chinese pianist. Freed from its customary ponytail, Sian's thick, sun-bleached blonde hair seemed to ripple with each turn of her head, brushing the low-necked, pale lemon blouse that her posture was causing to gape provocatively. Her blue eyes were watching me with amusement, and her Nordic beauty and the clear fresh scent of her warm skin — so close I was tempted to touch — made me think of sea and sand under a hot sun.

'I've noticed her,' I said softly, 'but with you this close do you really think I care?'

'Well, you should do,' Sian said, glancing across my shoulder and narrowing those

---

[1] See *Rock to Death*

beautiful blue eyes. 'You see, on second thoughts I don't think she's looking at you at all. For some reason, that young woman is scared stiff. She's pale beneath the beginnings of a tan, and those looks she's throwing this way are — I'm sure — a cry for help. I think she's weighing us up as a team.'

'Surreptitiously.'

'Stop it. This is serious.'

'What, you really think she wants to hire us? The *nonpareil*. A team battered but unbowed, bruised but still functioning.'

'Yes, and when you've quite finished trying to be clever, our drinks need refreshing. While doing that, make it obvious you've seen her. Nod in a friendly way, lift your eyebrows questioningly, give her a warm smile that manages to convey supreme confidence in your undoubted talents.'

'Do all that at once,' I said, 'and it'll be me falling down stairs.'

I pushed back my chair and with our empty glasses held low down between finger and thumb made my way casually over to the bar. I couldn't get close to the brunette's table, but did cast an encouraging smile in her direction while safely negotiating the three steps to the lower main floor. It was wasted. Her back was to the jazz trio playing on the other side of the ornamental wood and wrought-iron rail, and with dipped head she was concentrating on the Toshiba laptop standing open on the table. There was a camera close to the computer. It looked like an expensive, modern Nikon digital SLR.

There were a few suave characters with rich tans and colourful snoods tucked into the collars of open-necked shirts touched by their longish greying hair. They stood with their backs to the bar, squinting at the trio through the smoke curling from their cheroots. While the barman mixed fresh gin and tonics, I hoisted myself onto a stool. I was now much closer to the music, and the sound rolled over me in waves as the trumpeter pointed his instrument in my direction and embarked on a brassy solo he'd decided didn't call for a mute. It had been my intention to turn and study the intriguing brunette while looking casually about the room, but I was foiled. By the time I'd settled, she'd left her table and was standing right behind me.

I sensed the warmth of her presence. When I turned on the stool she was so close my knee brushed a thigh that had spent a lot of time on the track or in a gym. Tall and slim in faded jeans and a dusky pink cotton top, she wore the dark hair Sian had noticed cut in one of those modern styles that leaves it high at the nape of the neck and sweeping forward to finish in points below and in front of both ears. Her brown eyes were huge and liquid. The assumed boldness in them failed to hide uncertainty and, yes, unmistakable fear.

'Excuse me, but you are Jack Scott?'

I caught most of what she said; lost some in the noise as the drummer began earning his fee. I leaned forward, smiled, frowned.

'Sorry . . . ?'

She stepped very close, bringing with her more warmth and the scent of musk.

'I said, are you Jack Scott?'

'I am indeed.'

'I . . . need to talk to you.'

'Surreptitiously?'

'Pardon?'

'It's all right, that was me being silly, trying to put you at ease.' I smiled. 'Are you in some kind of trouble?'

'I . . . ' She hesitated, cast a nervous glance sideways at the men propping up the bar, looked back at me and pulled a face.

Her meaning was clear. Though she clearly knew where I'd been sitting, I stretched out an arm to point and said, 'Why don't you join Sian at our table? I'll bring you whatever it is you're drinking and we can talk there.'

'What you're having will be fine,' she said breathlessly.

I watched her walk away, her stiff shoulders screaming tension, then turned back to the bar to order the extra drink. The music finished, Applause rippled in the silence. Heels clicked on the floor as the brunette negotiated the three steps. I heard her laptop snap shut. The barman, following her every move, managed to pour most of the tonic into the glasses. Ice crackled. Lime juice oozed from fresh slices, began trickling deliciously. He touched his moustache, rolled his eyes. I nodded agreement, carried the drinks back to the table on a tray. When I sat down, Sian was watching me.

'This young woman — '

'Prudence,' the brunette said. 'Prudence Wise.'

'Prudence has got herself in a bit of a pickle,' Sian said.

'Inadvertently,' Prudence said. And she looked at me from under raised eyebrows, her lips curved in a brave attempt at a smile.

'If you can indulge in banter,' I said, 'it can't be all that bad.'

'Oh, but it is. Inside, I'm shaking like a leaf.'

'So why us? If it's that serious, why not the police?'

'The first reason is because, if I'm wrong, I don't want to end up looking foolish. The second is, you two have made quite a name for yourselves. My father told me how both of you helped DI Romero. You're real-life knight-errants — or should that be knights-errant? Paladins, anyway, both of you, risking life and limb fighting those crooks up the Rock in the middle of a raging summer storm. Well, this pickle I've got myself into may be serious in the same sort of way. I think there are crooks involved. One in particular, who for some reason doesn't want his face to be seen.'

'Not many of them do,' Sian said.

'I know, but . . . ' she hesitated, her lips pursed.

'Take your time, there's no hurry.'

'But that's just it, there is. I've taken photographs that other people seem desperate . . . ' She trailed off again, sighed deeply. A degree of disconcerting turmoil was created under the pink cotton blouse. I struggled not to drown in her dark eyes.

'The thing is, I'm determined to become a successful freelance photographer,' Prudence said. 'I'm from Liverpool, as you've probably worked out from the accent, but Mum and Dad live here and Dad got me a wonderful commission. There's a bloke called Bernie Rickman. He's got a huge yacht called *Sea Wind,* so he must be mega rich. I think he's

10

one of those crooked expats, and that makes him the usual poser: sun-washed jeans, rope-soled yachting shoes, all-over tan with gold chains clinking and bouffant greying hair, you know the type.'

'Only too well,' I said. 'Most of them have permanently stiff necks from looking nervously over their shoulders.'

'Right now you could say that of me too,' Prudence said, and proved it by twisting in a couple of directions to see what was going on behind her.

I thought that odd, but let it slide.

'Anyway,' she went on, 'Rickman wanted photographs taken on board this enormous boat of his. Dad phoned me, and I took the first available Monarch flight out of Manchester. When I got here, Dad drove me straight down to Marina Bay and did the introductions. Rickman was impressed with my professional manner and the expensive equipment, and we were off. The weather here is perfect, of course. On the day of the shoot we were protected from the sun by those droopy white awning things they drape over the smaller decks on huge yachts — the shade underneath it made photography a doddle. Natural light worked perfectly. Bernie Rickman was flashing his teeth and his glistening tan; blonde bimbos wearing bits of string were languidly twining their limbs about his person — '

'*Caramba*,' I said.

' — and I did the job and he gave me three thousand quid.'

'Goodness,' Sian said softly.

'Then, of course, he wanted to see the slideshow.'

'And it all went wrong.'

'Not all. I was very proud of the photographs I'd taken. But the mistake I made was in letting him view the full slideshow before I'd done any editing. I don't mean retouching or anything like that. It's just that, if I'd taken the time, I would have removed the pictures I didn't want him to see.'

'Which, until you ran that slideshow for Rickman,' I said, 'you didn't know you'd taken.'

'Exactly. Well, I knew I'd taken them, but not what I'd accidentally included in a couple of the frames.'

'And that's this particular person you mentioned — a crook, you say — who doesn't want his face to be seen?'

'Well, I don't know he's crooked, but . . . He wasn't doing much at all, just sitting in the shadows looking completely out of place and . . . darkly sinister. That's what makes the — ' She bit her lip. 'That's what makes the threats,' she said faintly, 'so convincing and utterly terrifying.'

'Threats of any kind are rarely welcome,' I said. 'Can we see the offending pictures?'

Sian moved the drinks to make space. Prudence opened the laptop and switched it on. She'd been looking at the slideshow and gnawing at her lip when I went to the bar, so it came up on the screen straight away. She swung the computer towards us. I leaned close to Sian.

'There are just the two,' Prudence said. 'You can see what happened — or, at least, I can. We were all gathered under that awning, there was this wonderful reflected light with lots of flicker coming off the water and Rickman and the girls were doing exactly what I told them to do. Act daft, I said. Do some giggling and laughing, a bit of playful squealing to add some zest. I suggested they hold their drinks up in the air so the glasses created glistening rings of fire in the bright sunlight, do some smooching if that's what Rickman fancied. While that was going on I was snapping away, but changing my position to catch him from different angles. Which was fine while the background was mostly the open blue waters of the bay with just the smudge of Algeciras and the Spanish hills in the distance. But then I moved to the group's left. That meant my camera was pointing along the boat towards the bows, as it were. There was a bit of a cabin or whatever they call those things, and suddenly mystery man was in the frame.'

I had very little experience of luxury yachts, but the man she had inadvertently photographed was sitting in, well, let's call it a cabin. And I could see what Prudence meant by darkly sinister, because she'd described the whole situation beautifully.

Rickman was in washed-out denim shorts and a sleeveless white T-shirt, a tall man shaded by the sagging awning but with his oiled skin splashed with the reflected light from the sea. Prudence had made sure that everywhere in the photographs there were patches of white hull, with rails of gleaming brass and chrome sweeping gracefully towards the raking bow. Tanned, lissom girls dressed in scraps of coloured cloth were trailing crimson-tipped fingers across Rickman's pecs and sinewy thighs, and he looked for all the world like just another millionaire whooping it up aboard a yacht moored in any one of the harbours along the Mediterranean coast.

But it was all an illusion that didn't quite come off. The cheapness beneath the gloss was mercilessly exposed by the too-heavy gold chains at wrists and neck, the blue of tattoos on both forearms and a grin that was not upper-class insouciance but rich, expat cocky.

In such a world, illusory or real, the man in the cabin looked as out of place as an undertaker at a wedding reception. He was sweating copiously in a dark business suit, and with his pale hands and sleek, slicked-back hair he would have been more at home sitting at an all-night poker table in any cheap inner-city nightclub.

'Death warmed up,' Prudence said.

'I haven't heard that description for ages,' I said, turning away from the laptop. 'You said mystery man. So you don't know who he is?'

'Haven't a clue.' She looked straight at me, and shook her head.

'But you've definitely been threatened?'

'Mm. After about fifteen minutes of photographs I decided I'd got enough, and called time. The girls wiggled away to do some serious drinking and tanning on an upper deck. I copied everything from the camera's memory card to the laptop's hard drive, and by then Rickman was back carrying a cold drink for me and yet another stiff one for himself. And off we went with the slideshow, Rickman standing with his hand gently squeezing my shoulder. Bastard!

Anyway, when those pictures appeared on the screen, suntanned Bernie did such a violent double-take he almost ended up flat on his back. He staggered a bit, glared and immediately afterwards there was a narrowing of those pale blue eyes. Then he cast a baleful look in my direction that was so cruel it made my knees weak.'

'And that's when he threatened you?'

'Gosh, no. He recovered quickly. We lounged about in the shade on seats with huge pink and lemon cushions like dimpled pillows and guzzled our drinks while wilting in the heat. Then he handed me a gin-soaked brown envelope containing all that cash in used notes and, very much richer, I tripped gaily down the gangway.'

'And then . . . ?'

'A white Mercedes overtook me and pulled up.'

'The door flew open and an evil-smelling thug with a scarred face dragged you inside and a pad soaked in chloroform was — '

'Cut it out, Jack,' Sian said.

'It wasn't that bad,' Prudence said, smiling weakly at me, 'though the effect was almost the same.' She shut the laptop with a click, her face troubled as she sipped her drink without really tasting it. 'A woman was driving. She leaned across to open the door

16

for me, and we drove off. Beautiful long hair, greyish-blonde, bleached by the sun and sweeping, naked tanned shoulders. She was wearing — just about — the most expensive casual clothes I've ever rubbed up against, and the diamond rings she was flashing on fingers like talons were causing oncoming drivers to swerve. It's not far into town from the marinas, as you know, but in that time she managed to scare me rigid. She told me Rickman wanted those pictures. She didn't need to specify. If I was stubborn, she said with a sweet smile, I would wake up one morning in hospital wearing a different face, and would henceforth refuse to look in mirrors.'

'D'you know who she was?'

'I assumed Rickman's wife, Françoise. While we were sitting drinking he mentioned that she'd just returned from a trip to England.'

'Why send her, I wonder, and not the thug with the chloroform?'

'I suppose because Rickman knew using his wife would be more effective. Give the threat emphasis. I'm, well, you know — '

'Young and beautiful,' Sian said.

'And struggling to make a living, while she's beautiful and rich and there she was suggesting someone could take away what little I have going for me with a couple of strokes of a cut-throat razor.'

I nodded, frowned into my drink and rattled the ice. The sound, in the circumstances, was . . . chilling.

'When was this photoshoot, and the threats?'

'Yesterday.'

'Did this beautiful woman tell you what to do? How to get the incriminating photos to Rickman? Because they must be incriminating in some way, mustn't they?'

'Absolutely. And, no, she didn't, because there was no need. I know where *Sea Wind*'s moored, don't I? I suppose all I have to do is toddle down there and hand them over.'

'But you haven't, not yet — and you haven't been . . . approached?'

'By someone wearing brass knucks or waving a shiv?' She grinned a trifle sheepishly. 'Actually, I've been keeping my head down. As in, staying in my room with the door locked and my head in a book.'

'And the room is where?'

'This hotel.' She pointed at the ceiling. 'Up there somewhere.'

'Which should mean that you're reasonably safe.' Sian pursed her lips. 'When are you going back to the UK?'

Prudence shrugged her shoulders. 'I was

hoping to stay here for a while — blue skies and hot sun, breathtaking scenery, do some work on my website and portfolio.'

'You're here on your own, I take it?' Sian said, frowning. 'Look, if you really feel that you're in danger, that Rickman means business, you've got two obvious choices.'

'Well, I suppose I could always take the easy way out and do as he says . . . or, what's the other, get on the first plane home?'

'Why don't you go and stay with your parents for a while?'

'Oh, I'd love to, but they're in Tangier. I think they intend staying there indefinitely.' She was beginning to look embarrassed. 'I didn't mention it, but Adele and Charlie — Mum and Dad actually live aboard their yacht. The *Alcheringa*. It's a Sunseeker 66 Manhattan Flybridge, if you want the full title.'

'Can't say I've considered buying that particular model,' I said, straight-faced, 'but I suppose that means Mum and Dad are . . . what, filthy rich?'

'I suppose so. They're retired, but Charlie was a successful Liverpool businessman. He made a small fortune in bathroom tissues. A polite term for you-know-what.'

'What do they do now, Prudence?'

'Pru, please.' She shrugged her shoulders.

'Well, apart from cruising the Med posing in expensive togs from fashion houses like Gucci, Versace and Jimmy Choo, not a lot.'

There was a sudden silence. Pru's cheeks were pink. She was staring down into her glass, watching the ice melt, the lime wilt. She seemed to be waiting, with considerable unease, for . . . a decision? And it suddenly occurred to me that the uneasiness could be caused by something other than fear, or that the fear itself could have a cause unrelated to her story. I'd asked her if she'd recognized the man she'd accidentally photographed. She'd looked straight at me when she said no — and wasn't that a sign that someone is striving to convince you they're telling the truth? But if she was lying, to what purpose? She'd told a very pretty tale, embellished with lots of colourful characters and detail, but she hadn't yet told us precisely what she wanted us to do.

Were we to be bodyguards? If so, for how long? Or was she asking us to trot along to Marina Bay, confront Bernie Rickman and his heavies and possibly end up under tons of liquid concrete in one of the expensive new waterside developments?

The quiet was broken by Sian, who, as always, came up with an intelligent suggestion suitably masked by the mundane.

She said, 'Jack, it's still only 8.30. I know you want to get the latest on Eleanor, so perhaps now would be a good time to head up Europa Road and talk to Reg.'

2

Sian's idea was that Reg Fitz-Norton, a retired diplomat who adored my mother, Eleanor, would listen to Prudence's story, dip into his vast experience and come up with words of wisdom that would solve all her problems. I thought it unlikely, but it was at least worth a try.

As it happened Prudence was tired, edgy and in no mood for going over her story yet again, which made it a non-starter anyway. So we compromised.

The young woman from Liverpool left the laptop in our care and made her way to the lifts, followed by the barman's dark, lustful eyes. Sian and I stopped at reception. There, I made it clear to the wide-eyed receptionist that if anyone came to the hotel asking for Prudence Wise's room number, she should refuse to give it to them. If they insisted, became awkward or threatening, she should pick up the phone, call Prudence first to warn her, then phone the police.

That done — which was about as much as we could do — we left the hotel by the side door opening into Library Street just as the band started up again. It was, I thought, like the exit of the toreadors, but the insistent beat had us walking as if we had two left feet. As the music faded behind us we strolled the short distance to the taxi rank, and there jumped into a cab that would take us the mile or so up the hill to Reg's house.

We'd zipped up Eliot's Way where it skirted the car parks and Alameda Gardens and were passing the Rock Hotel when a car came up fast behind us. It nosed in dangerously close. Headlights on full beam lit up the inside of the taxi. Our driver swore softly and reached up to adjust his mirror. For the next fifty yards I could see his eyes darting from that to the off-side wing mirror. Then he exploded.

'Come on, you dipstick,' he growled, 'what are you playing at?'

'Just a couple of drunken youths winding you up,' Sian said, twisting so she could look back. 'Ignore them, they'll go away.'

'I think you are wrong,' the driver said. 'This does not happen, here, in Gibraltar.'

Even as he spoke there was a roar from the following car's engine and it pulled out to overtake on a tight bend where, in normal daytime traffic, overtaking would have been suicidal. It hurtled past. There was a tinny scratching sound as the vehicles briefly touched. The cab driver swore again. His knuckles were white on the steering wheel. I leant across Sian. The overtaking car was a rusty old Datsun. The man in the driving seat was grinning across at us. He wore a wide-brimmed bush hat. His teeth were startlingly white in a tanned face.

'Not drunk, not young,' I said.

'But they *have* gone away,' Sian said as it raced ahead with a series of mocking toots on the horn, 'so that makes me half right.'

The driver grunted his disagreement.

'I think maybe not even that,' he said.

He was proved right. The taxi had rounded a bend and was coasting down a slight slope that took it onto the flat. As the driver pulled to a halt, I saw the Datsun's brake lights glow fifty yards ahead of us. Then, with a squeal of tyres, it did a careless three-point turn that must have added to the dents in the rear bumper, drove a short way towards us and pulled in tight up against a stone wall. The headlights were switched off.

Pale exhaust smoke drifting towards the clear night skies told me that the engine, clearly souped-up, way too powerful for such a shabby body, was still running.

'They're watching us,' Sian said quietly, turning away from the driver.

'Looks like it,' I said. 'But why?'

'A cheap crook's after a young woman's

blood. She's just spent the best part of an hour pouring her heart out to us.'

'So now the shock troops are after our blood?'

'Perhaps they think we now know something they don't. And they're wondering what we're going to do with it.'

The driver was getting impatient, tapping his fingers on the wheel. I shrugged.

'Well, if that's what they're wondering,' I said, 'let's show them,' and I got out of the taxi.

⋆   ⋆   ⋆

There's really just that one reasonably level section of Europa Road, and the expensive houses in the prime position along its western edge cling to slopes that fall precipitously to yet more houses along South Barrack Road. Several of those residences along Europa Road have a small parking area — and for small, read tiny. Room for two small cars, with a squeeze.

Reg had recently downsized, and was now driving a new Nissan Micra. Sian was staring at it while I paid the driver, and when the taxi drove off she turned to me, wide-eyed.

'What on earth,' she said, 'is Reg doing?'

'Fishing.'

'Yes, I can see that, two rods like long whips on his roof rack — but I mean, what does he know about fishing? Does he go out on a boat, or — '

'He fishes off the rocks at Europa Point. Late evening, usually, watches the sun go down, communes with nature. It's his way of chilling.'

'Well, glory be,' Sian said softly, and turned towards the house.

From the tiny parking area the houses are reached by a gate through rustic stone walls, and by stone steps leading steeply down. Like most, Reg's living areas are on the upper floor, bedrooms and bathroom on the lower.

He answered the door with a tall glass of gin and tonic tinkling in one hand. I looked at his eyes. It wasn't his first. Reg noticed the look, and winked. While the cat's away, he seemed to be saying, and I thumped him on the shoulder as the old diplomat stood to one side, grinning.

His grey hair was tied back in the usual ponytail, and he had on the blue tracksuit he'd been wearing when, not too long ago, he'd used a flying rugby tackle to knock me backwards down the steps of my mother's bungalow high up the Rock's slopes. He'd thought I was one of Ronnie Skaill's thugs. Typical ex-public school, he was as hard as nails and had come close to shattering my larynx with a sinewy forearm.

The living room's gold-shaded table lamps cast a warm light over thick Persian rugs, pale spruce parquet flooring, chairs and a huge settee upholstered in soft ivory leather. Reg's Bose stereo system was playing softly in the background: we'd travelled a mile or so and moved from the Eliott hotel's modern jazz to the tinkling flamenco guitars of old Spain, and were enveloped in the wild scent from small baskets of pot-pourri that Eleanor scattered about Reg's house to foster the illusion of fresh flowers.

Reg shut the door and followed us in, plonked his glass down on the coffee table then went to stare silently out of the wide picture windows that took up three sides of a sort of suspended sun room — with skylight — and afforded panoramic views over the town and bay.

Sian raised her eyebrows inquiringly at me, then crossed to the drinks cabinet and reached for the Bombay Sapphire. I put Pru's laptop on the settee and joined Reg at the window.

'Thoughtful, Reg. Or are you still concerned?'

He grunted. 'Life's too short to waste time worrying.'

In the circumstances, I thought that was an

odd, insensitive remark. Were we both thinking on the same lines? I was talking about Eleanor, but now he had me wondering. Reg Fitz-Norton is diplomatic but foolhardy, and has been known to tread on toes.

'What are you looking at? Or looking for?'

'Mm? Oh . . . ' He gestured vaguely at the twinkling lights, the reflections in the distant water.

'You can't see the hospital from here.'

'General direction,' Reg said, and pointed. 'She's somewhere over there.'

'But not for much longer.'

He nodded absently, his mind — I assumed — in that distant hospital ward. 'You know, Eleanor's a remarkable woman for her age. Mind's wonderfully alert, she's rock-steady on her feet.'

'She also,' I said, 'enjoys the occasional gin and tonic.'

'Even a young pup like you knows the old saying — '

'I'm in my fifties, Reg.'

'When the sun's over the yardarm. That's when the day's first drink is taken. It was ten in the morning when Eleanor was pushed; she'd not long eaten breakfast. Anyway, under the influence or sober she was pushed by a woman, or so she tells me — though her memory of the incident is understandably hazy.'

He took a deep breath, managed a grin, looked straight at me. 'Your face is looking better, old boy. Bruises fading to yellow, swelling around the hooter almost gone — '

'Eleanor, Reg.'

'She's fine. Home tomorrow. Here, not in her bungalow, so I can look after her while she reads magazines with her cast stuck up in the air and pops Ferrero Rocher chocs into her mouth at frequent intervals.'

'With her little finger daintily cocked,' Sian called, busy pouring, 'while poor old Reg rushes madly about vacuuming and polishing and seeing to her every whim.'

'What a life, eh,' Reg said, grinning.

'So you're not as miserable as you look?'

'If he is, we'll soon cheer him up,' Sian said, coming over to hand me a crystal glass containing smoky Aran single malt with ice and Reg a fresh gin and tonic. She flicked the diplomat's dangling ponytail, put a hand on his shoulder so she could get close to kiss him on the cheek. 'You love unravelling knotty problems, don't you, Reg? Dabbling in a bit of insider trading? Even poking about on the murky fringes of the underworld if there's profit in it — but preferably down at one of those sun-soaked marinas? Bit of an art expert as well, if I remember rightly.'

'I have my moments.'

'Well, have one now,' I said, 'because a young lady called Pru needs help.'

'Or something,' Sian said, glancing at me. 'She didn't exactly tell us what, did she?'

'Do go on,' Reg said. 'Who's this Pru when she's at home, and what's she been up to?'

'You ever heard of Bernie Rickman?'

'Of course I've heard of him, and so have you. That rakish black boat that nearly belonged to your dear departed brother is moored across the concrete from Rickman's huge yacht.'

'Bloody hell, you're right,' I said, amazed. 'Now you mention it I remember seeing the name, marvelled at its size, imagined it sneering at Tim's little canoe.'

'Sneering is what Rickman does to those lesser mortals he despises — and that's just about everybody. Does it because he's convinced he's the cat's whiskers, when actually he's the lowest of the low. *Sea Wind* and his whole flamboyant lifestyle are financed by illegal activities too numerous to mention. If I say soft drugs, you'll get a small part of a much bigger picture.'

While talking we'd moved down the three steps from the cool, starlit sun room. Sian curled up on the settee with the laptop. I sank into one of the huge chairs and watched Reg as he placed the drink Sian had given him on the coffee table alongside the one he'd abandoned. He now had two drinks, and he looked at me with a wry grin. Not his usual self, perhaps, but sharp as a knife and, as always, proving to be an excellent source of all kinds of information.

'If Rickman's that crooked,' I said, 'why isn't he behind bars?'

'Never been caught red-handed. His kind rarely are. Gibraltar's got water on three sides, a guarded border on the other, so all of Rickman's skulduggery is forced to involve boats of one kind or another. Needless to say, *Sea Wind* is not one of them.'

'The late Ronnie Skaill used to stay in the background while using Tim and his canoe,' Sian said. 'I imagine Rickman does the same.'

'Yes, and in much the same way,' Reg said. 'The men doing his dirty work are, on the surface — no pun intended — beyond reproach. Their vessels are a big step down from *Sea Wind* but still white, gleaming and very expensive. More importantly, they are also very fast.'

I glanced at Sian. She guessed at once what I was thinking, and lifted her shoulders, spread her hands.

'That would certainly seem to limit

Rickman's choice,' I said carefully. 'I mean, how many crooked owners of luxury yachts are out there cruising the Med?'

'There's one I can name straight away,' Reg said, coming in on cue, 'and that's cuddly Charlie Wise. His boat, the *Alcheringa*, is classy and swift, and Wise came here as a retired businessman with impeccable credentials. Rickman would consider that an asset, something he could use. Crucially, the grapevine was hinting years ago that Wise was fast running out of cash, and if Rickman showed him an easy way out of his troubles . . . '

'Yes, but isn't the boat Wise owns a Sunseeker 66? Worth a bloody fortune. If he's short of cash surely he could sell that rather than turn to a life of crime.'

'Except that what I just said was a trifle misleading. Charlie doesn't actually own the boat; he had one that was much smaller but apparently there's some sort of arrangement in place. Whether that's straightforward leasing, or the use of the Sunseeker for certain services rendered . . . '

Reg shrugged his shoulders. He picked up the old drink, drained it and leaned back in his chair holding the one in which fresh ice tinkled in time with his pulse.

'So who's the boat's real owner?' Sian said.

Reg grinned.

'Christ,' I said. 'Not Bernie Rickman?'

'Who else? But that's just another snippet of useless information. Interesting, yes, but I've been merrily digressing and you still haven't answered my question.'

'Pru,' I said slowly, 'is Prudence Wise.'

'Oh dear,' Reg said.

'Yes, Charlie Wise is her father, as you've no doubt twigged, and what she's been doing is taking risky photographs on board Rickman's *Sea Wind*.'

'Which brings us to why we're here,' Sian said. 'We've been ribbing you something cruel, Reg, but you know damn well we look on you as a respected father figure, a seasoned campaigner on the international financial and art markets, so let's put that to the test. Pru took pictures of a man aboard Rickman's yacht. Since then she's been threatened. We thought you might recognize him, so we brought along her computer.'

The laptop clicked. Sian swung it open, pressed a couple of buttons and patted the seat next to her. Reg looked at me, winked. He went and sat as close to Sian as he could, placed an arm around her shoulders, squeezed.

'By the way, I failed to mention that you're also an incorrigible womanizer unwilling to admit he's over the hill and well down the slippery slope,' Sian said, and pointed at the screen. 'That's him, on Rickman's boat, sitting in the shade. What d'you think?'

'I think it's amazing you've come all this way.'

'Why?'

'Well, if you click on the BBC News website, you'll see why.'

Sian did as instructed, waited a few moments — then her eyes widened.

'Bloody hell,' she said, and cast a startled look in my direction. 'That bloke Pru photographed is someone called Karl Creeny. This is an old picture they've dug up, looks like a mug shot, but it's him all right. He's a Liverpool hoodlum, Jack, and he's wanted in connection with a recent robbery. Two million quid's worth of precious gems was stolen from a well-known diamond merchant in Liverpool city centre.'

★　★　★

'You know,' Reg said, 'you two really must be very, very careful.'

'Us?' I looked at Sian in mock amazement. 'Really, Reg, I think you're the one who should be watching his back.'

Reg looked stunned. 'Go on, tell me why.'

'You operate on the fringes of a murky

world and must run the most awful risks. Haven't you ever badly miscalculated and brought the wrath of underworld villains down on your head? Gone desperately running for cover?'

'The short answer is that perhaps I have, but I'm still here and in no danger, whereas at the moment you two are exposed and vulnerable.'

'This is Gibraltar, Reg,' Sian said, 'sun-soaked outpost of the British Empire, tax haven — '

'Yes, all right, safe as houses and I know you're the bee's knees, the dream team and all that rot, but sooner or later you're going to come to grief. Everybody tends to snigger at those ex-pat crooks living in their white villas on the sunny Spanish Costas but, you know, they're all pretty unsavoury characters. That's how they make their dough. No scruples, and bloody vicious to boot.'

'But we've done nothing to upset them, Reg.'

'How d'you know?'

'Well . . . '

'Rickman's after that young woman's blood. He's desperate to get his hands on those pictures she's taken. That tells me he's bound to be having her watched.'

'Ouch,' Sian said, grimacing. 'So the

watchers watching her will know we've got her laptop and they'll now be watching us.'

'Which explains the rusty Datsun,' I said.

Reg raised questioning eyebrows.

'It sped past, headlights full on, the driver grinning like someone bloodthirsty looking forward to a killing. When we stopped here it pulled in ahead of us, turned around. It's probably still there . . . waiting.'

'There you are then,' Reg said bluntly. 'So, forgetting for the moment that your lives are in danger, what about it, old boy? Do you believe her story?'

We'd already told Reg about our eventful evening, starting with Prudence Wise approaching me at the bar in the Eliott hotel, and finishing as the lift doors slid to behind her and Sian and I walked out into the night with her laptop. Reg's sharp blue eyes had got brighter and brighter as the hint of intrigue began lifting him out of the minor doldrums, and he'd listened attentively to everything I said.

And now he'd come up with a good question — the same one, in fact, that I'd asked myself a little earlier in the Eliott. We'd listened patiently to Pru Wise, smiled and nodded acceptance and understanding — but were we foolish to take her word for what was going on?

36

'Well, the one thing we can't dispute,' I said, 'is that she's got photographs of Karl Creeny. So she was on Rickman's yacht, she spent a couple of hours in the sun for which she got paid three thousand quid, and there's no reason to doubt that the commission was arranged for her by Charlie.'

'Yes, but if I'm right,' Reg said, 'then Charlie Wise is a bit of a shady character. Let's assume Pru did take those pictures, and since then she's been threatened. If the negotiations for the photographic session were done for her by her father, it would be interesting to know who first brought up the idea of a photo shoot.'

'You mean did Rickman approach Charlie Wise, or was it the other way round?'

'Exactly. And if it was Charlie's idea, then we have to ask why he wanted his daughter clicking away on board Rickman's yacht.'

'If he had somehow heard in advance that Karl Creeny was, at some point, likely to be on board,' Sian said slowly, 'then an innocent young woman taking pics in the sun would be an excellent way of getting confirmation. She wouldn't need to know her dad's motives for getting her the job. She'd just merrily take a series of photographs. In the course of doing that, her dad hoped she'd provide him with proof that Creeny was there. Which she did.'

'Ah, yes,' Reg said, 'but that brings me back to the point about believing the young woman. If Charlie did want photographs of Creeny, then surely hoping his daughter would get them by accident was a bit hit and miss? So, did she accidentally take those shots of Creeny lurking in the background, or was she working with her dad from the outset, and know exactly what she was after?'

'And whether she was or she wasn't,' Sian said, 'we already know why the photographs were taken, don't we? Karl Creeny was involved in a Liverpool jewel robbery, was almost certainly Mr Big, the mastermind. So there can be only one reason for his sudden appearance here in Gibraltar.'

'Because, one way or another,' I said, 'this is where the diamonds are going to turn up.'

'And they,' Reg said, 'are what Charlie Wise is after.'

'All very logical, very straightforward,' I said. 'But if Charlie Wise is after those stolen gems, what the hell are he and Adele doing umpteen miles away in Tangier?'

Reg downed his drink, rattled the ice and looked thoughtful.

'According to those news reports, Karl Creeny is known to have left the UK before the police could block all exits. He used his own passport, boarded a plane at Manchester, and he's now reckoned to be somewhere in Morocco.'

'Except that he's not,' Sian said, 'but Charlie Wise is. So, same question: if Charlie really is after those diamonds,' she said, 'then what the hell is going on?'

3

Reg phoned for a taxi to take us back into town. Then we all descended the steps from the house. Trailing fronds of bougainvillea glistening with night dew brushed our shoulders, planted cool wet kisses on our cheeks. We emerged on the tiny off-road parking area, and sneaked a look to our right. The Datsun was still there. Reg stepped out into the road, stretched to his full height, and gave it the finger. The headlights flashed mockingly. Reg chuckled.

'I wonder if it's the local vicar waiting for his maiden aunt to finish a rubber of bridge?' I said, grinning at Reg.

'Wearing a bush hat, and driving a rust bucket with a souped-up engine?' Sian said. 'Yes, very likely.'

Somehow, that short exchange between Reg and the Datsun had dispelled any sense of danger. Reg kissed Sian, slapped my shoulder and went back home while we waited under the stars in the scented cool of his off-road parking area. Sian gazed up at the luminous night skies, enchanted. They seemed to be rotating lazily above the Rock's heights, and she swayed dizzily against me with a warm, tipsy giggle. I hugged her, my face nuzzling the warm silk of her hair.

The cab arrived, different vehicle, different driver. The nearly new minibus with sliding side doors took perhaps three or four minutes to whisk us from Reg's house down the long hill past the Rock Hotel to Main Street. On foot it would have taken at least four times as long, and at that time of night Europa Road was deserted. With the rusty Datsun purring somewhere behind us and the threat of hoodlums lurking in the shadows, it was definitely not worth the risk.

At the taxi stand by Trafalgar Cemetery we left the cab. I dropped a jingle of pound coins into the driver's palm and, feeling much safer in the bright lights of town, we walked without haste through the old stone arches of Southport Gates and along Main Street. There were plenty of people about, the air alive with talk and laughter, heady with the fragrance of flowering wisteria, trailing bougainvillea, and body lotion that had been liberally splashed on the heated skin of both sexes.

Opposite Library Street, the Copacabana restaurant and bar was warmly lit and buzzing with life. Insisting she needed the exercise to clear her head, Sian pushed me down at one of the outside tables and set off briskly for the Eliott Hotel.

By the time the two espressos I'd ordered had been placed in front of me on dainty paper doilies, she was back. Still carrying the laptop.

'Don't tell me,' I said as Sian dropped into her seat, 'Pru's asleep, she wouldn't answer the phone.'

'Guess again.'

'Different receptionist. You couldn't convince her you were legit, and she refused to phone the room.'

'You're right, she wouldn't. But why should she? The room's empty. Unoccupied. There's nobody there.'

Daintily, Sian sipped her espresso and wiggled her eyebrows at me.

'You're kidding. You mean she's checked out?'

'I mean she'd already checked out when she was talking to us.'

'So, when I was ordering drinks and she came tip-tapping over to lean close and appeal for help . . . ?'

'It was all part of a well-orchestrated scheme. As was her pretence at taking the lift. Her one piece of luggage was in a room behind reception. As soon as she thought we were clear of the hotel she collected it and walked out.'

42

'Going where?'

'Christ knows, but wherever it is she's going by car. She had a hired Nissan Micra tucked away under the trees in the hotel's small car park in Library Square.'

'Well, I don't know where the Micra's taking devious Pru Wise, but it seems pretty clear we've been taken for a ride.'

'Played like fish.'

'Netted, landed, left pop-eyed and gasping.'

'But not gaffed,' Sian said, shuddering.

'Don't speak too soon.' I grimaced. 'That Datsun wasn't hanging about for nothing. And you heard Reg. He's convinced there are some evil characters out there, and thanks to Pru we've still got our sticky little hands on an incriminating laptop.'

'But why did she do it?' Sian said. 'What was her game, what was it all in aid of?'

'That's more or less the same question you asked when we were leaving Reg. Her latest antics leave us even further away from the answer.'

'So what do we do?'

'What we don't do is stroll casually down to Marina Bay. Rickman's *Sea Wind* is moored next to Tim's canoe. Flashing the Toshiba that close to the mob would be asking for trouble.'

Sian chuckled. 'The mob, he says, blasé. So, all right, what do we do, get rid of it? And

I don't mean drop it in the sea.'

'I know exactly what you mean.' I glanced at my watch. 'It's almost eleven. Think he'll still be in his office?'

'You know Romero. He considers any time before midnight to be early afternoon.'

'Then let's go to Irish Town and disturb his extended siesta,' I said, and reached for my mobile phone.

★　★　★

The heavy brass inkwells on DI Luis Romero's antique mahogany desk glinted like tarnished gold in the green light from his banker's lamp. The dapper Gibraltarian detective was sitting back in his leather swivel chair, just outside the circle of light. The shadows emphasized the expensive grey suit and crisp white shirt, his glossy black hair, the intelligent eyes with all the comforting softness of shiny agate.

The laptop was open on his desk. The light from the screen flattened the hard planes of his lean face. It had taken us just a few minutes to tell him how we'd spent our evening. He had now been staring pensively at the photograph on the screen for more than a minute, one hand toying absently with the gold pen on his blotter.

'It is a pity,' he said at last, 'that you did not bring this to us much earlier in the day.'

'Couldn't,' Sian said. 'If you'd been listening, darling, you'd know we didn't get it ourselves till after dinner.'

I was sitting in a hard chair some way back from Romero's desk. Sian was curled languidly in one of the comfortably padded rattan chairs up against the dusty bamboo Venetian blinds covering the window. Her blue eyes were dancing. She was gently mocking Romero. He smiled benignly at her, shrugged his shoulders.

'In any case,' he said, 'I am talking a lot of hot air. If, as you say, these pictures were taken yesterday and their existence quickly discovered, the jewel thief Karl Creeny will no longer be with us, the bird will have flown.'

'He's not the only one,' I said.

'Ah, yes, of course, there is this young woman . . .'

'Her name is Prudence Wise.'

That got an unexpected reaction. Romero shot me a surprised glance, then a deep crease formed between his dark eyebrows as he frowned. He rocked his head from side to side, lips pursed, and there was a distant look in his eyes.

'And this . . . Prudence,' he said thoughtfully, 'she was here in Gibraltar especially to take these photographs, and was staying at the Eliott hotel?'

'I can't be sure of anything. If what she was telling us was all a pack of lies — '

'Actually,' Sian said, 'we don't know that she has lied to us at all. She told us her story, and at least part of it is backed up by those photographs Luis has been studying. Also, she looked really scared, and I'd say that was genuine. Okay, so she didn't tell us she was checking out — but why should she? I mean, can't you imagine the way her mind was working? She probably thought, sod this, if there's somebody out looking for me with a razor, I'm going home.'

Romero raised his eyebrows. 'And she set off to drive all the way to England?'

'I thought Malaga,' Sian said. 'There are more flights from there, and if it's a Hertz rental she's driving she could leave the car at the airport.'

'What about this?' Romero said. He flapped a hand at the computer, looked questioningly at me.

I dismissed it with a shrug. 'The photographs she needs will be on the camera's memory card, and she'll have them backed up on a flash drive. That Toshiba's an old model. Prudence has been well paid, so why not dump it? It would get Rickman and that Liverpool villain off her back, which is what she wants.'

'But it has not been dumped. She has given it to you, and with it, a big problem. I know for sure that Rickman is a crook who employs others who delight in using violence. If he is desperate to get his hands on these incriminating pictures — '

'He's out of luck. The problem is now sitting in the middle of your desk.'

Romero snorted. 'My desk is already overcrowded. I am here tonight because a body was discovered near the airport. The death was suspicious; there is the question of identification of victim and perpetrators.' Again he shrugged. 'But that is neither here nor there, it is not your concern. This, however' — he flicked a finger at the screen — 'despite your casual dismissal, is not something you can easily walk away from.'

'Eleanor will be out of hospital tomorrow,' I said carefully. 'As far as I can see, with my dear old mother's leg on the mend there's nothing stopping us from returning to the UK.'

'Are you foolish enough to imagine that, by leaving Gibraltar, you can put all of this behind you?'

Sian sighed heavily.

'Damn,' she said softly. 'It was bloody obvious that girl was up to something. We couldn't work it out, thought she needed a couple of bodyguards for an hour or so — something like that. Were we miles out? Is there much more to it?'

'Perhaps when looking for an answer you should take into consideration her parents.'

'Charlie and Adele.' Sian nodded. 'She mentioned them — and I must admit she looked either acutely embarrassed, or plain blooming guilty. Jack and I were trying to work out why. Well, you're acquainted with ex-diplomat Reg Fitz-Norton. That crafty old sod has his fingers in all sorts of pies, some of them with nasty smells, and Reg has Charlie down as seriously broke. With that in mind, Pru getting aboard *Sea Wind* to take pics just when this bloke Creeny was on board seemed like too much of a coincidence. We know her dad fixed it, so we were beginning to think Charlie might be after those stolen gemstones.'

'Which are, however, believed to be still in the UK,' Romero said.

'But not for long. Karl Creeny is suspected of masterminding the robbery. There's surely no mystery about why he was sitting there like an out of work undertaker on Rickman's boat.'

'No, the inference is quite clear,' Romero said. 'Rickman and Creeny are in some form of collaboration. Sooner or later, those stolen jewels were to be delivered into their hands. However, the question we must ask ourselves — if your theory is correct — is could Charlie Wise somehow skip jauntily onto *Sea Wind* and snatch a fortune in stolen gems from under their noses?'

'The blunt answer is no, he couldn't do it,' Sian said flatly. 'Not a chance.'

I looked long and hard at Romero, then shrugged off my disappointment. 'It didn't really add up anyway, because when we suggested Pru stay with her parents for safety, she told us they are in Tangier. Miles away from the action.'

'She was almost right,' Romero said, and he closed the laptop with a snap.

I stared. 'Well, they're either in Tangier, or they're not,' I said. 'Which is it?'

'Shall we say they appear to have made it halfway?'

'Oh dear,' Sian said, 'that sounds ominous. So, halfway — then what happened?'

'They left this evening and were undoubtedly on their way to Tangier. It was a trip they had planned, they had talked about it incessantly. There are excellent restaurants overlooking the marina, so several people saw them leave. But just a few hours later, in the red glow of a brilliant sunset, their boat was spotted in the straits. It was wallowing in a heavy swell about a mile off the Spanish coast. Coastguards from Gibraltar were called. When they boarded the vessel, they found no sign of Charlie Wise or his wife.'

'What about the crew?'

'When going on a long Mediterranean cruise, he employs a couple of local lads so that he and Adele can happily stay loaded to the gills. This time, perhaps he and his wife needed their wits about them — and no witnesses. There was nobody on board that boat. The vessel was deserted.'

'Poor Pru. If she really has left Gib she won't know, will she?' Sian was frowning. 'What are your thoughts on this, Luis? Charlie weighed down by a mountain of debt so they sailed away into the sunset to end it all?'

'A tragic, romantic scenario, but alas, pure fantasy.' Romero smiled grimly. 'If Charlie and Adele killed themselves, how can we explain the fact that the hull of their beautiful yacht was riddled with bullet holes.'

'Bloody hell,' I said softly.

'Above the waterline,' Romero said. 'A neat dotted line, leading up towards the flybridge. It would seem that the weapon was fired from another small vessel as it approached the *Alcheringa*. Perhaps it was meant as a warning: an old-fashioned shot across the bows, heave to or be scuttled. After that . . . well, who knows? There was no sign of a desperate struggle for survival, nothing was broken or disturbed, there were no pools of blood.'

I frowned. 'So what was it, a kidnapping? Or do you think they *have* been murdered? Knocked unconscious, then lashed to the anchor and thrown overboard?'

Romero was sitting back again, his arms folded. 'Come on, Jack. You are an amateur detective. You were skilful in your handling of the Skaill affair. Instead of asking questions, let me have your thoughts. It is a wonderful mental challenge for you. We have a deserted vessel on the high seas; it is the *Marie Celeste* all over again.'

'Well, there's never an hour out of any twenty-four when the straits are empty of ships. You mentioned a small vessel, so you must have found a witness. Someone who saw or heard something.'

'A series of brilliant flashes were seen from the bridge of a cargo vessel on an easterly course through the straits. The captain has been in war zones. He knew what was going on and immediately alerted the coastguards here in Gibraltar. He then ordered a special watch to be kept. A short while later the officer on lookout reported seeing a small boat. He said it was moving at speed away from what looked like an abandoned luxury motor cruiser, heading in the general direction of Gibraltar.'

'All right,' Sian said, 'so this is all we know for sure. Out in the straits, a boat opens fire on the *Alcheringa*. Soon afterwards, what has to be the same boat is seen heading at speed towards Gibraltar. That doesn't give us much to go on.'

'Except speculation,' I said, 'and we've got no idea why they were attacked.'

'But of course you have,' Romero said.

He had lit a thin cigar. He waggled it. The smoke shimmied upwards to be caught and swirled by the wooden blades of the gently rotating ceiling fan.

'Have we?'

Romero grinned, flashing his white teeth at me.

'Go back to your original theory.'

'Charlie was after the diamonds.'

'Aha, no, that's not it at all,' Sian said, realization dawning. 'Charlie's succeeded. Somehow he managed to snatch them, and they were tucked away in one of the boat's lockers.'

'Damn it, yes, of course,' I said, 'And Rickman discovered they were missing, and knew the thief had to be Charlie.'

'And he sent thugs armed with Kalashnikovs to recover them.' Sian looked at Romero. 'But did they or didn't they? Recover them, I mean. They must have done, surely?'

Romero shook his head reprovingly. 'You are not thinking. If Charlie was clever enough to steal those diamonds,' he said, 'why then would he be stupid enough to take them with him on a trip to Tangier that everybody in Gibraltar knew about?'

A silence heavy with concentrated thought settled over the office. It was broken when the door clicked and a policeman in shirtsleeves came in with three china mugs on a silver tray. He placed the tray on the desk, winked at Romero, and went out. I reached across, took two mugs, handed one to Sian. She tasted it, rolled her eyes in ecstasy. It was rich, ground coffee, scalding hot, very sweet.

'Obviously because he never intended to go anywhere near Tangier,' Sian said, and she sat back with her coffee as Romero chuckled. 'It was a bluff from the start. Charlie planted the Tangier idea in everybody's minds. That's what he wanted everyone to think. What he and Adele actually did was' — she glanced at Romero, squeezed her eyes almost shut, wrinkled her nose, then opened her eyes wide to see him nodding encouragement and said — 'jump ship.'

'Using the tender,' I said. 'Those boats have a fast inflatable that can be stored deflated or

ready to go on the stern swimming platform.'
I looked accusingly at the detective. 'You knew
it was missing, but didn't let on?'

'But no,' Romero said, 'the tender was not
missing. For safety on those long cruises,
Wise always kept it ready on that swimming
platform. It was exactly where it should have
been, and so the thought that the Wises had,
as Sian puts it — jumped ship — never
occurred to me.'

'What if they had a second inflatable and
used that to make it to the Spanish coast with
the gemstones, leaving those gunmen to attack
an empty vessel?' Sian said. 'That would mean
my idea of Pru making for Malaga could be
wrong. The opposite direction now seems more
likely; she could have left Gib and headed
west. And it might not be 'poor Pru' either.
It's 'clever Pru', isn't it? She really was in it
with mummy and daddy, and she drove across
the border to join them.'

'But not clever Sian,' I said. 'Sorry, but to
me the idea of a second inflatable just doesn't
seem right.'

Sian nodded slowly. 'So . . . what are you
saying? That they are dead? They really were
consigned to a watery grave?'

'No. I don't think that happened. It was
a well thought out plan to escape with the
diamonds. I think they had help to get clear.'

'Which really puts the cat amongst the pigeons,' Romero said. 'If they were taken off the *Alcheringa* by another vessel, then it is quite possible that they did after all make it all the way to Tangier. And, unfortunately, Morocco does not have an extradition treaty with the UK.'

With great delicacy he tapped the ash from his cigar into a solid brass ashtray, then pushed back his swivel chair.

'So let us hope that Sian has found the answer,' he said, coming round the desk. 'They headed for the Spanish coast, and will be joined there by their daughter. However, even that does not help us a great deal. We do not know where they are, or what they will do next. Charlie Wise will be aware that airports in Spain and Portugal will be watched. Wherever he is he is now safely beyond the reach of the police here in Gibraltar, so — '

'If I was in Charlie's shoes,' I said, 'I'd simply cause the family to disappear. Go to ground. Come back to life in twelve months' time with new identities and those glittering baubles to be sold to the highest bidder.'

'And at the present time, for that kind of deal, the mind immediately considers oil-rich Arab sheikhs,' Romero said thoughtfully. 'Sooner or later, that, I am sure, is how Wise could do his trading.'

He fastened his jacket's single button, ran a hand across his already smooth hair. 'And I will leave you with this thought, Jack: despite my earlier pessimism, I believe that when tomorrow you return to your stone farmhouse in the Welsh mountains, you will be very well out of this whole affair.'

Yes, I thought, reaching for Sian's hand and making for the door, *that would be very pleasant — but I wonder if what you have just done with those words, Luis, is put paid to any possibility of that happening?*

4

'Christ, you took your bloody time.'

He was sitting on a bollard close to Tim's boat, *El Pájaro Negro*. Ragged blond hair shone in the moonlight. Shadow, cast by the wide-brimmed bush hat, hid the man's eyes but left the lower half of his face exposed. His mouth was split in a sardonic grin, his teeth white against the suntan. Sinewy forearms rested on his spread knees, wrists slack. The pistol dangling casually from one of his hands was a sinister black shape, silently menacing.

Sian's hand tightened, crushing my fingers.

'And you're a long way from a sunburnt country,' I said. I took a pace forward, so that Sian was partially shielded by my body. 'Shouldn't you be bent over shearing Merino sheep? Straddling a surf board off Bondi, waiting to catch the next big wave?'

'Mate, with my luck what I'd be waiting for is the parole that'd get me out of Long Bay jail.' He winked. 'That's just to let you know I'm a tough cookie it'd be a big mistake to mess with.'

'Wouldn't dream of it,' I said. 'And talking of dreams, it's way past our bed time.'

'Tough it out. You walked into the police station in Irish Town carrying a laptop. Sashayed out a while later, empty-handed. Rickman's confused, and when that happens he gets upset. You're about to clarify matters.'

The pistol came up, waggled.

Sian's breath hissed softly, a controlled intake that was the prelude to action. She let my hand drop, stepped lightly to one side. I sensed her tension, knew she had her eyes fixed on the pistol and was estimating how fast she could get to the Australian.

'All right,' I said quickly, 'let's go and comfort Rickman,' and my hand shot out and grasped Sian's arm in a grip that caused her to wince.

'Jack, if he gets us on board that boat . . . ' she said softly.

'There's not an if in sight, darling,' said the Australian. 'This little Glock makes it a foregone conclusion.'

He was up on his feet, tall and lean, casting a long shadow. The pistol was used to point the way. Still keeping a tight hold of Sian's arm, I turned and walked towards the gangway leading up to the big white boat moored on the other side of the concrete strip from my late brother's much smaller black yacht.

When I stepped onto *Sea Wind*'s deck a section of shadow separated from the mass and became a stocky, muscular black man with a polished skull. He led the way past curved steps leading up to the bridge and on into a saloon where black leather and American walnut gleamed in the soft lighting. Blue smoke from a thin cigar clung like skeins of mist to the over-long greying black hair of a big barefoot man in chinos and T-shirt. He was standing by a cocktail cabinet. When he turned, glass in hand, I caught the faintest of clinks from the heavy gold bracelet encircling his wrist, saw the light winking on the gold neck chain.

Reclining on one of that luxurious saloon's sensually curved seats, a woman with streaks of grey in her long blonde hair was using a slender holder to smoke a black Russian cigarette. A flowered drawstring kaftan had the sheen of shot silk, suitable wrapping for an expensive toy. She was as lazily relaxed as a contented cat, her grey eyes amused.

'Welcome aboard,' the big man said, and his cold eyes drifted past me to strip Sian of her clothes. 'I'm Bernie Rickman. My wife, Françoise, is here to make sure I behave. Sit down, tell Clontarf what you'd like to drink.'

'Now, that really would be a fuckin' waste of time,' the Australian said.

He'd remained behind us. To get out of the saloon in a hurry we'd have to go over, around, or through him.

I suppressed a smile.

'Ebenholz?' Rickman said.

The black man, a prowling threat in sleeveless black shirt and jeans, didn't bother to answer. His weapon, which to me looked like an old Heckler and Koch P7, was carried in a worn leather shoulder rig, the holster under his left arm.

Rickman followed his restless movements for a moment, then registered indifference with a shrug of his shoulders.

'So, if you want a drink to calm your nerves, it looks like you'll have to help yourselves. Otherwise — '

'It's otherwise,' I said, 'and our nerves are fine. Why are we here?'

'Sit down.'

'Like hell — '

'If we're going to spend time doing serious talking, Jack, we should be comfortable.'

Sian's turn to exercise control. She dropped onto a long, richly upholstered seat, pulled me with her. I took a deep breath, ran fingers through my hair.

Rickman was leaning against the sleek walnut panelling close to the big flat-screen TV. He sipped his drink, let his eyes linger on Sian. The question, when it came, took me by surprise.

'Where is Charlie Wise, Scott?'

I frowned. 'In Tangier — isn't he?'

'I know where my ruined boat is, but not the man who was renting it from me.'

'He shot through.' The Australian, Clontarf, was grinning. 'An Aussie term, Jack. Means he's left in a hurry, gone bush, no forwarding address.'

'So now it's up to you, Scott,' Rickman said.

'Why?'

'Because you're in it with them.'

'It? I don't know what you're talking about. Pru Wise came to us this evening. We looked after her until she left. She'd been threatened by your wife.'

I glanced across at the woman. She winked, mimed a kiss.

'Do I really look like a femme fatale, a gun moll?' she said. The voice she'd chosen was straight out of a 1940s Hollywood gangster film, her eyes suggesting she was mildly amused but bored out of her mind.

Rickman shook his head, grinning quirkily.

'The truth is, you're all in it together, probably over your respective heads, and what you were doing is looking after each other,' he said. 'Before today's events it was nothing more than a get-rich-quick scheme, a game, something played out on the Xbox.

Now it's desperation; Charlie working out how to keep hold of ill-gotten gains when the pack's baying at his heels. The Yanks would call it exit strategy. It's possible when Charlie worked that one out he was thinking only of self and family. But I've got a better idea.'

'Get rid of it. It's worthless.'

'Where's the laptop?'

'Ask your pet Digger.'

'I told you, he took it to the cop shop,' Clontarf said as Rickman flashed him a look. 'Expect an early call from the boys in blue.'

'Yes, and that'll be another waste of time,' Rickman said.

'Not theirs,' I said. 'With the laptop they have proof Karl Creeny, a man wanted in connection with a very big jewel robbery, was here on this boat.'

'So what? He was, but now he's not. What does that have to do with me? Gibraltar is a million miles away from the scene of his alleged crime. And if I did know Karl Creeny — again, so what? I haven't left the Rock in months.'

'Unlike Creeny,' I said. 'Here today, gone tomorrow. Seems to me his exit strategy was pure self. But who can blame him? He was in Gibraltar for the diamonds, wasn't he? And if Charlie's got them — which is surely what this is all about — then why hang around?'

'From certain information we were given by DI Romero,' Sian said, 'this Creeny's not letting the grass grow. Sounds as if he recruited a small army and went hunting for those jewels.'

The man called Ebenholz laughed softly. I looked at him, at the blank eyes and the glistening muscles, at the weapon carried as if it were an essential but perfectly natural part of his attire, a useful fashion accessory. Then I glanced across at the other man, the Australian who had moved away from the entrance, poured himself a drink and was watching proceedings with that sardonic grin. And I remembered the boat out in the straits, stitched with a neat line of bullet holes, and I wondered . . .

'I'm making it all sound very simple,' Rickman said, cutting across my speculation, 'but in real life it doesn't work like that.'

'All right,' I said, 'then tell us how it does work, and then maybe we can all get to bed. I don't know about you, but tomorrow Sian and I have a plane to catch.'

'Which will remove both of you from the scene of the crime,' Rickman said, 'but will do nothing to change the situation.'

'Meaning whatever you have planned for us can be activated here, or wherever we decide to go?' I nodded. 'DI Romero said something along those lines. Perhaps that's something you might bear in mind.'

'Why? You think that'll save you? If you're in the UK, that Gib cop's hands are tied.'

In the sudden silence a faint, distant creaking could be heard as the big boat moved gently at its moorings and a rope tightened. Ebenholz had stopped pacing. The restlessness had gone. There was a sense of purpose in his movements as he leaned back against the panelling and used his right hand to move the shoulder holster to a more accessible position.

Clontarf began whistling tunelessly through his teeth.

'Shut up,' Rickman snapped.

'Mate, I'm just wondering when you're going to get to the point.'

I nodded approvingly. 'My feelings exactly. So tell us, Rickman, what is this situation that won't be changed by a move to colder climes?'

'You are now working for me.'

'Explain.'

'Karl Creeny came here via Tangier. One of his men was bringing certain goods to Gibraltar. This morning he flew in from Manchester — '

'At last,' Sian breathed, 'an admission of guilt.' She looked at me. 'Didn't Romero say something about a body, found near the airport?'

'You're right, he didn't make it,' Rickman said, nodding. 'And yes, the goods were diamonds and they were in the man's cabin baggage. He carried the small case off the plane. Somewhere between arrivals and the waiting car he was attacked, beaten about the head with a well-known blunt instrument. When he was found in a narrow passageway, his skull fractured and his blood seeping away through cracks in dirty concrete, the case was missing. Now Wise has disappeared. Karl Creeny sees me as responsible for his financial loss, reckons I should have had men closer to that courier when he came off the plane. Consequently, I am now being threatened. You are in this with Wise — '

'I told you, that's nonsense.'

'Whatever. Wise is missing. You've been seen with Prudence. That's a connection, however loose. So now you're being threatened, Scott. By me. To remove that threat, you recover the diamonds.'

'But the diamonds,' I said, 'were taken here in Gibraltar. Wise sailed for Tangier with them on that Sunseeker and disappeared down a big black hole. What possible use can I be if I'm in the UK?'

'I'm getting tired of repeating myself.

You're in it with Wise. You know exactly where he is now.' Rickman shrugged. 'Maybe that's the UK, I don't know or care. But, believe me, *you* should.'

'What if I call your bluff? March straight from here into Irish Town police station?'

'Then you put yourself and people close to you in great danger. You have a mother, a colleague in Liverpool by the name of Calum Wick.' He noticed my look of surprise, and grinned. 'And then, of course, there is the lovely lady sitting by your side.'

My skin was prickling.

'So it's up to you,' he said. 'And you'd better make sure the answer comes fast, and it's the right one, or the danger your lovely lady's in could be . . . how shall I put it? Imminent.'

I watched Rickman pad across the carpet, pick up a bottle, unscrew the cap and take a long pull at what looked like tequila. All done. Terms stated. Without turning my attention to them I was acutely aware of the muscular black man's watchfulness, the Australian with a crystal glass in his left hand and a Glock 19 tucked into the waistband of his jeans.

Rickman's put himself out of the way, I thought. Behind both of the heavies, he was out of the line of fire. He'd cleared the field for action. In case. And, realizing that my hot-blooded Soldier Blue would be looking at possibilities, weighing up the odds, I reached to the side and grasped her hand.

She twisted it, pulled. I gripped harder.

'Bugger this useless talk,' Sian said. 'Look, Rickman, we agree, okay? We'll be on the first plane out tomorrow, and when we get where we're going we'll do what we can to find those bloody jewels. But not for you. They're not yours. We'll find them because there's a couple of good friends you didn't mention, and they're Liverpool cops. Those jewels will be put back where they belong.'

'A big mistake.'

'Why? What can you do? Once you let us go, we can do what the hell we like. Keeping us here indefinitely achieves nothing.' And then she smiled sweetly. 'More to the point, neither you nor those two pistol-toting losers have a hope in hell of holding us against our will.'

Rickman opened his mouth. Sian ripped her hand from my grasp and sprang to her feet. The black man pushed away from the panelling, eyes shining. One glance at him warned Sian what she was up against. She looked across at Rickman, grimaced and shook her head as if realizing instantly that she was being foolhardy. I knew different, and felt my mouth go dry. Still looking at Rickman, Sian spun and launched a vicious kick. Her heel rammed into the softness below Ebenholz's belt. He grunted, instinctively made a grab for his groin with one hand, his pistol with the other, and began to fold. The glistening skull came down. Sian spun again, kicked again, met the descending target. Her foot exploded against Ebenholz's jaw. His head snapped back. Blood sprayed. He went down with a thud.

Clontarf hadn't moved. Now he lifted his hands and clapped slowly, mockingly.

'You beauty,' he said. He looked at me, and shook his head. 'Mate,' he said, 'that girl of yours is one holy terror.'

'That's the truth,' Sian said. 'And I think you should bear that in mind, because we're leaving now so I'd like you to get out of our way.'

And with that she brushed past the Australian and walked out of the saloon leaving me stranded in her wake.

5

A single light illuminated the elegant timber panelling and brass fittings on a smaller boat — the carpet from which older bloodstains had so recently been cleaned — and bounced off the crystal glass of Islay whisky that was a little unsteady in my hand. I could hear the soft whisper of the shower, the faint sound of Sian singing. A slightly twisted smile lightened my face.

I remembered a similar situation a short while after my brother, Tim, had been shot dead in this same saloon. Sian had emerged from the shower, and we had sipped gin and tonics while debating — perhaps agonizing — over whether a return to the UK was a good idea. Well, that decision had been made some time ago, but in the space of twenty-four hours the world seemed to have slipped on its axis. Suddenly we were off balance, struggling to keep a hold on reality when the solid ground beneath our feet was beset by tremors.

Or perhaps, I thought wryly, it was just me feeling that giddy sensation of everything being out of kilter. Sian, if her recent actions were anything to go by, was serenely unaffected.

★ ★ ★

I had met her in Norway; Sian taking a break from military duty — instructing an intelligence cell on deep water exercises in high-speed inflatables — me on holiday and stepping gingerly onto skis for the first time since my own stint in uniform. Over many pleasant evenings seated before a roaring fire in the ski lodge I learned that this young woman who looked as warm and soft as honey and melted butter had seen her Scottish seafaring father lost overboard in an Arctic gale when she'd been ten years old and illegally aboard his ship, had returned to nurse her dying mother in the Cardiff slums and, years later, with a university degree under her Shotokan karate black belt, had moved north to become something of a legend among the high peaks of the Cairngorms. From there the army had seemed the most natural next step on her climb to the top.

Some time before the holiday that had brought us together I had bought Bryn Aur — the hill of gold — a stone farmhouse set against the foothills of Glyder Fawr and

Glyder Fach in North Wales. Across the yard from the main house, set beyond a massive oak tree, there was a workshop where I set out to design and manufacture what had since been acclaimed by purchasers as the world's finest toy soldiers. It was there that I took Sian Laidlaw at the end of the skiing holiday (the house, not the workshop), and over the years since then my blonde Soldier Blue had shared my home and frequently my bed. But on more than one occasion I had caught myself reflecting that nothing's settled until it's settled. The move to Gibraltar — mutually agreed — had proved to be yet another thorn, another fly in the ointment, another twist in a relationship in which the plot was always thickening.

We had moved to the iconic Rock towering above the narrow strip of water separating Europe from Africa to take over a security business from a Gibraltarian friend who wanted to spend the rest of his days fishing from a lazily rocking boat, cans of beer clinking in a net submerged in the cool blue sea. But we had almost come to grief when I was dragged into a murder inquiry where I would have been the chief witness for the prosecution. Before that could happen, we took on the villainous Skaill family. We had both been injured, my brother murdered in cold blood.

And now? Well, now there was another puzzle to unravel. But unlike our usual investigations involving a crime and a perpetrator, this one seemed to have several of each, and each one seen through a glass darkly.

Which, I thought ruefully, might be a warped misuse of a biblical quotation, but it seemed the only one I knew that ideally fitted the circumstances.

Deep in thought, I lifted my glass and almost chipped a front tooth when a damp and perfumed Sian Laidlaw came padding in from the shower.

★　★　★

'How's the foot?'

'I have two.'

'You balanced ballerina fashion on one, kicked hard with the other. You kicked again, and that one connected with bone and could have caused damage.'

'Oh, it did.'

'I mean to your foot.'

'Ebenholz has lightning fast reactions. I doubt if anyone noticed, but as fast as I attacked, he'd already begun riding the blow.'

'Yet even so you knocked him cold.'

Sian grinned. 'If he'd stayed stock still, he'd be crawling around that gin palace looking for his head.'

'You must think . . . ' I hesitated. 'Well, I really don't know what you must think of me.'

'I think your reactions are somewhat slower than Ebenholz's. And I took you by surprise. By the time you realized what was happening, mulled over the situation and decided to come heroically to my aid, it was all over.'

'Mm, slow but steady. Yet I seem to remember that a long time ago when we came up against Dakin, the taxidermist turned killer, I saved your life with a similar skilful martial arts manoeuvre.'

'That was then, this is now.' Sian smiled sweetly. 'You're a lot older.'

'Than you, or than then?'

'Both.'

I sighed. 'Damn it, but you were impressive. That raw-boned Digger said it all didn't he?'

'Yes, he did. But I have the uneasy feeling that if ever I were to come up against him, he'd be a damn sight more dangerous than his bruiser of a colleague.'

'Why uneasy? It's not likely to happen.'

'You don't believe Rickman?'

'I don't understand Rickman. We spoke to Prudence Wise at, what was it, eight o'clock or thereabouts? It's now a little after midnight. In that time, a man we don't know has used threats to force us to find another man we don't know. From him we're supposed to recover stolen jewels, and hand them over to — guess what — yes, another man we don't know.'

'I think the idea under all that talk is that we should give them to Rickman.'

'Yes, well, we know where they'll end up after that — or do we?'

'If we don't, it's about time we sat down and worked this out.'

So saying, Sian flopped down on one of the soft seats and cast a meaningful glance towards the cocktail cabinet. I rolled my eyes, got up, refreshed my own drink and mixed a gin and tonic for her. There was a board, with ice barrel, knife, and half a lime. I rattled ice, cut a slice of fruit, perched it on the rim of the glass. When I held it out to her she grasped my wrist, touched the tips of my fingers with her lips, pressed my knuckles against her still-moist cheek.

'What's that for?' I said softly.

'For understanding. For not being the ultimate macho male. For not angrily berating me.'

'Ah. You mean when you emasculated me, metaphorically speaking, by taking on that muscular thug?'

'Something like that.'

'No, nothing like that. It's teamwork. You're the brawn, I'm the brains.'

She pouted, took the drink then slapped my hand away.

'Then do some, big boy. Thinking, I mean.'

'Mm. All joking aside, you were right. We really must sit down and work this out.'

I plopped down opposite her, shook my head. 'For a start, I meant it when I said I don't understand Rickman. And the bit I don't understand most is why we've been dragged into this. Looked at logically, we're surplus to requirements. If he wants to find Wise, he's got two armed men working for him who are well capable. I'm sure they got within a whisker of catching Wise when they riddled his Sunseeker with bullets.'

'You think it was Clontarf and Ebenholz with a Kalashnikov?'

'Of course.'

Frowning, Sian sipped her drink. Sucked the slice of lime. Dropped it into the glass and swished it around.

'If we don't understand what's going on,' she said, 'it's because we don't have enough information. We're in the dark. So what we do is go along with Rickman's weird ideas — or act in a way that makes it look as if we're doing that — and then . . . well, we see what transpires.'

I smiled. 'I can't see much transpiring when I haven't got a clue where to start. Wise's boat was found rocking in a heavy swell out in the Straits of Gibraltar. Bad place from which to start following a trail.'

'That's not like you.'

'I've got no starting point, nothing to go on.'

'Are you sure?'

'Charlie and Adele jumped ship, went Christ knows where. Same for Prudence. She checked out of the Eliott, and disappeared.'

'Yes, but although Prudence drove her little Micra off into the sunset, she left something behind. Her laptop. There must be some personal information on that hard drive.'

I closed my eyes, disgusted with myself.

'You're right, I'm being stupid. And, actually, so are you. We don't need her laptop. When Pru said she was staying here for a while, she mentioned a website. Her website will have contact information.'

'Yes, you big pudding, but you can't look at a website without a computer. You have to go to Romero, get the laptop.'

'Mm, I don't know. We have to assume every move we make will be watched. If we're really doing Rickman's bidding — and that's the impression we want to create — we should stay well away from the police.'

'In that case, I know where there's an internet café. You can pay to go online for as little as fifteen minutes.'

'Hang on a minute. A thought has occurred. While we've been soaking up the sun, Calum's been installing a modern computer system in the office at Bryn Aur.'

Sian groaned, 'Now he tells me.'

I looked at his watch.

'Which way does this hour's difference work?'

'It's earlier in the UK.'

'Then Mr Wick will have finished his day's work casting toy soldiers, and is probably sitting in my living room drinking my fine liquor. Now's the perfect time to get him up off his backside.'

Digging my mobile out of my pocket, I keyed in the number and winked at Sian as I listened to the landline telephone ringing in distant Bryn Aur.

6

Calum Wick looked around the big living room with an unexpected feeling of . . . fondness? Love? Well, maybe he wouldn't go quite that far, but he had been so many times to the big stone farmhouse owned by Jack Scott that simply walking in through the front door and across the porch's quarry-tiled floor was like slipping his arms into an old, shabby, very snug overcoat.

Shabby? Well, no, hardly that either. Completing the fantasy of wrapping that imaginary overcoat around him came when he passed the stairs where glossy toy soldiers stood in stone niches, and entered Bryn Aur's living-room. It had been built in the late nineteenth century, had improved with age and was now stamped with the character of the ex-soldier who created exquisite military miniatures and helped the police solve intriguing mysteries. Twenty-five feet long and half that broad, the room had a floor of massive slate slabs scattered with rich Indian rugs beneath a low-beamed ceiling. Wall lights with tasselled red shades warmly illuminated white stone walls lined with bookcases. The door leading through to the kitchen and office had black iron hinges. There was a cavernous ingle-nook with iron dog grate, a basket of cut logs shedding dry bark, an Ercol coffee table and, well . . .

Thoughts drifting, feeling a sudden and most unexpected warm glow, Wick kicked off his shoes, lifted his long legs onto the leather Chesterfield and stretched out luxuriously.

'You all right there?' Stan Jones said.

'And why shouldn't I be?'

'Yeah, I suppose you're right. This must be dead luxurious to a Scot used to livin' in a stone bothy with a few scraps of peat smoulderin' in a rusty iron basket and the smoke goin' out through a black hole in the roof.'

'My dear old friend, you are labouring under an awful misapprehension.'

Jones, an incorrigible Liverpool scally who was balding, whipcord thin and could have been fifty or ninety, scratched at the white stubble that he designed by the occasional trim with nail scissors, and grinned.

'I was wonderin', that's all. I mean, what is it with you and Jack Scott? He makes toy soldiers; you paint them, but how did that come about? Did you come together with a bump, like, accidentally, and get stuck in a fuckin' time warp?'

'Fortuitously, not accidentally,' Wick said. 'And your suggestion of a bump is close to the truth, but much milder than the reality. To explain, I'll need to go back a bit. Are you up for it?'

'Sure, take your time,' Jones said. 'As long as there's brandy in the bottle.'

Behind his paint-stained, wire-framed glasses, the bearded Scot's eyes became thoughtful.

'Scott was in the army,' he said. 'Royal Engineers, Paras, doing very well indeed. But something went wrong for him in Beirut. I don't know the full story, but he killed an innocent man, decided enough was enough and at thirty he walked away and spent the next five years wandering aimlessly downhill in a hot climate.'

'Cornwall?'

It was Wick's turn to grin. 'Actually, it was Australia. Jack Scott did everything from painting fences in the outback to conducting coach loads of tourists around Alice Springs and selling accident insurance on the streets of Sydney. Luckily for me, it didn't work out. One rain-swept night soon after he returned to the UK he strolled into a spit-and-sawdust pub on the glistening streets of Brixton and saved me from a savage beating by three huge Yardies.'

'So why were you being thumped? I

suppose it was them not takin' kindly to racist remarks made by a man with a funny accent — and maybe wearin' a skirt.'

'A remark of that nature may have been uttered by me in the heat of the altercation but, no, it started because they were desirous of making a wee profit from my wheeling and dealing.'

'What was that?'

'Driving stolen Mercedes saloons from Germany to Liverpool for a bent detective sergeant whose contacts had no scruples but very fat wallets.'

'Oh yeah, I remember hearin' about that one. Scott ended up involved, didn't he?'

'Eventually. I told him about it that night, in an evil smelling public toilet where we were groaning into a cracked basin stained with our blood.'

'Cue violins, eh? But the scam didn't last, did it?'

'For him, no. I think it was conscience. He opted out and began to frequent the American Bar on Lime Street where he habitually sank into dark, alcoholic brooding. The owner was an ex-boxer.'

Jones nodded. 'I know him. Or did. He fell off his perch.'

'As we all do, eventually, some of us with nary a flutter. Anyway, this former pugilist told me my friend was heading for a fall and so I led Jack next door to see our private investigator friends.'

'Short fat and greasy. An' that's just the gaffer, Manny Yates, with his waistcoats and those same skinny cigars you're always suckin' on.'

'Schimmelpennincks. At the time Manny was looking for a man with experience in investigative techniques. Jack had been in the army's Special Investigation Branch, so he was a natural.'

'So if he was good, why isn't he still there with Manny?'

'He stayed five years, which I suppose he considered long enough. Then he drifted away, discovered military modelling and a skill he hadn't known he possessed.'

'And along the way he also discovered Sian Laidlaw.'

'I imagine there's a crude connotation to what you're suggesting,' Wick said, 'which I will ignore. The truth is, that meeting with Sian in an Austrian ski lodge is the event that not only changed Scott's life — '

He broke off.

On the other side of the white door with its black iron hinges, a phone had begun to ring.

7

'He did it with one hand,' I said, 'while holding the phone with the other.'

Sian had swished out of the saloon while I was making the call, cheekily flapping the hem of her towelling robe to allow me a brief glimpse of naked thigh. Now she was in the big double bed in the yacht's only stateroom — or whatever they call bedrooms on boats, I thought — and was sitting back against plumped-up pillows, her face shiny with grease. Or expensive night cream.

'What are you grinning at?'

'I'm wondering,' I said, 'if other portions of your anatomy have had the same tender care as your face.'

'You mean those portions you cannot reach?'

'Cannot, or must not?'

'Proscribed, is a good word. Another is *verboten*. Sounds much more severe. What did Calum say?'

'He said Prudence Wise has an excellent website. Her Liverpool address and phone number are there on her contact page.' I flapped the scrap of paper on which I'd hastily scrawled the details. 'She lives in Seaforth, t'other side of Bootle.'

'As does my sister.'

I blinked, then cautiously sat on the corner of the bed.

'We haven't been in touch with Siobhan since that trouble she had when we were playing detective up in Scotland.'

'You haven't.' Sian reached across, picked up her mobile, waggled it. 'We talk from time to time.'

'Then in that case,' I said, 'I have an idea.'

'I'm ahead of you. Two birds with one stone, that sort of thing?'

'What's she got, house or flat?'

'End terrace, with three bedrooms. And she'd love to see us, put us up for a few days. I'll sort that end out, but you know what you must do?'

'Well, as those worldly possessions we brought with us or have acquired while here will be shipped out tomorrow, there has to be somebody there at the other end when they eventually arrive.'

'That's easily done. You get back to Calum, I'll phone Siobhan.'

'Er, yes, but on one condition.'

Sian slid down in the bed, yawned, snuggled into the pillows.

'I tell you what I'll do,' she said. 'If you can tell me what's the opposite of *verboten*, I'll consider — '

'*Erlaubt*,' I said, and with a broad wink I headed for the bathroom.

Or, I thought, whatever it is they call them on boats.

8

One week later

'Considering the length of time we've been together,' I said, 'in what might be described — a little indelicately — as an on and off relationship, I think we should be thinking seriously about marriage. Ours, I mean. I'm in my fifties. You're . . . well, thereabouts. So I think we should do it, get married, tie the knot, splice the mainbrace — something like that, anyway, but I'm sure you know what I mean.'

Silence.

Well, not quite. There was some noise, but put it all in a pot and stir it with a wooden spoon and it would still amount to little more than the low kitchen humming of a fridge-freezer.

The speedometer needle was flickering on sixty-five. Cold rain was pattering the Audi Quattro's windscreen, combining with the swish of the windscreen wipers to emphasize the warmth and comfort of the speeding car's interior. The heater control was three-quarters into the red segment, the fan on two — a mere whisper of sound. A jazz CD was playing, just loud enough to be heard. I had an idea it was Stan Getz, one of his slower pieces, equivalent to being stroked with a warm velvet glove. I grinned at the thought. On the wet roads winding through the Welsh hills, even the monotonous hiss of tyres on slick tarmac — carrying with it a subtle warning that care must be taken — couldn't cut through my mood of quiet contentment.

After all, I might be pushing hard through a cold autumn evening, but wasn't this why we'd returned to the UK? Four recognizably different seasons? And didn't that entail taking the rough with the smooth?

I glanced sideways. Sian was flat out in the fully-reclined passenger seat. Her feet, snug in bright red socks, were up on the dash above the glove compartment. Zipped up inside a matching fleece, she'd taken off the restraining rubber band and her hair was loose against the seat, behind and around her head, a halo glowing golden in the dim light from the dash. Her eyes were closed.

I faced front again as the road took the sweeping rise past the T-junction in Capel Curig. The car rocked sideways. Sian rolled against the door with a bump, then stretched and yawned. She cleared her throat. I felt her looking at me. Kept calm. Wondered if she'd heard.

'Where are we?' she said, her voice soft and warm. Her hand dropped to her side. The seat's back rose slowly and smoothly to forty-five degrees. I thought of Frankenstein's monster awakening, and pushed my lips forward to ward off a grin.

'You fell asleep when we left the coast,' I said. 'You've just missed Capel Curig. Not that far to go now. One more lake. A few twists and turns.'

'I've been dreaming.'

'That's what we do, when we sleep.'

'Let me refine that. It was either a beautiful dream, or a scary nightmare.' She chuckled. 'I thought I heard you propose, Jack. Ask me to marry you, all of it mixed up with something to do with sailors and grog. That's what I thought I heard.'

I watched the headlights sweeping across dripping hedges, trees caught in the main beam, tossing in the wind.

'And if it was something more than a thought,' I said, 'something that might have to be taken seriously, how would you classify it? Scary nightmare, or beautiful dream?'

'Oh, it doesn't really matter, does it?' she said, and I flashed her a glance. She winked at me. 'Because, actually, I wasn't asleep. I've done little more than doze. Enjoying the ride.' She giggled. 'I always do, don't I?'

'Invariably.'

'And not infrequently.' She reached across, rubbed my arm, squeezed it gently. 'I was awake, Jack, so I know exactly what you said. And I was touched by that tremor of emotion in your voice. What was it, undying passion or chronic nervousness? Anyway, I don't know why it's taken you so long.'

'From Seaforth in Liverpool to where we are now in North Wales,' I said, 'has taken us little more than an hour.'

'But from a certain Austrian ski slope where a maker of toy soldiers met his young — youngish — Soldier Blue, it's taken us all of . . . what? How long have we been together?'

'I'd say five or six years. Could be much longer. I'll ask Calum. But surely you know the old saying?'

'Which one? An Englishman needs time? Which is always a convenient excuse.'

'I was thinking of better late than never.'

'Ooh, that's a double-edged sword, that one — or something. I mean, a little bit late's all right, but some people leave things so long they miss the boat.'

'And is that what I've done?'

There was a long silence. I negotiated a few more tricky bends without seeing them, without slowing. Felt the car's rear end slide just a little, corrected it without thinking.

'I think we should leave this intensely personal conversation,' Sian said at last, 'till later on this evening. I mean, I know you're an excellent driver, but my answer — either way — could leave you emotionally unsettled. That would be dangerous on these roads. We might be forced to continue our little talk while hanging upside down from our seat belts in a dark, dank ditch.'

'Reluctantly, I agree. Another maxim I always go by — along with the better late than never bit of nonsense — is never make important decisions during the hours of darkness. They're best left until dawn has well and truly broken. With that in mind, let's change the subject to safer ground. Have you got any ideas on the mysterious disappearance of Prudence Wise?'

'Only that it's not mysterious. We were at Siobhan's for a week; we knocked on Pru's door several times and got no answer. But why were we expecting her to be there? After all, you phoned Louis Romero after a couple of those fruitless visits, and he told you Pru's hired car had definitely been logged passing through customs into Spain. If she didn't take a flight from Malaga, as I'd suggested, well, she's still there somewhere and southern Spain's a long way from Seaforth.'

'And Bryn Aur, nestling beneath the Glyders,' I said, 'is a long way from Gibraltar. What I mean by that is that now we're very close to home, Bernie Rickman's threats seem laughable.'

'Yes, we'll soon be in our own stone fortress and safe from all those with evil intentions,' Sian mused softly.

The possessive pronoun, so casually uttered, set my heart a-fluttering. There was also something in her voice that told me, without glancing at her, that she was looking to her left across the stone walls that separated the road down which we were now cruising from the valley of Afon Ogwen and beyond that the stone farmhouse known as Bryn Aur. All was in darkness. The lowering clouds that were the source of the incessant rain cut out moon and stars, but that valley was in her thoughts and mine and, when I slowed, turned left and took the big car dipping down the road to double back and along the river towards home, I was engulfed by a wave of emotion that was shocking in its unexpectedness and brought with it the threat of tears.

We had been away for more than a year.

Homecoming had never felt so good.

But when I took the car rocking across the bridge and the heavy tyres crunched up onto the stone yard fronting the house, that wonderful feeling of well-being was shattered just as easily and as swiftly as a hammer shatters fragile glass.

A new Vauxhall Astra was parked under the big oak tree. Rain dripping from the tree's branches and dancing leaves was splashing onto the bonnet where it was quickly and perceptibly transformed into thin vapour that rose into the cold air to be whipped away by the wind.

I pulled to a halt, applied the handbrake. Sat back. Looked out of the window and whistled softly through my teeth.

'That engine's still warm,' I said, turning a puzzled glance towards Sian and stating the obvious. 'Now who the hell's come calling, when not a living soul other than your sister knew we were coming home today?'

* * *

The house, set back against the almost vertical hillside, was in darkness. Not a sound could be heard but the soft patter of rain on stone, leaves, metal, the faint crackle as the Quattro's engine began to cool.

'Jack, don't do that. You'll have the alarm howling, irate farmers in wellies rushing round here with loaded shotguns.'

I was out of the Quattro, peering in

through the Astra's passenger window. Ignoring the warning, I tried the passenger door. Locked. I kicked at the front tyre, shook my head.

'Welsh farmers don't rush. And there isn't a house within half a mile. Anyway, who takes any notice of car alarms?' I stepped back, hands on hips. 'What the hell's going on, Sian?'

'You seem to be stuck in a groove with that question. Nothing's going on, other than it's raining and I'm getting wet. If you're going to stand there admiring that thing, throw me your keys.'

'Haven't got them. There's only one set, and Calum's been here. He'll have left them under the stone pot by the porch.'

'Yes, for nosy strangers in shiny new Vauxhall Astras.'

'Who even now are lurking in the dark living room waiting to waylay us. As if.'

Sian had slipped on a pair of sandals, left the Quattro ahead of me and had been waiting by the front door. I walked across the yard's wet stone flagging, reached her as she tipped the mossy stone pot with its dying geraniums, found the keys. Sian pulled a face. Her hand was wet with leaves and mud. She looked around for something to wipe it on, shrugged, held it daintily to one side as she switched the keys to her other hand and opened the door. She pushed. It swung wide. Something tinkled.

The porch's red and black quarry tiles were lost in the gloom. Sian stepped inside out of the rain, pulled the door away from the wall, bent to look behind it

'Whoever it is, they must have shoved these through the letter box,' she said. She held up a set of car keys. They jingled, ghostly chains clanking in the dark.

'Go on in, get the coffee going,' I said. 'I'm already wet so I might as well have a look, see what's what.'

I took the keys, waited for her to turn away and go on into the house. She shook her head. In the gloom, her face looked pale.

'No . . . No, I'll wait for you.'

'I don't really think there's anyone in there.'

'No,' Sian said. 'Neither do I — and that's what bothers me.'

'And the car's empty.'

'Yes.'

'So . . . ?'

'Just hurry up. Or, better still, as I'm wet too . . . '

I saw the uneasiness in her eyes, saw the effort she made to replace it with the steely look I knew so well; saw the effort fail. I touched her hand briefly, turned away. A gust of wind blew icy rain into my unbuttoned shirt collar. I hunched my shoulders and trotted across to the car, aware of Sian's feet slapping wetly behind me. I pointed the key fob, tried the remote. The car's lights flashed, and there was the reassuring clunk of the central locking. The interior light came on. Sian moved quickly. She opened the driver's door and slipped inside. I watched her grasp the wheel with both hands, look around, slide a hand across the top of the dash then stretch across to the passenger side and open the glove compartment. She pulled out a grained faux-leather folder. Flipped it open.

'Car's handbook, documents. Nothing else.'

I nodded. Heavy droplets from the oak tree plopped onto my head as I opened the rear door, leaned into the new-car smell; into emptiness. Slid inside. Felt along the floor, twisted awkwardly to feel around under the front seats.

When I straightened, Sian had turned to watch.

'Nothing?'

'Nope.'

'Try the boot.'

'Yes, I will, and there'll be nothing there. Do you know why?'

'Go on.'

'I've worked it out. This car has obviously

been bought by a local farmer. It's been in to the main dealers for its first service, the farmer told them when they'd finished to deliver it and pop the keys through the letterbox.'

Sian visibly relaxed, picked up the story.

'The farmer always deals with a local garage,' she said. 'That means the main dealer doesn't know him from Adam — '

'And a lot of Welsh farms, in the same area, have similar names,' I finished. 'Or they sound similar, if you happen to be English.'

'Right car, wrong farm,' Sian said. 'Or something.' She grinned. 'Look in the boot, Jack. I'll get the coffee on.'

She was skipping in a fine spray across the yard to the front door as I got out of the car. The porch light came on. I heard the front door open and seconds later the living room's red lights glowed warmly behind the closed curtains.

I slid out of the car, slammed the rear door. Pulled a face as more rain dripped under my collar and trickled down my back, then went around and opened the boot. The automatic light came on. Wind gusted, lifted the lid hard against the stops. Rain lashed the boot's interior. I leaned in. Swore softly. For a moment I stood there, frozen, not believing what I was seeing. Then, reluctantly, I reached in, grasped a small, wet, furry object between thumb and forefinger and slipped it into my pocket. I straightened, took a deep breath of the cold air, then reached up and slammed the boot. Pressed the remote. Heard the clunk and watched the lights flash, then ran across the yard and into the house.

I kicked off my shoes in the porch, toed them alongside Sian's sandals. When I padded through into the house the light in the hall was on low, a lambent moon illuminating the red-coated miniature soldiers standing on night guard in their stone niches all the way up the stairs.

Red tasselled wall lights in the living room turned Sian's loose hair to a creamy strawberry blonde. Her feet in their wet socks were planted firmly on the Indian rug in front of the leather Chesterfield, and she was shrugging out of the red fleece. Still holding it, she looked across at me, smiled brightly and raised her eyebrows.

'Nothing — right?'

'Something.'

I'd stopped. My hands were thrust into my pockets. My shoulders were stiff. I could imagine what my face must look like, saw the horror Sian could see there reflected in her blue eyes.

'Oh Christ, Jack, what is it?'

I took a deep breath. 'There's a body in the boot.'

Sian nodded, nodded again, jerky movements, her mind racing ahead.

'Prudence Wise?'

I nodded. 'Yes. It's Pru.'

And in a seemingly callous remark of the kind anyone might make when knocked sideways and left stunned by the shock of the unexpected, Sian said, 'Well, at least we now know why she wasn't answering her door.'

*   *   *

'The house is lovely and warm. Why is that?'

She was still standing on the Indian rug. I thought she seemed dazed. She was looking in an absent way at the cold logs piled in the stone inglenook's iron dog grate.

'That's something else Calum fixed,' I said, 'He got central heating installed. The electric kind, with storage heaters. They take in half-price electricity during the night. Any other kind is inconvenient. Out here in the sticks gas has to be ordered, and stored in ugly tanks. Same for oil.'

'Well, he used his head, then — or was that you?'

I shrugged stiff shoulders. I watched impassively as Sian balled up the red fleece and flung it at a chair. Her hand came up, covered her mouth. She stood there for a long moment, staring as the fleece uncurled and slid onto the floor. Then with a shuddering sigh she let her hand drop. When she looked at me her haunted blue eyes were welling with unshed tears.

She shook her head, angrily, and swung on her heel.

'I'll see to that coffee.'

I followed her through. A switch clicked and the kitchen was filled with white light. Sian filled the kettle, went to the cupboard and began rattling crockery. I crossed to the sink, stared out of the window. Light was spilling out, the wet stone flags shining in the rain. Away to the left, my stone toy-soldier workshop was on the very edge of the pool of light. The Vauxhall Astra was a gleaming blue shape under the oak tree. Once a family saloon, now a hearse.

I turned away. The kettle was singing. Sian had spooned instant coffee into cups and was staring broodingly at nothing. I wandered into the adjoining office and looked at the shiny new computer system; checked that there were no messages on the answering machine; looked at the invoices, orders and notes on the desk, neatly sorted by Calum.

And all the while I was only half-seeing,

half-aware of where I was and what I was doing, because it was impossible to forget the object in my pocket that was cold and wet against my thigh, how it had got into that condition, and what it meant.

'Jack.'

The coffee was in china cups and saucers on the pine table, black and steaming. Sian was reaching into another cupboard for a bottle. The top squeaked as she unscrewed it. She poured liberally. Brandy slopped into her saucer. She sat down, dipped a finger into the spilled spirit, tasted it, closed her eyes.

'Romero was right; returning to the UK has solved nothing.'

She looked at me blankly. 'What?'

'We spent time with your sister, we're home now and convinced we made the right decision, so the mild dilemma we were facing in Gibraltar has been solved. But the other, the serious business — Rickman, Wise, that Creeny bloke lurking like a Hollywood gangster — they're not going to go away.'

'You really think this' — Sian nodded her blonde head towards the window — 'is their doing? Isn't that you being a bit paranoid?'

'No, it's not. You know this cannot be coincidence. And you know you're being defensive, backing away from unpalatable facts.'

'Probably. But that poor girl out there in the boot of that car gives me a damn good reason. For just about the first time in my life I'm feeling scared stiff.'

'I can understand that.' I hesitated. 'Rickman has to be behind this gruesome business. We didn't come straight here, so it looks as if he's been following our movements ever since we left Gib — and that's creepy.'

'The age of technology. Calum traced Pru through her website.'

'But only Calum knew we were visiting Siobhan. The only way Rickman could have known that is if he had us followed from the airport. But even if he'd had us watched for a week he couldn't possibly know we were coming here today.'

'So it's back to my earlier doubts. For a start, why would Rickman murder Pru? Or have her murdered?'

I sighed. 'I don't know. But stepping back in time, we have Pru Wise coming to see us in Gibraltar. She told a convincing tale of accidental involvement in intrigue on board Rickman's yacht, and claimed she'd later been threatened with bodily harm by Rickman's wife. Then we're taken aboard that same yacht and threatened by Rickman. A week later Pru Wise is as good as dumped on our bloody doorstep, as dead as a doornail.'

'Yes, it all sounds clear cut; everything slots neatly into place. Rickman's behind it and that's that. But while you seem utterly convinced it's Rickman, I'm willing to consider other possibilities. Why? There's something you're not telling me, isn't there?'

Sian was watching me closely. I avoided her eyes, looked down, slowly sipped my coffee.

'How did she die?'

'I don't know. I opened the boot, took the . . . I don't know.'

But I'd been unable to prevent a slip of the tongue, and Sian didn't miss much.

'Took the . . . what? What was it you took?'

I put the cup down and reached into my pocket.

'D'you know what this is?'

I held the object between finger and thumb. It was tiny and plump, glistening with the slimy sheen of a garden slug. Sian pulled a face.

'Something wet and soggy and not very nice. Furry. A . . . toy. Is that what it is?'

'It's a souvenir.'

'From?'

'Someone's holiday, usually, but not this time. It's got spring arms so it can be attached to something. The stem of a table lamp. The edge of a curtain. It would look quite realistic, because that's what they do in the wild. Or in sanctuaries. Cling to trees, the eucalyptus kind, or to their mothers.'

'Oh, Jesus Christ,' Sian said, and again drink slopped into her saucer as her hand came up to cover her mouth. 'Jack, it's a bloody koala.'

'Yes, it is.'

'Where was it?'

'Whoever murdered Prudence Wise,' I said, 'wedged this cuddly little object in her open mouth.'

9

'How long has she been dead?'

'You keep asking me questions I can't possibly answer.'

'All right, then look at it this way,' Sian said. 'That . . . thing, that koala, it was in Pru's mouth. Put there — as we no doubt both agree — by that Aussie bastard who calls himself Clontarf. But the koala's wet, Jack. Slippery. So if that's saliva . . . '

She took a deep breath, shuddered, almost knocked her chair over as she stood up and stumbled with her cup to the sink. She threw away the coffee, returned to the table and splashed brandy into the cup. Lifted it to her lips. Drank deeply.

'Sian — '

'Shut up. Listen. If that thing is wet with saliva, then . . . well, you tell me, you're the sleuth. How long after a person dies does it take for the body's fluids to begin to dry? Especially those in the mouth, when it's wide open and it's blocked with — '

'I don't know. Or, I know as much or as little as you. We're both army trained. So if we don't know the answer with all that expertise behind us, then we call in someone who either does, or can find out.'

'Alun.'

'Yes. We have to call the police anyway, and Alun Morgan's the local cop. But he's also a friend, and in your state you need somebody who will be efficient but compassionate.'

'My state?' Sian's laugh was harsh. 'Then get it done, Jack. Call the local detective inspector. I'll sit here and get well and truly pissed. Now, that really will be a state.'

★ ★ ★

DI Alun Morgan of Bethesda was the proud owner of a Volvo Estate so old that its rear number plate was usually lost behind a cloud of blue exhaust fumes. Illegal, the dour Welshman would say, but if a policeman couldn't break the law then what the hell was the point in joining the force. Spoken tongue in cheek, I always believed, but the imp of mischief that forever lurked in the detective's dark eyes meant that, until proof was forthcoming, listeners were inclined to take whatever he said with several grains of salt.

In my voice when I telephoned there must have been echoes of a funeral bell darkly tolling that advised Morgan to choose more reliable transport, and possibly a driver

105

guaranteed to get him to his destination. And so, twenty minutes after my call, it was a police Land Rover with headlights blazing that rocked across the bridge, roared up the slope into the yard and slid to a halt alongside the Vauxhall Astra.

The detective was stamping his feet, scrubbing the soles of his black police-issue shoes on the outside mat and brushing rain from his dark hair when I went to let him in. The living room lights had been switched off, and Morgan preceded me through to the kitchen where Sian was still sitting at the table. Pink-cheeked, her demeanour maudlin but her blue eyes remarkably clear, she looked up and managed a wan smile.

'Hello Alun.'

'Well now, that's not what I was expecting,' Morgan said, the Welsh lilt in his voice like music to my ears. 'After a year away I was expecting a warm embrace, but I suppose, in the circumstances — '

'Can't manage it,' Sian said. 'Probably fall down if I stood up. Jack will tell you why.'

'He's done that already over the phone, though not in detail,' Morgan said. He pulled out a chair, sat down. 'A body, isn't it?' he said, still talking to Sian. 'In that car out there. And this person who has died, she was no stranger to you.'

'We got to know her briefly in Gibraltar. Her name is — was Prudence Wise. I suppose the car's hers, although — '

'That's being checked now,' Morgan said. 'In the age of the computer, my uniformed colleague will have the owner's name within minutes. It will take a while longer for the doctor on duty to get here, for he lives some way away and was having an early night, bless him. So,' he said, casting a sidelong glance at the bottle next to Sian's cup, 'as there's some waiting to be done . . . '

'I'll pour,' I said.

'It would be best,' Morgan said, 'to dilute it with coffee.'

'And a couple of butter shortbreads so the drink isn't being taken on an empty stomach?'

'There now,' Morgan said, grinning at Sian, 'isn't that thoughtful of him?'

'Not really. The best we can manage is cheap custard creams.'

'Picked up from a garage on your way here, no doubt. When was that, by the way? I mean, when did you get here? If I know that it will at least tell me when the body was discovered.'

'Jack?'

I looked at my watch. 'It would have been just before nine when I opened the boot.'

107

'And you took which route from Liverpool?'

'The M56 from Runcorn, through Queensferry to the A55, followed that to Abergele, then Llangernyw, Llanrwst and on to Betws-y-Coed and the A5.'

Morgan was making notes. 'Not important, any of this, but it always helps if I have a clear picture in my mind.'

There was a discreet tapping on the living room door, and a uniformed constable came through, cap in hand, wet jacket glistening.

'The car's owner, sir,' he said, and handed Morgan a slip of paper.

'Thank you, Ellis,' the DI said. 'The wonders of modern technology.' He unfolded the paper, gave what was written on it a fleeting glance, then turned to Jack and said, 'Did you lock the Astra?'

'I'm sure I did.'

'If you have the keys, Ellis here can hand them to Dr Barnard when he arrives so that he can do the necessary.'

I had dropped them on the coffee table. I went through to the living room, handed the keys to the constable and let him out, then returned to the kitchen. Morgan was sipping his coffee with relish, but looked reflective. His hand was resting lightly on the paper, which he'd turned face down.

'Does the name ring bells? Are you any the wiser now you have it?'

The dark eyes looked thoughtfully at me.

'You mean is he or she a known criminal? Well, no, and so I'm more confused than anything.'

'When Alun read the name,' Sian said, 'he looked at me. I wonder why?'

'It was a perfectly natural reaction,' Morgan said. 'That Astra out there is your car, Sian. But you know that, of course.'

'That's ridiculous.'

'I'd like to think so, otherwise everything becomes complicated and distasteful. But according to what PC Ellis discovered, you registered it in your name, with this place as your home address, exactly one week ago to the day.'

10

Two hours later the police surgeon had come and gone, and an ambulance had taken away the body. The Astra had been covered with a tarpaulin and fenced off with police tape tied to the oak tree and various fence posts. It would be winched onto a low loader in the morning. PC Ellis, after standing close to DI Morgan in the rain and listening carefully to what he had to say, had driven off alone in the police Land Rover. Morgan, Sian and I had moved into the living room. Though it was cosy and probably much too warm — in that hour I had lit the fire, and flames from crackling logs were flickering and dancing in the dog grate — the atmosphere was stiff and uncomfortable.

'You see,' Morgan said, looking pensively into the fire, 'until this is sorted out one way or another, I have to treat you as a suspect. That being the case, I don't give you information; it's the other way around.'

Sian, sitting on the edge of the Chesterfield, shook her head in frustration.

'All I asked was how long has she been dead.'

'Impossible to tell until the post mortem.'

'Then if you want information from me, I'll repeat what I've already said. We flew in from Gibraltar a week ago, yes, but it's not my car, Alun. I've got a Shogun parked behind the house. Calum's been looking after it for me. Why the hell would I need a bloody Astra?'

'Then you're insisting that you travelled from Liverpool, with Jack, in that powerful rally car he runs on public roads?'

'Yes. How many more times must I tell you?'

Morgan sighed, let his gaze drift searchingly from Sian to me.

'As far as I can tell, you've both been honest and open. To put it another way, you're sticking to your story — which could mean something else entirely. But, summing up, there were various goings on during your last day in Gibraltar, you spent a week at Sian's sister's house and this evening you came here and discovered the Astra and the body in the boot. You've handed over that horrible little creature you found in that poor girl's mouth and told me it could link the crime to an Australian going by the name of Clontarf. But now I need to know more.'

'There is no more,' I said.

'There's always something, and anyway I'm talking about this end, not Gibraltar. Nowadays DNA can prove guilt but, as you know, it can also prove innocence. So if Sian has never been inside that car — '

'I have. I slid in, grabbed the steering wheel, looked in the glove compartment.'

'That's a pity. Your fingerprints will be all over the place. Be nasty if they're the only ones there.'

The glare from Sian drew no comment.

'I got into the back seat,' I said. 'I also opened the boot.'

'Jack, Jack,' Morgan said chidingly, 'surely you both know — '

'It was a car, Alun, not a crime scene. It didn't become a crime scene until I found Pru.'

The DI had taken off his jacket. His white shirt was dazzling in the room's soft lighting. He sat back in his deep armchair and shook his head.

'So, moving on, you found her, and we know from our medical expert that Prudence Wise died from strangulation. Is that some-thing you noticed?'

'She was wearing a high-necked sweater. I couldn't see her throat.'

'Her eyes would have given some indica-tion — '

'They were looking at me. They were very dead. I felt sick, closed the boot in a hurry.'

'Understandable, Jack. I also like the symbolic

act of making the whole affair a closed book, if you want an analogy. Shutting the boot marks the end of it, as far as you're concerned.'

'If only.'

'Well, ignoring for the moment the question of the car's ownership, there's absolutely no need for you to be involved. The body was discovered here, in Wales, and so the investigation will be in the hands of the North Wales police. That koala sounds like a genuine link to the Australian, Clontarf, so I'll pass the information to your friend DI Romero in Gibraltar. If this Charlie Wise is in Spain, then getting news of his daughter's death to him is up to the Spanish police. As for the suspected jewel thief, Karl Creeny, well, nothing has changed. The hunt for him began in Liverpool and was being led by your other police friends, Mike Haggard and Willie Vine. Then that girl Pru took her photographs, and no doubt when Creeny discovered what had happened he quickly went to ground.'

'Good for him, but it still leaves us exposed. Sian in particular.'

'Meaning what, exactly?'

'What if the people who are almost certainly responsible for Pru's murder don't consider our involvement in the affair at an end?'

'Rickman? His bully boys? Why shouldn't they?'

113

'We told you a good story, but the story was incomplete.'

'Dammit,' Morgan said, 'why am I not surprised?'

It was Sian who answered. She was now stretched out on the Chesterfield, and had been quiet for a while.

'Without going into details, I can tell you that one bit we left out of our story was that we were threatened,' she said. 'Also, if Clontarf murdered Pru Wise, he's likely to be here, not in Gibraltar. And there must be a reason for the body being dumped here, on Jack's property.'

'That being?'

'I don't know.'

There was a lull in the conversation. It was late. The police constable had taken the Land Rover away because I had offered to drive Alun Morgan the short distance to his home on the outskirts of Bethesda. The rain had ceased. Outside, all was quiet. Inside that hot living room, three weary people were gathering their thoughts, trying to make sense out of the bizarre.

I dropped into a chair, kicked off my shoes.

'No more questions, Alun?'

'Not just now.'

'Then it's a lecture?'

'And not before time.'

'Something you've been thinking about?'

'Well, not recently. It's more a reawakening, if you like, of past concerns that have come bubbling to the surface with your return.'

'Okay, then let me guess. You're our friend, Alun, but we have a professional connection too, and that's crime investigation.'

'Professional on my side, yes. On yours, it's strictly amateur.'

'But is that the problem?'

'It's been a concern. For a long time. After all, we first met when Gwynfryn Pritchard came rattling across your bridge in his Land Rover with the belief that his wife had not drowned, but had been murdered — and that was some years ago. Ever since then I've believed that you treat such investigations in a cavalier manner. And I've worked out why that is.'

'Cavalier it may be, but we get results,' Sian said.

'You go in blind, hoping for the best, and more by good luck than anything else.'

'We solve the crime. Is that what you've worked out? We're blasé because we know luck's on our side?'

'You're two misfits.'

Sian raised her eyebrows at me. 'I'm not sure if that's an insult, or a compliment. I quite like not conforming. Anyway, I think I see what he's getting at.'

'Army barmy,' I said. 'That's what he's saying.'

'Army conditioned,' Morgan corrected. 'Weren't you both very young when you enlisted?'

'I was fifteen,' I said. 'Sian — '

'Seventeen.'

'And, all right, neither of you stayed in for the full twenty-two years, but in my opinion you served long enough to make your return to civvy street feel like stepping onto the surface of Mars.'

'Mm. There's a lot of truth in that,' I said.

'Look at it this way,' Morgan said. 'Someone in their forties or fifties gets picked up by a giant hand and, without any training, is dropped into army life. How would they cope?'

'With great difficulty,' Sian said. 'Or not at all.'

'There you are then. You were a couple of squaddies, and a giant hand picked you up and deposited you on those mean streets out there. And before too long, there you are, strutting in that cavalier manner after hardened criminals as if you're God's gift because that's the way soldiers think of themselves — '

His mobile phone interrupted him. The ring tone was a sea shanty, and I wondered at the detective's choice. If we were misfits, what life was it this earnest Welshman was yearning after?

Morgan had picked up his jacket, walked away from the seating around the coffee table and was facing the wall covered with packed bookshelves as he took the call. He paced, spoke little, listened intently then closed the call with a curt 'Thank you' and stood for a moment in silence before returning to his chair.

'Good news?' Sian asked.

'The usual answer to that is, "it all depends".'

'On whose side you're on,' I said.

'Exactly. That call was from PC Ellis. I asked you which route you took getting here so that he could begin sorting information from CCTV cameras along the way.'

'Wouldn't that take weeks?' Sian said.

'If all the cameras were checked it would take some time, yes. But there was no need for that. Your Audi Quattro was picked up by the camera on the A55 near the marble church at Bodelwyddan. That same camera also picked up the blue Vauxhall Astra. It was one hour ahead of you. The driver had blonde hair. Almost certainly a woman.'

'Was it now?' I said softly.

'Has to be Françoise Rickman,' Sian said. 'She was the one who threatened Pru.'

'And now she's over here with Clontarf.' I nodded. 'I remember you saying he was the more dangerous of those two men.'

'Well, at least we have a genuine name to play around with,' Alun said. 'I'll inform everyone concerned; the woman's name will be flagged at ports and airports and we might just get lucky.' He hesitated. 'I can see how you come to all these conclusions, you're both very credible. But are they genuine, or are you trying to pull the wool over my eyes?'

'I don't like that look,' I said, 'and I don't like the tone. What's up, Alun?'

'You came along in your rally car an hour after the Astra. The camera was quite clear. Excellent picture.' Morgan paused. 'You were alone in the car, Jack.'

'Rubbish. Sian was with me.'

'You were driving,' Morgan said, 'no doubt about that. But the passenger seat in that Audi Quattro was empty. Empty, I suggest, because Sian was one hour ahead of you driving the Vauxhall Astra we already know is registered in her name.'

11

'Don't leave town.'

'What?'

'That's what Alun Morgan said. It was a condition he made for unlocking my shackles and opening the cell door.'

'You, or both of us? Not to leave town, I mean?'

'I'm the one who's suspected of driving that Astra; they couldn't see me in your car because I was lying down.'

'Listening to a proposal of marriage.'

She smiled fleetingly. 'Yes, well, you're not under suspicion because you were recorded on camera. Although, as you're my known associate, you're not completely in the clear. But that's all. They've got nothing against you.'

'Nor you. Nothing concrete anyway, or they wouldn't have let you go.'

'Ah, well now, that's where the plot thickens.'

It was noon on the day following the discovery of Prudence Wise's body. Because Alun Morgan was a friend he had reluctantly — at risk to his career prospects, the ageing detective inspector had suggested, tongue in cheek — allowed Sian to spend the night at Bryn Aur. However, a telephone call soon after breakfast had invited her to the police station — Alun Morgan's front room — to make a statement and hear the strength of the evidence against her, and she had driven down the A5 in her Mitsubishi Shogun.

I had watched her go then crossed the yard, opened up the workshops and spent the morning familiarizing myself with all that I had left behind when we moved to Gibraltar. The whole toy soldier business known as Magna Carta had been in the capable hands of Calum Wick. Although Wick painted toy soldiers for me in his first-floor flat overlooking the River Mersey in Liverpool's Grassendale area — and was involved in dodgy business interests with our mutual scally friend Stan Jones — for the past twelve months he had spent at least half of each week in North Wales.

And couldn't be faulted, I'd decided after an hour or so inspecting new castings, checking clipboards hung on hooks from shelves where ranks of soldiers, ordered by regular business customers in the States, stood ready for painting, and looking with feelings of intense pride at glossy soldiers tissue-wrapped in red boxes ready for dispatch.

Then I sat down at a bench and started on work that had become urgent after my twelve months away: the creation of a new line of figures which I would sculpt from scratch, using various spare legs, arms, heads and weapons and the essential epoxy resin that could be moulded and left to harden like stone.

Later in the morning I went back to the house and prepared ham sandwiches, thick with mustard, and a large flask of coffee. I was back in the workshop with lunch ready on one of the benches when the Shogun roared at speed over the bridge and up the slope and rocked to a halt beneath the big oak tree.

'Have a sandwich,' I said.

'Actually, I was expecting a warm, welcoming kiss.'

'Prisoners recently released find that sex after a long period of celibacy can be — '

'Exhilarating?'

'Exhausting. And be careful how you eat the sandwich; too much rich food when you've been used to a prison diet can — '

'Shut up.'

'I've also heard that, for those held in isolation, socializing can be a considerable problem — '

'Jack!'

I grinned. 'All right, then tell me why they let you go.'

'Because they found that there was good reason to be interested in not two cars, but three.'

Sian took a bite out of a sandwich, grimaced as the mustard started a fire in her mouth, and reached for the flask.

'Careful, that's also hot.'

'But wet.'

'Yes. You know, I'd thought about another car,' I said. 'The blonde who dumped the Astra had to make a getaway, and it's a long walk from Bryn Aur to civilization.' I watched her splash coffee into a mug, and pushed mine over for a refill. 'But how did the police home in on one particular car, and connect it to the crime?'

'CCTV cameras again. They looked at a few more. They came up with pictures of the Astra at several locations on its way through Wales. Each time it was caught, there was a silver Audi close behind.'

'That's not enough to raise suspicions, surely? In bad weather, at night, cars will often stay close so that those following the unlucky leader can relax.'

'Number plates lead to the owners, as we discovered to my cost, and this Audi is owned by a well-known Liverpool villain who's been

122

in and out of jail since his teens. Also,' Sian said through a mouthful of ham sandwich, 'there were two men in the following Audi. Those cameras are good. Alun's men were able to tell that the passenger had fair hair, and was wearing a hat with a wide brim. Which confirms what that horrible little koala had already told us.'

I nodded. 'Which brings us to poor Pru. On the face of it, her murder seems pointless. But that's because we think like law-abiding citizens. In the world where men like Rickman and Creeny operate, if Charlie's gone into hiding with the diamonds then an excellent way of bringing him to the surface would be to kill his daughter.'

'Well,' Sian said, 'in my opinion it was Karl Creeny who came up with the idea of doing that — drawing Charlie out by killing his daughter. And I'm sure it will work.'

'And now we come to the bit that doesn't make sense.'

'Why here?'

'Exactly. Why dump Pru's body here? And why go through that elaborate procedure of registering a car in your name, which is what they must have done?'

'That's bad enough, but what's really creepy is that someone must have been watching us ever since we stepped off the plane. Otherwise how could they possibly arrange for the body to be dumped here just an hour before we arrived?'

'I'm not so much concerned about the how, as the why. It was dumped here and we're being targeted — but for what reason? What can they possibly have against us? They were upset by our half-hour chat with Pru Wise? They didn't like our handing her laptop over to Luis Romero? I think that's nonsense. And if it was neither of those things then I have to go back a bit further for the reason — and that brings me to my mother's accident.'

Sian looked startled. She was standing up, brushing crumbs from her jeans. She stopped, stared at me, then leaned against the bench with her coffee.

'Yes, but, hang on a minute, I know Eleanor's your mother but surely we're now talking about unrelated crimes. The attack on Eleanor has nothing to do with us. Surely that's somebody choosing a horrible way to get at poor old Reg. Or am I being monumentally stupid?'

My empty mug was on the bench. I used my finger in the handle to rotate it on the worn timber. I stared into space, lost in thought.

'Well, Reg is certainly a wheeler dealer,' I said at last. 'The money involved in his little

. . . ventures . . . is surely not chicken feed, and I'm quite sure he's capable of dodgy tactics. If he's trodden on someone's toes, it's reasonable to believe they'd hit back in a way that issues a severe warning.'

'And yet,' Sian said, 'it still leaves a big question unanswered. A blonde woman pushed your mother down the steps by the American War Memorial on Line Wall Road. A blonde woman drove a blue Vauxhall Astra into North Wales. The same woman? Or not?'

'If we rule out my pet hate of coincidence, then yes, it has to be. And in that case, however far-fetched it may sound, then everything must be connected. But how? Eleanor was pushed. Then Charlie Wise steals Creeny's diamonds. Sian, I think I'm going bonkers, because the timing of those events makes any link impossible.'

12

'Some of the whys are easily explained, laddie,' Calum said, a Scotsman in Wales deliberately exaggerating the brogue. 'The body was deposited on your territory so that when Charlie and his wife hear about it, and surface, they'll come here. When they do, the hunters will be close behind. That means you and Sian are in danger.'

'It's been a week since Pru was murdered,' I said. 'So far, not a sausage.'

Wick chuckled. 'Very well put, but can you not see? They're making you wait. Cranking up the nerves. Softening you up so that when the blow comes you'll offer little more than a whimper of protest before capitulating.'

'I could put up with an indefinite wait if we knew what was going on, where Sian and I fit in.'

'Or your mother's broken leg, if it comes to that. From what you've told me the sequence of those events makes any connection wildly improbable.'

'So we wait for the blow to fall, and at that point realization will dawn on us,' I said, and tossed a warding file noisily onto the bench.

'Small consolation, wouldn't you say, if we're drawing our last, dying breath?'

Wick was still smiling, taking none of it too seriously. His teeth were a sparkling white in the depths of his salt-and-pepper beard.

The light was reflected from his glasses so that his dark eyes were hidden.

His Mercedes was parked under the oak. He'd driven from Liverpool then straight through the nearest car wash and the Merc was black and gleaming in the autumn sun. And he was right about jangling nerves. After seven days of puzzling over an insoluble problem while waiting for the roof to fall in, I'd cracked, and in the evening had rested my weary head on Sian's bosom. Not for the first time, but definitely for a different reason. She'd patted my head without sympathy, and told me to snap out of it. Or summon some male company.

Calum had arrived as we were finishing breakfast, and dumped his overnight bag in the spare bedroom. We'd shared a cup of coffee with Sian before she tootled off in the Shogun, heading for the nearest gymnasium with Nautilus machines, then crossed the yard to the workshop. Now Calum was at one bench, working on unfinished toy soldier castings, using snips and a sharp knife to cut bits of unwanted metal from glittering Black

Watch Highlanders. I was at another, putting the finishing touches to an original of a 95th Rifleman I had sculpted from scratch. It was almost ready for the next process. The original would be encased in fast-setting silicone rubber, and from the resulting mould a hard metal master figure would be cast.

'This fellow, Creeny,' Calum said, squinting across at me through his stained John Lennon specs. 'Stan the Van did some digging in the gutters. That man moved to Liverpool from Scotland; he's a Glaswegian of the very worst kind. Bemoans the passing of the cut-throat razor. Frequently used one himself when he was, as it were, carving out an underworld empire.'

'So the threats to alter Pru's face were delivered by Françoise Rickman, but came from Creeny.'

'Of course. He'd masterminded a robbery, sneaked into Gib and was suddenly exposed by that wee slip of a girl.'

'Then got blind-sided. Charlie Wise nipped in, stole the diamonds and vanished in several puffs of smoke from a Kalashnikov's muzzle.'

I looked towards the window, at the oak moving gently in the mild breeze, and said softly, 'I wonder where Creeny is now, if he's made it back to the UK, if he's mustered his troops.'

But Calum was pushing his lean frame back from the bench and uncoiling, his ears tuned elsewhere.

'I wonder if, like me,' he said, 'you've been listening to the purr of a distant vehicle which faded as it hit the valley floor but has suddenly become much louder.'

'If it's Creeny,' I said as we made for the door, 'the battle will be like something from a Stephen King novel up there in the backwoods of Maine. Three middle-aged men facing each other across a sunlit yard, armed with tin snips, a file and a cut-throat razor.'

Despite the sun, the air was chill. The breeze ruffled my hair. Calum moved away towards the oak tree. Determined to protect his Mercedes? A cunning outflanking man-oeuvre? I grinned absently, walked along the stone front of the workshop and so nearer to the house. As I did so I realized I'd left my file on the bench. Unarmed, I faced the approaching hordes driving up the slope from the stone bridge in their war wagon: a red Nissan Micra.

For one horrible moment I recalled the transport Prudence Wise had driven from Gibraltar into Spain and thought she'd come back from the dead. Then the Micra pulled to a halt. Alongside Calum's Mercedes it appeared to diminish in size. Calum was watching from the other side of his car, arms folded on the roof. Like me he'd seen the Micra's occupants, and relaxed.

The little car's doors swung open. A man and a woman slid out awkwardly, straightened with difficulty, looked across at me with faces lined with recent tragedy.

In the circumstances, it didn't need a detective of any kind to work out who had finally come calling.

★　★　★

It was as if they had stepped down from their yacht in the Mediterranean — soon afterwards riddled with bullets — and landed in my slate-floored, black-beamed living room without time passing or distance being crossed. They were suntanned, dressed for hotter climes, and I'd swear I could smell warm salt air and a whiff of Ambre Solaire sun oil. Pru had mentioned togs by Gucci, Versace and Jimmy Choo, and while I'm no fashion expert I could recognize style, and imagine the cost. Summer togs. Mediterranean, any-time togs. Unsuitable for a North Wales autumn.

The introductions had been done as we clustered in the yard. We'd shaken hands, remarked on their journey and the weather. Then the visitors, turning blue, had made a break for the house.

They were both well into their sixties. Charlie was about five nine, overweight and balding, and had a rust and red patterned snood tucked into his open-necked shirt, a gold ring in his left ear. Adele was tall and still willow-slim, with long fair hair bleached a streaky blonde by her years in the sun. A simple flowered sun dress exposed tanned shoulders. She'd slipped on a wrap that must have cost the earth, but Bryn Aur's new central heating was doing nothing to ease her shivering.

She was standing with her back to the inglenook, hugging herself for warmth, and she turned as Calum came through with a wooden tray laden with drinks and a couple of bottles and placed it on the coffee table. Charlie had dropped onto the Chesterfield and looked exhausted, but wasn't too far gone to grab a glass of whisky and knock it back in one go.

'Needed that,' he said.

'But it's not your usual tipple, darling.'

'Close.' He grinned wanly at me.

'He's most particular,' Adele said. 'Always drinks Laphroaig Quarter Cask single malt Islay Scotch whisky — '

'Or whatever local brew's on special offer. Do me a favour, darling, cut the crap. We're

131

broke; our daughter's dead.'

Calum threw himself into a chair and stretched out, ankles crossed. I had been standing by the window with the bright sun at my back. Now I crossed to a free armchair, picking up a drink on the way.

'I am so sorry for your loss,' I said.

Charlie shrugged, clearly wanting his grief to remain at the back of his mind where it had been dumped. Adele looked down into her drink and registered sorrow with a sniff.

'We flew in today, from Spain,' Charlie said. 'Came straight here instead of to the cops because we're mystified. Can't see where you fit in, why you were the chosen ones.'

'Before getting to that, how did you find us?' I shook my head. 'No, what I mean is how did you connect my name to Prudence?'

He looked at me as if I was thick. 'Brit newspapers. We get 'em in Spain.'

'Yes, but — '

'Yeah, yeah, it's been more than a week. So we get them, but not every day.'

'And they're days old anyway,' Adele said. 'I read them now and then, and he only reads the sport.'

'You do know police from Gibraltar and Spain are looking for you?'

Charlie nodded. 'Not working too hard at it, though, not making it a priority. No crime's been committed. Just a couple of ancient Brits have gone missing. And I'll guarantee Rickman's already recovered his boat.'

'That's true, but you must surely understand,' I said, 'that this happened to Prudence because of . . . of what you did?'

Charlie stared. 'But that's a load of bollocks. You saying Rickman killed her because I got tired of carrying drugs and illegals across the Med?'

'On the night you sailed,' I said, 'he sent two men after you. With guns.'

'We did hear some shooting from afar, didn't make any connection,' Adele said, both hands wrapped around her empty glass. 'By that time our friends had got us very close to Tarifa.'

'That's where you went ashore?'

'Oh yes. All planned in advance. Even the villa we were renting — '

'Ignore that,' Charlie said. 'I'm not ashamed to say I'm skint. For villa, read tatty one-bed terrace in a town still in the Middle Ages.'

'As you are, darling,' Adele said sweetly. 'Just.'

'Anyway,' Charlie went on, 'what I'm saying is Rickman wouldn't commit murder just because I called his bluff.'

'Cross purposes is a phrase that springs to

133

mind,' Calum said, stirring from his repose just enough to place his glass on the tray. 'Something like that, anyway, but we're certainly reading from different pages. So tell us, Charlie, what's with the bluff and how did you call it?'

'By goin'.' He looked at Calum, back at me. 'Rickman warned me, but I took no notice. I was workin' for him, and now I'm not. If he doesn't like that, well, tough titty.'

'Is that what you think this is about?'

'Yeah, well . . . what else?'

'Stolen diamonds,' I suggested.

'What fuckin' diamonds?'

I looked at Adele. 'You told me you read the papers; you must have seen the story.'

'Now and then, I said — and no, I didn't.'

'Charlie,' I said, 'who dreamed up that photo shoot aboard *Sea Wind?*'

'Rickman. He's the ultimate poser. He was wettin' himself at the idea.'

'And you didn't know Karl Creeny was going to be there?'

'Couldn't, could I. I've never heard of him.'

'Well, I find that hard to believe, and from the look on her face so does Adele.'

'Just get to the point, if there is one,' said Charlie, irritably.

'The diamonds I'm talking about are the ones recently stolen by Karl Creeny from a

134

Liverpool diamond merchant. The ones that were carried to Gibraltar by one of Creeny's men. Now very dead. As you know. Because that's how you got your hands on them, and that's why you planned that elaborate disappearance.'

Charlie's mouth fell open. He went pale beneath his tan. Adele wobbled. Her empty glass hit the rug in front of the dog grate, and rolled. She dropped to the Chesterfield alongside Charlie, and grabbed his hand.

'Where in God's name,' Charlie croaked, 'did you get that idea?'

'From Bernie Rickman. He took us aboard *Sea Wind* and threatened us in your absence. He's convinced you stole Creeny's jewels. That's why he sent armed men after you. And that's why it didn't end there, as you thought it might. We're pretty sure Prudence was murdered by people working for Rickman, One's an Australian going by the name of Clontarf.'

I looked questioningly at Charlie. He shook his head.

'Okay, well, the others were a Liverpool crook, and Françoise Rickman.'

Charlie swore softly. 'Christ, I might've known that cow'd be involved,' he said.

'We believe your daughter was killed to draw you out of hiding,' I said quietly. 'If we're right, it's worked a treat.'

'Bloody has, hasn't it?' Charlie said.

'And there'd be no point doing it unless a careful watch is then kept to see if the suckers walk into the trap.'

'Right. So they must be out there now, somewhere in those fuckin' hills, blokes with guns just waiting for us to turn up.'

There was horror in his voice, and Adele winced as, in his despair, Charlie's grip on her hand tightened like a vice.

13

'I didn't steal the diamonds,' Charlie said.

'We didn't even know there'd been a robbery,' Adele said huskily, 'let alone that someone was bringing the diamonds to Gib.'

She was still clinging to Charlie's hand. When she'd dropped down beside him it was as if her legs had given way. It was Adele's collapse more than Charlie's desperate denial that was planting doubt in my mind. They looked genuinely shocked, and that shock was making them look their age. Middle-aged jewel thieves? I couldn't see it.

'But you must have heard about the robbery. It was on television.'

'Come on, Jack, the first you heard of it was from Reg,' Calum pointed out. 'Not everybody watches the box.'

'Dead right,' Charlie said. 'And we were busy, weren't we, planning the great escape. That took time, ingenuity and a lot of courage.' He looked proudly at Adele. 'Just like all those years ago, eh? It took guts to get from the daily grind producing poxy bathroom tissues to living the life of Riley on the Med, so we knew we had it in us.'

Adele seemed to soften at the memories. She'd released Charlie's hand, and her eyes were distant.

'One day we were slaves to industry,' she said, 'the next we'd retired. We toasted our freedom with foaming glasses of Krug Grande Cuvée champagne, spent the rest of that same night loading up our black BMW X5 SUV.'

'God, yes,' Charlie said. 'Pru was at uni, so there was nothing holding us. Made do with a couple of snatched hours of sleep, then headed south with thumping heads and bleary eyes. And it was two fingers to Spain's sprawling, crowded holiday Costas, I tell you. Went like an arrow for the Rock of Gibraltar. British, a tax haven, which is always handy, and as a bonus it's basking in the Mediterranean sun. Crossed the airport's sun-baked runway, booked in at the Rock Hotel and settled down to plan the next move.'

'You hadn't thought further ahead than that?' I said quietly, fascinated by the story and what it said about the man telling it.

'Well, sort of,' Charlie said. 'It was a no-brainer, really, because from the moment we crossed the channel we'd been chasing a very special dream.' He chuckled. 'The way I saw it, an overpriced apartment in one of the white blocks soaring from all that reclaimed land in Gib would have been like going from rat-race to mouse-hole. So we bought a boat, a small one but big enough to live on, and then . . . '

He trailed off. Adele's posture had once again become stiff with tension for, like Charlie's, her thoughts had raced ahead from memories of their own small boat to the big one that had come at a hell of a price. A price which had eventually become too much to handle.

'Going all that way overland,' I said, 'was a strange decision.'

Charlie shook his head. 'Absolutely not. It's like all those motor homes you see nowadays. People love 'em because of the freedom. And it's not just the fact that you really can go where you like, stop when you like, it's that indescribable feeling you get . . . ' He shrugged, at a loss for words. 'I'd do that trip again,' he said finally. 'Do it tomorrow.'

'Aye, well,' Calum said, 'the courage it took could come in handy just now, because unless my ears are deceiving me there is a car getting closer by the second.' He didn't move when he looked at me, but there was a new tenseness in his lean frame.

'Oh, Jesus Christ,' Charlie said. Pressing her face to his shoulder, Adele whimpered like an animal in pain.

I crossed to the window, listened to the purr of the approaching vehicle.

'It's all right, it's the Shogun.'

I heard Calum explaining what that meant as I watched Sian's big 4x4 rock up into the yard and pull to a stop by the Micra. She got out, stared at yet another strange car, then glanced with a frown towards the house. I gave her a wave. She nodded, and I turned away.

'Even if you didn't steal the jewels,' I said, 'you're still in deep trouble.'

'Like, trapped, you mean?' Charlie said, surprisingly astute.

'Let's just say that coming in was easy; going out could be more difficult.'

Even Charlie smiled at that. Colour was returning to his face. Adele bent to recover her glass, then splashed whisky into it from the bottle on the tray. Footsteps sounded on the hallway's tiled floor. The door clicked open and Sian swept in. She was flushed from her work with weights. Her tied-back damp hair suggested fifty or so lengths of the pool. She wore her red fleece draped like a shawl over a pale yellow T-shirt. Quick as a flash her blue eyes took in the newcomers. They switched to Calum — who nodded at her unspoken question — then she padded across the Indian rug to Charlie.

'Sian Laidlaw,' she said, holding out her hand. 'I'm here to save you.'

Charlie and Adele shook hands, consternation mingling with bewilderment, putting blank looks on their faces.

'I've spotted the men watching the house,' Sian explained. 'They're up on the hillside, about half a mile from here. You know the spot, Jack. They're using binoculars, but being very careless with them in this bright sun. The lenses are flashing like a bloody heliograph.'

'So with them up there, how do we get out?' Charlie said.

'The easy answer is, don't bother,' Calum said. 'Stay here until they run out of food and water, make a break for it when they head for the shops.'

Sian shook her head. 'They've been out there waiting for Charlie and Adele to show up, so it can only be a matter of time before they storm the house.'

'Then we think fast, and outwit them,' I said.

'Easy for you to say,' Charlie said. 'What brain I've got left has gone numb.'

'Try subterfuge,' Calum said, uncoiling from his chair, yawning, and stretching his long arms towards the black beams.

'Eh?'

'Leave here in disguise. Or rather, don't leave here, but look as if you are because people who look like you are away like the wind in your wee car.'

'That's excellent,' Sian said. She'd been in the kitchen and was back swigging long draughts from a tall glass of water. 'Also, it will work a treat because there's rain coming and those people who are not Charlie and Adele can throw jackets or something over their heads. Their faces will be hidden, without in any way looking suspicious.'

'Problem is,' I said, 'that when those people who are not Charlie and Adele leave they'll be followed by those armed men up there on the hill who think they are, and will be in the trouble meant for — '

'Charlie and Adele,' Calum said. 'However, trouble for gallant amateur detectives would be all in a day's work, and taken in their stride.'

'You three,' Charlie said, 'are completely bonkers.'

'Not at all.' Calum stroked his beard, poked at his glasses. I thought he looked a bit embarrassed. 'We tend to laugh and joke a lot out of habit,' he went on, 'which can be a wee bit off-putting to strangers. But today I think we've all got a special reason. We're so sorry for your loss, but rather than get maudlin, lightening the mood seems like a much better idea.'

For a moment there was silence. Then Charlie gestured helplessly.

'Yeah . . . and thanks for that,' he said gruffly. Adele made some kind of appreciative sound, but her eyes were damp and she was again looking into her glass.

'Anyway,' Calum said, working his shoulders to ease the tension, 'to keep the light-hearted bit going but append to it a serious note, I think the idea of Jack and Sian rushing out of here wearing your clothes is not only hilarious, but workable.'

'The biter bit,' I said. 'Rickman's mob used a murder to draw you here; we use cunning to draw them away. And once they're on our tails, you leap into Calum's Mercedes and head for . . . well, where would they go, Sian?'

'Calum's flat in Liverpool?' She looked at the lanky Scot. 'You've got a spare room, Calum, so what d'you say?'

'It cannot be used.' Calum shook his head. 'Hell, didn't Rickman mention my name when he threatened you? If he knows that, he'll surely know where I live.'

'Okay, well, as we've decided on Liverpool I've got a better idea,' I said. 'Eleanor lives in Gib, but she's kept her flat in Booker Avenue, and I've got a set of keys.'

Sian frowned. 'But won't Rickman have that address in his notes?'

'No. He knows Eleanor lives in Gibraltar, and he won't have looked beyond her bungalow.'

'Yes, all right, that sounds like an excellent bolt hole,' Sian said, a twinkle in her eyes, 'but do you really trust Charlie and Adele?'

'Calum will take them there, with a week's supplies,' I said, deadpan, 'and lock them in.'

'But if we don't move fast it'll be too damn late,' Calum said. He grinned at Charlie. 'That was another example of their weak jokes, as you've no doubt guessed, but I think it's time you all rushed upstairs and changed clothes.'

And so we did, Sian and I had plenty of spare jeans and sweaters that were roughly the right size for our two visitors. I wore Charlie's shirt — we were both wearing jeans, so didn't need to swap — and Sian slipped Adele's dress on over her T-shirt and jeans. The rain Sian forecast had already come sweeping in along the valley and was hissing through the big oak and turning the yard's stone flags to cold grey mirrors. Visibility from the mountain's slopes would be severely restricted. Looking through misted binoculars and sheets of fine rain the watchers would spot bits of shirt and quick flashes of the

144

brightly-coloured dress, and draw the wrong conclusions.

Downstairs again, I said, 'If I've got this right there's a rough track leading to their lookout position. In theory they could watch us leave here, race down and cut us off. But I think we're safe enough; in this weather and on those slopes they'd need four wheel drive to manage that.'

'And with me driving,' Sian said, 'we'll be ahead of them at the main road.'

'We'll head for Bethesda. You never know, we could reach Alun Morgan's cosy police station before they catch us.'

'Good thinking. Right, are we ready?'

The keys to Eleanor's flat were on a hook in the office. I told Calum where they were. He nodded, and went through to get them.

Charlie said, 'And you'll need these.'

He threw the Micra's keys to me. It crossed my mind then that we hadn't thought further than the switch of clothing, and the Wises' getaway. We'd have their hired car. If we survived the next half hour, our next task would be to take it to Liverpool. After that, well, to me another trip to Gibraltar seemed inevitable . . .

Then Sian and I were at the front door. In the porch we both grabbed waxed Barbour jackets from pegs. When we ran out into wind-blown rain smelling of cold wet heather they were over our heads but not completely hiding our borrowed clothing. Indeed, we lingered over opening the car, keeping our heads hidden but making sure the watchers got a good eyeful of the rest. Then, already soaked around the nether regions, we ducked into the Micra and slammed the doors.

'You realize this could all be for nought, a waste of effort?' Sian said as she gunned the little car down the slope over the bridge and onto the road running alongside the Afon Ogwen. 'Those folk on the mountain could have been farmers with shotguns, after rabbits, or lost hikers looking for the way home.'

'But we know they weren't,' I said, gazing in dismay at the wet slopes, 'because that surely has to be the bad lads in that Land Rover rocking and rolling down the track to our left. Two of 'em in there, as far as I can make out.'

'Damn, they heard all about the mountains and the rain and brought a suitable vehicle.'

'Yes, and if you don't put your little clog down they really will cut us off at the pass.'

Stones and wet gravel flew into the air like grapeshot as Sian pushed the accelerator to the floor. The front wheels spun, gripped, and we took off. Almost literally. Never more than ten yards from the river, the road that would take us up to the A5 was a trail of potholes held together by patches of tarmac. We spent a considerable time airborne. Our seat belts prevented us from crashing through the windscreen in a shower of glass. My fingers hooked on the underside of my seat stopped my head from breaking through the roof. Sian had the steering wheel to hang on to, but she was smiling and leaning back in her seat with the relaxed confidence of a rally driver.

We jolted past the track coming down from the mountain with no more than twenty yards to spare. I reached up and pulled down the sun visor. Through the vanity mirror I saw the Land Rover hit bottom and bounce. In mid-air, the driver spun the wheel to the left. When they touched down, the front wheels gripped while the back end slid on the gravel. The rear wheels hit the wet grass sloping down to the rushing water. Then the four-wheel drive took over and pulled them clear.

'That's some driving.'

'Clontarf,' Sian said, eyes flicking to the mirror. 'Thinks he's on a dirt track in Queensland, chasing bloody kangaroos.'

A quarter of a mile ahead the road did a sharp right turn into a steep up-slope. At the top there was a dry-stone wall, with an opening onto the main road. In the hair-raising seconds it took us to reach that turn the Land Rover was up close enough to nudge the Micra's bumper. In my vanity mirror I could see Clontarf grinning through the windscreen behind the wide sweep of the wipers. He could see my eyes watching him. He lifted a hand, sliced his finger across his throat.

'I wonder what Crocodile Dundee will do,' I said quickly, 'when he realizes he's been tricked, that Charlie and Adele have slipped through his fingers.'

'Not a damn thing, because I'm going to make it to Alun's place.'

'Sublime confidence in the face of overwhelming odds.'

'Why, how many are in that Land Rover.'

'Can't see. I know there were two.'

'Then we're not outnumbered. And if the other one's that useless thug Ebenholz . . . '

The turn loomed. Sian hit it at fifty. The car slewed as if on ice. She fought the wheel, used the heel of her hand to change down to third, accelerated hard up the hill. In the mirror I could see billowing blue smoke from the burning rubber. Then I closed my eyes. She went through the hole in the wall onto the London to Holyhead main road without looking right, and spun the wheel hard left. On the smooth wet tarmac the Micra slid sideways onto the wrong side of the road. Down a gear she went, into second, and with a howl of protest the little car shot back across the road. Just in time. A camper van coming up from the coast rocked to a screeching halt, horn blaring, the woman driver's eyes like saucers.

'Goodness me,' Sian said mildly, and I looked at her innocent expression and started laughing.

Two hundred yards later I was still chuckling uncontrollably when she fiercely banged my shoulder with her fist.

'Here we go.'

There was a roaring in my ears. For a moment I was disorientated. Were we being buzzed by one of the low-flying jets from RAF Valley on Anglesey? Then the Land Rover drew level with us. Too close. At fifty miles an hour on a not very wide road the vehicles touched with a squeal of tortured metal. The big one leaned on us. Sian hissed like a snake, said something rude and forced the Micra to lean back. Then Clontarf changed tactics. He accelerated and looked as if he would complete the overtaking manoeuvre he'd begun. Instead, with half the Land Rover past us, he simply slowed down again and began cutting across Sian's path.

There was a way out. Sian found it. We were down to a crawling twenty miles an hour when she slammed on the brakes. The Micra stood on its nose. Clontarf was caught out. The Land Rover pulled ahead before he could react. Sian dropped to first, spun the wheel right, banged on the accelerator and pulled out to overtake. The small engine's revs were up in the red as it drove the lowest gear. There was a high-pitched howl, the reek of hot oil. Then we were past the now stationary Land Rover and pulling back into the left lane as a fast Ford Mondeo came up the hill with horn blaring and headlights flashing.

But we were still a long way from that homely police station and our friendly detective inspector. This time Clontarf didn't pull punches. Half a mile further on down the hill he brought the heavy Land Rover roaring up behind us. Without slowing down, the big 4x4 slammed into the Micra's rear off-side wing. The impact knocked the little car so far off line it almost rolled. Sian held it by wrenching a hard right lock, but momentum defeated her. She swore as there was a horrible crunch of metal and the tinkle of breaking glass. Then, with a teeth-on-edge grating we juddered to a halt, the nearside front wing crumpled against the jagged stone wall. We were sticking out at forty-five degrees, the Micra's boot on the road's centre line.

My ears were ringing. Sian was biting her lip, looking in the mirror while unclipping her seat belt. There was the flat sound of someone running: Clontarf was coming fast around the Land Rover to my side of the car. Then something rapped so hard on my window the glass starred. When I looked, the muzzle of his Glock 19 was glaring at me like an evil black eye.

'What d'you reckon?' Sian said. 'Sit here until hell freezes, or open the window to see what he wants?'

'Neither holds much attraction,' I said, and reached across to press the button.

The window slid down at its own pace. A gust of wind drove cold rain into the car. Then Clontarf was peering in.

'Christ,' he said, 'it's Scott of Gibraltar and the karate kid.'

Then he rammed the cold muzzle of the Glock into my ear and bared his white teeth in a grin that reminded me of a hungry shark.

'Where are they?'

'I honestly don't know,' I said, and eased my head away from the Glock. Clontarf shook his head, tutted, and grabbed me by

Charlie's colourful collar.

'Not a good move, not a good answer,' he said. 'How about you, darling, you got more sense than this feller?'

'I have, actually,' Sian said, and turned to smile sweetly at him.

'Yeah, and that's not exactly the answer I wanted either,' he said, and he turned and spat into the road. 'I'm getting soaked out here, so let's hurry this up. Charlie Wise and that Sheila of his swapped clothes with you two, and you led me a dance. My guess is they waited a while, then piled into that big Mercedes with your oppo and set off at great speed in the opposite direction. Doesn't take a genius to work out they're making for Liverpool. So it's back to the question, slightly rephrased: we all know where they are now, but what I need to know is where they're going.'

'A long speech,' I said, 'for the same short answer: I don't — ' The strong hand moved up and grabbed my hair. The cold muzzle twisted further into my ear, and I winced, clenched my teeth.

'You've got ten seconds,' Clontarf said, 'then the karate kid gets blood and brains all over her borrowed dress.'

And then we all heard the patter of many feet splashing down the hill and a strange and breathless voice from Sian's side of the Micra called, 'Is everything all right here? Anybody hurt?'

Clontarf eased back. The Glock disappeared. He straightened, and moved away from the window. Around the middle-aged man who had spoken several men and women in running kit were bouncing on the spot, jogging up and down the road or doing stretching exercises in the rain as they waited for their friend. He was steaming in the cold, wet hair stringy, bare legs beneath running shorts streaked with mud.

'I was just asking these people the same question,' Clontarf said. 'They're fine, so — '

'Hit them from behind, did you? Understandable in this weather, but doesn't give you a leg to stand on, does it? Unless they're not bothered, but with that damage — '

Sian's window whizzed down. 'It's a hired car. It's their insurance so we couldn't care less,' she said, 'and we're certainly not going to get this poor man into trouble.'

The wet runner had a moustache that was drooping in the rain. He grinned at Sian, looked across the car at Clontarf.

'Lucky you, eh? The best you can do now is jump in your motor and buzz off smartish. Scrape the blue paint off your bumper. Plead ignorance, if questioned. We'll help separate this wreck from the wall and check the damage.'

He waited.

I said, 'That's very good of you.'

Then I looked innocently at Clontarf.

Rain was dripping from his bush hat. His teeth were bared in what could have been a friendly smile but was more likely to be a silent snarl of frustration. There was nothing he could do. He'd ended up surrounded by steaming members of a local athletics club out on a training run — Runners in The Rain, The March Hares or some such — and the only luck to come his way was bad.

He gave me a stare from hard blue eyes that held a clear promise. I thought of General Douglas MacArthur's words when he left the Philippine Islands, and I knew that Clontarf was telling me he'd be back. Then he splashed away through the rain, the door of the Land Rover slammed and the runners scattered as the angry Australian did a three-point-turn at racing speed and drove back up the A5.

'Notice anything?' Sian said.

'We're still alive.'

'Clontarf was alone.'

'No. I definitely saw two men — '

'Look,' the moustachioed runner said, watching cold wet runners taking off in ones

154

and twos and vanishing downhill in the spray, 'we can help if you're desperate, but you'd better speak up or there'll be just me left.'

'We're fine,' Sian said, and to prove it she started the Micra and gave the engine a couple of blips. Then, for emphasis, she pulled away from the wall with a scraping and a tinkling that made the runner screw his face in anguish.

'Right then.'

'Thank you for stopping.' Sian smiled. 'I know it sounds dramatic, but you saved our lives.'

'I — ' He frowned, looked at the wall, looked at the car, looked at Sian and in utter bewilderment said, 'Yes, well . . . '

And he was off, a middle-aged jogger some fifty yards off the pace and with a conundrum to work out.

'Turn now,' I said, 'while the road's empty.'

'I thought we were going to see Alun?'

'There were two men in that Land Rover — '

'No, Jack, not when Clontarf drove off.'

'I believe you. I'm talking about earlier. The second man must have rolled out when they were coming down that track. There could be only one reason for them splitting up, and that's why we're going back to the house.'

The explanation was unnecessary. As soon as I mentioned the second man's fast exit

Sian was into a three-point turn that made Clontarf's look like something executed by a learner driver on his first day. And the road was no longer deserted. Cars coming up and down with windscreen wipers flapping slowed and beeped horns or flashed lights, and as we raced away and Sian waved a hand airily out of the open window I saw heads turning to look at the gouges in the stone wall and scattered fragments of headlight glass shining in the rain.

Sian took the Micra up to sixty, then seventy. I was waiting for a wheel to fall off, or something filled with petrol to explode and finish what Clontarf hadn't managed. Sian, arms as straight and as twitchy as a Formula One driver's, kept casting glances to the right of the road looking for the opening in the wall that led to the road down to the river, and home.

She said, 'Was the other man Ebenholz?'

'Don't know. They were bouncing down that track; the second man was just a vague shape.'

'Well, we were posing as Charlie and Adele, so he would have made for the house hoping to catch the real us with our pants down.'

'As it were. And, yes, he would have done that, on foot. But if it is Ebenholz, he'll be fast. Also, if he stays on the road by the river he'll be in the right place to wreck our clever plans. Calum doesn't know him, hasn't seen him. If a stranger stood in the middle of the track waving the Mercedes down, Calum would be forced to stop.'

'And with Ebenholz brandishing that Heckler and Koch it'd be all over. Damn, damn, damn.'

'Yes. He'd see Charlie and Adele with Calum and know at once how we'd worked it. He'd take them back to the house.'

'Where Clontarf,' Sian said, 'will very soon join him — '

'Whoa, whoa, we're there,' I yelled.

Sian slammed on the brakes. We slid on the wet road, sort of sideways, which pointed the Micra's damaged nose where Sian wanted it. Once again, without looking anywhere except where she was going, she accelerated across the road, bounced through the opening in the wall and suddenly we were careering down the stony slope.

'You lead a charmed life,' I said, opening my eyes.

'Long may it continue.' She flashed me a look. 'But isn't going back to the house pushing our luck? Surely a better idea would have been to go to Alun's and get backup?'

'If it was just Charlie and Adele, yes, but Calum's involved.'

'Ah, yes.'

She was quiet for a moment. The car rattled and bounced. Afon Ogwen, already swollen by water rushing down from the heights, was a fierce roar that could be heard above the whine of the engine.

'You're still in third.'

'Better that way, unless you want to end up in the river. I'm thinking hard, wondering what lies in wait for us.'

'If Calum *was* stopped by Ebenholz, they'll all be at the house. If he got past Ebenholz . . . well, who knows? Ebenholz must have seen the Merc. If he couldn't stop it he'd have watched to see which way it went, then waited for the Land Rover so he and Clontarf could give chase. In that case they'll be hot on Calum's tail and we'll have the house to ourselves. Or perhaps Clontarf got back in time to see Calum turn up the hill, and went after the Merc on his own.'

'Leaving Ebenholz stranded, in which case, again, he probably went for the house,' Sian said. 'Well, we'll soon know,' and she twitched the wheel to take the turn onto the stone bridge, bounced, then roared up the slope into Bryn Aur's yard.

She pulled to a halt alongside her Shogun. Beyond the big silver 4x4 there was a space where the Nissan Micra we were in had been parked, then my Audi Quattro.

'The Merc's not here,' I said.

'Nor is the Land Rover.'

'So . . . ?'

'I don't like it.'

'Don't blame you. It's a repeat of the other night, isn't it?' I said. 'We got here in darkness and rain. That strange blue Astra was parked where we are now. You said something about nosy strangers, and I suggested they were lurking in the dark living room waiting to waylay us. They weren't then, but now . . . '

'Yes,' Sian said, 'but before we find out the hard way I'm going to look behind the house.'

'Excellent idea.' I clicked open my door. 'Stay there and keep your eyes skinned.'

'Hey, hang on — '

But I was already out and jogging across the yard to the side of the house furthest from my stone workshop, closest to the porch and front door. The wind had dropped; the rain had eased to a fine drizzle. Watching the house, fully expecting the front door to burst open and a man with a gun come charging out, I slipped on the wet stone and almost fell. Then I was around the side of the house and on the gravel incline that led to what would have been a back yard or garden if there'd been room. But this was an old farmhouse in North Wales — hill country. It backed onto sheer rock that had been eroded by centuries of water cascading down from the high peaks. Between the house and the cliff face there was a space some six yards wide. We had left the cars there, under covers, while we were in Gibraltar. It stretched for the full length of the building. Underfoot was solid rock. On it a shed, a couple of bins, lots of empty flower pots, some sacks of compost.

But no Land Rover, and no Mercedes.

I walked back to the car, slid in, sat with my legs out in the drizzle and dug out my mobile phone.

'Not there?'

'No. All clear. Which means Calum made it and is on his way to Liverpool with Charlie and Adele.'

'And is almost certainly being followed.'

I nodded, clicked the speed dial, listening to Calum's phone ringing far away in the snug interior of the Mercedes.

'Yes, Charlie?'

'Ha,' I said, 'very funny, but that subterfuge worked well and is now over. However, if there's a green Land Rover behind you, with a damaged front bumper, you could be in trouble.'

'It's been there for a while. Two men. One blonde, suntanned; one black and hairless.'

'Where are you?'

'Through Queensferry, approaching the M56, which is bathed in brilliant sunshine.'

'Clontarf and his pal know you're heading for Liverpool.'

'Of course. But not the exact location, and I will endeavour to make sure it stays that way.'

'Well, you're in a Merc, they're in a 4 x 4, so on the motorway you should lose them.'

'Aye, in normal circumstances, but traffic's heavy and slow. Looks like roadworks ahead, or an accident, so there's very little chance of zipping down the fast lane.'

'So how will you work it?'

'If they're still with me when I hit the metropolis I'll simply cruise around to the Admiral Street cop shop and introduce them to Mike Haggard and Willie Vine.'

I chuckled. 'Tell Charlie his hired car is looking the worse for wear. We'll bring it in tonight, and see you all at Eleanor's.'

I clicked off, told Sian the situation.

She grinned, 'Trust Calum to think of that way out. Knowing him, he'll get Haggard to take the Wises round to Eleanor's in a police car.' She clicked open her door and got out. 'Anyway, I'm going in, I'll change out of these ridiculous clothes and make a hot drink.'

'Be with you in a minute, I've one more call to make.'

'Yes,' Sian said, poking her head back in and giving me a knowing look, 'and when you do come in I'll tell you who you phoned, and what you said — word for word.'

The door clunked shut. She walked away, blonde hair shining, looked back and pulled a face. I waved, dialled, again listened to a distant phone ringing.

'Eleanor,' I said, 'how's the leg?'

'All white and crinkly.'

'And that's the plaster?'

She chuckled. 'Yeah, but inside it the leg'll be headin' that way.'

'And heading that way is what Charlie and Adele Wise are now doing. Gibraltar's probably all abuzz about the mystery of their whereabouts, so you'll be pleased to know they'll very soon be in your Liverpool flat.'

'Bloody hell. Are you off your rocker?'

'Not at all. And talking of rockers, where are you now?'

'At home. Reg was getting on my nerves. For some reason he's all uptight. And, as it happens, I haven't got a rocker.'

'And even if you had you couldn't use it, because you're moving out.'

'Am I?'

'Yes, you're going back to Reg.'

'Oh, and why am I doing that?'

'Because we need somewhere to stay.'

'Who's we?'

'Well, there's me, my bride-to-be — '

'Bloody hell, you always were a polished bugger. Go on then, you've finally asked her to marry you, and you're saying she's said yes?'

'Not exactly.'

'And what exactly does that mean?'

'We were in a speeding car, rain sweeping across the Welsh hills, and Sian had just woken up. We both wanted clear heads in a romantic setting, a crackling log fire in the inglenook, warm lights, soft music — '

'And a couple of stiff drinks for courage — but you said clear heads, so that wouldn't do, would it?'

'No, but preferable to what we did get.'

'And what was that.'

'To put it bluntly, what we got was a stiff.'

'Oh, God, Jack, that's bloody awful. Are you talking about that young girl you met in the Eliott? It was in the papers, but I was too sickened to look at the details.'

'Yes, and there's really no other way I can put this. She'd been stuffed into the boot of a car, she was dead and cold and . . . well, you can see why talk of wedding bells was put on hold.'

'Sadly, yes, I can, but I still think you could've phrased that more delicately for your fragile mother.' Eleanor sighed. 'But if you're coming back to Gib, why my house? If you're after a really romantic location, what's wrong with the boat?'

'It's up for sale — ownership passed to me when everybody else faded away, and I placed it with an agent before we left Gib. Didn't I tell you? A big chunk of the proceeds will go to needy causes. I know of an ex-pat Liverpool pensioner with silver hair who's living in penury in a run-down shack in one of Britain's overseas territories — '

'God, you do go on.'

'Mm. But it's a nice thought, isn't it, all that lolly? Anyway, another reason for us staying in your bungalow is that a certain Bernie Rickman's gin palace is moored close to Tim's canoe, and he's almost certainly involved in another murder we're . . . well, investigating.'

'No need to be shy; Reg has been telling me all about Rickman and this feller Creeny. So the other murder you're . . . well, investigatin', wouldn't by any chance be linked to a recent jewel robbery?'

'Mm, well, yes it could be.'

'God, listen to Mr Uncertainty. Okay and as there's likely to be blokes comin' after you with guns and those brass things they put on their fists I suppose that bearded, brainless

164

Scotsman will be coming with you to hold your hand?'

'He thinks the world of you, too, Eleanor,' I said, with a smile in my voice. 'And I'm so glad I phoned. I didn't really have a plan — still haven't — but bringing Calum into the mix is a terrific idea. What the three of us did to Ronnie Skaill and family is still in the news, and our being back on the Rock will send shivers down several crooked spines that are already tinged with yellow.'

Part Two

14

'I have been talking frequently on the telephone to DI Haggard in Liverpool,' Luis Romero said. 'He in turn talks to Alun Morgan in North Wales, and from those conversations I have learned a great deal. For example, I was under the impression that you are still a suspect.'

'Not really,' Sian said. 'That was a crook concocting a crafty plot aimed at achieving something or other we haven't yet worked out. I told DI Morgan where I'd be for the next week or so, and he was happy to let me go.'

'That's good,' Romero said, 'but I thought also that both of you would be needed as witnesses at the inquest into the death of Prudence Wise?'

'Her parents are there,' I said, 'and as Sian just pointed out, if they need us they know where we are.'

Romero smiled. 'A rather cavalier attitude, Jack, wouldn't you say?'

I grinned. 'That's what I am, a cavalier.'

'Buccaneer,' Sian said.

'Buccaneer my arse. He's nothing but a damn mountebank, and a Sassenach to boot,' Romero said, then opened wide, innocent eyes as I looked at him in amazement. 'I have not slipped a cog,' he said, 'I am merely paraphrasing your wonderful friend Calum Wick. Incidentally, I thought he was coming with you?'

↝ 'That was the plan suggested by Eleanor,' I said, 'but the canny Scot decided it was unsafe to leave Charlie and Adele Wise alone in the big city.'

'Their city, surely?'

'Yes, but with non-indigenous villains lurking. It's easy to predict what home-grown crooks will get up to; not so easy when said crooks come from cultures on opposite sides of the globe.'

'Can a globe have sides?' Romero said.

'Well, there's the inside, and — '

'The outside, yes, of course.' Romero nodded, but his mind had moved on. 'You do realize that those of my investigations which might concern you here in Gibraltar are at an end. Charlie Wise and his wife are no longer missing. The boat they abandoned in the straits caused no damage to any third party, and has been recovered by its owner. Charlie and his wife could be accused of . . . I don't know, reckless driving?' — he looked amused — 'or of actions likely to endanger international shipping, but I'm quite sure that won't happen.'

'There's still the body at the airport,' I said. 'And surely you're working closely with the Merseyside Police in their efforts to locate those stolen jewels?'

'And Karl Creeny.' Romero nodded. His eyes had turned cold, and the atmosphere of relaxed good humour that had prevailed since the three of us got together faded away like early morning mist under a searing sun.

An apt simile, I thought. Through the wide windows of Eleanor's double-fronted bungalow high up the Rock's slopes I could see dazzling sunlight sparkling on the waters of Gibraltar Bay, the white houses and sand-coloured business premises in distant Algeciras softened by the heat haze. It was 10.30 in the morning and too soon for the sun to reach the Rock's west-facing slopes, but the temperature in the room was still comfortably warm compared to what might be expected at this time of year in my farmhouse in North Wales.

Until Romero's last words. Mention of Creeny's name had reminded me of why we had returned to Gibraltar, and suddenly there was an unwelcome chill in the air.

'I don't know about Creeny,' I said, 'but when we left Gibraltar your words were ringing in my ears. You told me in North Wales I'd be well out of it, but it didn't turn out that way. Prudence Wise's body was dumped in my front yard. Because a couple of blokes called Clontarf and Ebenholz, and quite possibly Rickman's wife, Françoise, were involved, we know Bernie Rickman must have ordered that girl's death. Charlie and Adele want us to bring the killer to justice. We'd do it anyway — that's really why we're here.'

Romero frowned. 'Do it anyway? But why? Because you have got into the habit? Because you cannot leave well alone?'

'Is that what you call it, leaving well alone? Far from it, I'd say, because not a damn thing's been settled to anyone's satisfaction. Besides, we liked that young woman, and we don't like being used.'

Astute as ever, Romero smiled crookedly.

'But there is more, of course.'

'Oh yes. The Wises also want us to clear their names: in your office we all reached the conclusion that they had stolen those jewels, but we were wrong.'

'You cannot be sure of that.'

'No.' I nodded acceptance. 'I understand that, and so we're back to keeping on keeping on: we all know that the only way of getting to the truth is by finding the real thief.'

'Who, I am quite sure, is enmeshed in a tangled web of intrigue and murder, which will be difficult and dangerous for you to unravel,' Romero said.

'There you are then,' Sian said, 'a perfect case for the deadly duo.'

She was curled up in a chair, looking tired. Three-hour jet lag? I was standing near one of the windows watching Romero. He wore his usual dark suit, but the jacket was open, his shirt startlingly white in the reflected sunlight. He was sitting opposite Sian, legs crossed, one glossy black shoe jiggling up and down.

'I have heard your story of what happened in North Wales,' the DI said, 'and of course your friends in the Merseyside Police are anxious to interview those two men, Ebenholz, and Clontarf. But — forgive me — up to now it is just an unsubstantiated story. The murder is fact, of course, but if my information is correct you actually came face to face only with Clontarf. He threatened you and Sian, you survived and saw no more of him. As for Ebenholz and Françoise Rickman, you believe they were in North Wales, but really that is pure speculation.'

'Surely provable,' I said, 'by a quick glance at lists of passengers flying out of Gibraltar?'

Romero shrugged. 'In the woman's case, possibly, though not absolutely certain. Her husband dislikes working within the law, so perhaps she slipped under the radar.' He shrugged, smiled a little at the term he had used. 'As for the other two, do you really think that those ridiculous names are genuine?'

'Clontarf is a Sydney suburb, so I'd guess he adopted that. Ebenholz? No, I think both are names are assumed. To know the real ones we'd need to look at their passports.'

'Which is impossible. Those men have vanished. Also, you will forget about chasing jewel thieves and attempting to solve murders. I do not want you under my feet, or treading on my toes.'

'We will act circumspectly,' I said. 'Do nothing drastic, leave justice unperverted, your toes unbruised — '

'Meaning he'll go charging in at the deep end, as per usual,' Sian said happily. 'And if I'm right, that means strolling down to the marina for a quiet chat with Bernie Rickman.'

I shot her a look. 'Is that a plan?'

She smiled. 'I thought we might ask him bluntly if, actually, it was he who stole those diamonds.'

'Damn, now there's an original idea,' I said. 'Have you been working on that theory?'

'Behind these limpid blue eyes,' Sian said, 'a razor-sharp mind never rests.'

Romero eased out of his chair and stood buttoning his jacket.

'You are both crazy, intent on acting with

great foolishness,' he said, 'but alas, despite my strong words I can do little to stop you. In your absence Rickman was questioned about Creeny's presence on his boat. He was apologetic, expressed ignorance, and as the bird has flown we had no option but to walk away, leave him alone. As for the other, the young woman's murder and what followed, well, we have only your word for the presence in North Wales of those three people. There is no way we can connect Rickman to that killing unless further proof comes from your Alun Morgan, or from the Merseyside Police.'

'Or unless we get that proof for them,' Sian said.

On his way to the door Romero cast her a dark look that was filled with warning, and not a little foreboding.

'As I recall, dear lady, in your last encounter with the underworld you were badly bruised and that canny Scot finished up hanging from a fragile tree, by his fingertips, over a yawning drop. Luck held out then — for all three of you. If I were in your shoes, I would not risk pushing it too far.'

15

The flat overlooked the River Mersey and from close range, if you squinted, gave a view of smudged Welsh hills. Penthouse, actually, Françoise Rickman thought, and she surveyed the interior with the critical eye of a woman accustomed to living a life of leisure on a luxury yacht, which for most of every year was bathed in hot sunshine beating down out of the clear blue skies over Gibraltar. And when life afloat with Bernie became . . . tiresome . . . then their nearby apartment was a welcome change, and was just as luxurious as *Sea Wind*. Top floor — so, penthouse — of a tall block that was dazzling white in the sun, and overlooked the flat blue waters of Marina Quay, the sports boats with their deep sea rods swaying and the huge, floating gin palaces. Which, when she was gazing out of those panoramic top-floor windows, Françoise decided, made her the highest of the low — and her chuckle was a deep gurgle of merriment.

As far as location and climate went, this Liverpool penthouse fell short of the required standard, but it was certainly a classy joint.

And at that her chuckle became rich and smoky. She remembered asking Jack Scott if he thought she looked like a femme fatale, a gun moll, and here she was thinking like one. A classy joint indeed — but why not? If the Yanks coined a fittingly descriptive phrase, then use it, and this place with its flat smoked-glass occasional tables, white Astrakhan rugs, original watercolours and a cocktail cabinet to die for — again the dirty chuckle — was certainly of a class. And hers for a couple of weeks if she wanted it — free, gratis, courtesy of a mysterious friend of a photographer called Penny Lane. Ryan Sharkey. Gambler, dilettante, whatever — but a man who certainly knew how to choose property.

And could afford the very best. In fact, the only jarring note with the place, Françoise decided, was the company she was keeping.

Clontarf, the Australian, had his dirty boots — caked in Welsh mud — up on one of the smoked-glass tables. Blond hair as unruly as a wet haystack, he was drinking from a stubby bottle of French lager and watching Françoise with amused blue eyes. Across from him, Ebenholz was a muscular shape, his glistening head wreathed in the blue smoke from a thin cigar. A glass of whisky rested on the arm of his chair. He was as motionless as a stone carving.

'So what was the point of that car business?' Clontarf drawled. 'Registering that blue Vauxhall in the Sheila's name, what was all that about? Anything? Nothing?'

'Nuisance value,' Françoise said. 'Wouldn't stick, obviously, but putting a body in the boot of what appeared to be her car showed what we were capable of. It was turning the screw, because at the time we were pressuring Scott and Laidlaw. They were useful then, now they're not.' She shrugged.

'Because of one phone call?'

Françoise jumped, startled as always on those rare occasions when Ebenholz opened his mouth to speak. His voice was deep — Arthur Prysock always sprang to mind, a jazz singer whose voice seemed to come from the soles of his boots.

'Yes,' she said, licking spilled gin from the back of her hand with the tip of her tongue.

'Which you're still keeping close to your . . . chest?' Ebenholz said, watching her.

Clontarf chuckled.

'Fuck off, both of you,' Françoise said, and smiled sweetly.

'I wasn't being suggestive,' Ebenholz said.

'I wasn't suggesting you were, merely that you're both working for me, not the other way around.'

'Can't work at all, darl, if you insist on

keeping secrets,' Clontarf said.

'*Private Eye* calls Rupert Murdoch The Dirty Digger,' Françoise said reflectively. 'A countryman of yours, isn't he?'

'What, and you're saying that's a fitting name for me, that we're all the same?'

'Under the skin, yes. And that was from Kipling, in case you're wondering. *The Colonel's Lady and Judy O'Grady*, sisters — '

'The skin'll be from a sheep if you tuck into some of Banjo Paterson's outpourings,' Clontarf said, grinning. 'But before this discussion gets entirely out of hand, how about giving us the good news?'

'Thanks to the phone call, I have an address where you will find an unsuspecting Charlie and Adele Wise,' Françoise said.

'Good on you.'

'Even better news is I'm getting out of here. Bernie misses me, so I'm going back to Gib. A woman with a passport identifying her as Fanny Roberts will leave Manchester for Malaga. She will hire a taxi to the Spanish border and will cross into Gibraltar as Françoise Rickman, returning refreshed from a few days' holiday at a friend's villa in Andalucia.'

'The scarlet fuckin' pimple,' Clontarf said, amazed. 'They seek her here, they seek her there, they seek that Sheila — '

'With you gone,' Ebenholz said, 'we do what, exactly?'

'Well, as I found Charlie for you — '

'An anonymous someone in Gib found Charlie,' Clontarf said. 'He told Bernie, Bernie phoned you — '

'I found Charlie and his wife,' Françoise said, glaring, 'now you take the two of them somewhere where their screams are unlikely to be heard, and you find out where they have hidden those diamonds.'

'Christ, you're a beauty,' Clontarf said softly, but the look on his lean, sun-lined face didn't quite match the words.

16

From time to time — well, actually most of the time — Sian, Calum and I talk a load of nonsense, which keeps us entertained but also serves to hide various weaknesses. Incompetence. Uncertainty. A realization that we're usually way out of our depth. Or perhaps most of the time the daft chatter is used to disguise a permanent blue funk. It always happens when we're deeply involved in the investigation of a puzzling murder case, of course, and what it boils down to is that although we may act tough on the occasions when we're hunting villains, we all understand there's always someone a lot tougher. That fact has been driven home to people as genuinely hard as Henry Cooper — though Rocky Marciano was forever the exception to the rule.

I told Sian that I would motor down to the marina on my own. I knew Clontarf and Ebenholz were still miles away, but for safety's sake (she asked whose? I said hers) I said she should either stay in the bungalow and keep the door locked, or drift on down to Reg's house on Europa Road and spend a pleasant morning chatting to the elegant lady with the wrinkled leg.

She refused.

I insisted.

The upshot being that we compromised.

She came with me, but promised she wouldn't kick anyone in the face. Which, I noted, was specific enough to leave other sensitive targets in bounds.

I parked the car we'd hired on Marina Quay where parking cars is impossible, and after a swift walk between gleaming white vessels, whose reflections shimmered in glassy blue waters rainbow-streaked with fuel oil, we clip-clopped up the gangway onto *Sea Wind*.

I'd phoned ahead. Rickman was expecting us, but not pleased. The sun had reached the marina and he invited us onto a deck over which an awning of light cotton duck billowed gently in a warm breeze. I was at once reminded of Prudence Wise and the photo session that had eventually led to her death, and it was with a feeling of unreality that I followed Sian's example and sank into pink and lemon dimpled cushions soft and deep enough to fold about my ears.

Rickman was in shorts and T-shirt and pink flip flops; amber liquid in an expensive glass loose in one hand and gold bracelets clinking on both wrists. He lifted his drink, waggled it with a question in his bloodshot eyes. We both shook our heads.

'You'll notice I'm on my own today,' he said, leering at Sian, 'for the safety of my staff.'

'Those would be your hired killers,' Sian said, and Rickman raised his eyes in mock horror.

'Do me a bloody favour, darling — '

'Prudence Wise died horribly. We know Clontarf and Ebenholz were involved. They're still in the UK. And your wife was there, too.'

'So they're all under arrest, is that it? Bin clapped in irons, loaded on the tumbril, on their way to the guillotine?'

'The police are looking for them.'

'Not them, actually. They're looking for several unidentified somebodies. So if you've come all the way down here to waste my time talking a load of rubbish — '

'Actually, we're here for you to confirm something that has suddenly become blindingly obvious,' Sian said.

'We worked it out, you see,' I said. 'Everything was getting so damn complicated it was clear someone was deliberately creating confusion to hide one very simple fact. Karl Creeny was using you as a middle man, letting you into all sorts of secrets, and you couldn't believe your luck. You stole those diamonds, didn't you, Rickman?'

'Oh yeah? Then what am I doin' having Wise chased halfway across Europe?'

'Covering yourself. Wise knows he didn't steal them, so he knows somebody else must be guilty. That somebody is you, so you need to silence Charlie and his wife. When that's done you'll let Creeny know that, yes, Charlie did have the diamonds, but they slipped through his fingers and have gone missing.' I stirred in my cushion. 'Only they're not, of course. You've got them.'

'I wish. Oh, and by the way, I'm waiting on a telephone call from Liverpool. When it comes, you'll be the first to hear the good news.'

I felt a sudden chill. 'Why Liverpool?'

''Cos you're talking through your hat. Charlie Wise has the diamonds. Charlie Wise is in Liverpool.' He sipped his drink, studied me as one would study a spider about to be crushed underfoot. 'Booker Avenue location. To be exact, a nice flat in an exclusive block up there on the corner of Booker Avenue and Allerton Road. What's your ma's name again? Eleanor?'

'How did you get that address?'

Rickman tapped the side of his nose. 'Tip-off. Anonymous. Someone heard I was looking for Charlie and was happy to oblige.'

'And this phone call from Liverpool?'

'Yeah, that'll be Clontarf, one of my 'hired killers', letting me know everything's under control.' He glared at Sian, and the shake of his head expressed disbelief. 'Ruffians I'll grant you, darling, a couple of rough diamonds would be an appropriate term in the circumstances, but calling them killers is a load of bollocks.'

'As is Charlie Wise having those diamonds,' Sian said.

'And round and round we go; you say yes, I say no. Which gets us nowhere, and if you remember, it was you two supposed to be finding Charlie and his woman for me.'

'Yes, well as it turned out, they found us. And it was refreshing to meet somebody who was telling the truth.'

It was a pointless conversation that looked likely to go on indefinitely, but I was concerned about the situation in Liverpool. I flashed Sian a quick glance. She wriggled her way out of the enveloping cushions, and was taking her mobile phone out of the cloth bag she carried slung from her shoulder as she stood up and walked out into the blazing sun.

'What's Reg Fitz-Norton done to upset you?'

Rickman frowned. I'd caught him off balance. He dragged his eyes away from Sian, who by now was talking on her phone, and shook his head absently.

'This and that. Wormed his way in on a deal, worked some financial black magic, walked away leaving others with burnt fingers.'

'So your lovely wife broke Eleanor's leg?'

'Your ma looked the wrong way, tripped, and fell down some hard steps. Maybe Reg sees it as something more than an accident.' He shrugged. 'Can please himself, can't he, but either way the uncertainty'll make him think twice.'

'You don't know Reg. One way or another, he'll make you pay dear for hurting the woman he loves.'

'Oh, yeah? What'll he do, hit me with his diplomatic bag?'

I fought my way out of my seat and looked for Sian. She was outside, hair glinting golden in the brilliant light, her back to the rail as she spoke into the phone.

Rickman tossed back the remains of his drink with a sharp twist of the wrist. He seemed to have forgotten all about us, and I heard him calling to someone as he walked away from me. There was a reply, muffled, a male voice, but by then I'd lost interest.

I walked out into the sunshine. I could feel the heat of the decking burning through the soles of my sandals. Overhead the sky was almost white. The Rock's green slopes and cliff faces towered above the buildings away to my right, its summit an uneven line against the bluer skies to the east. I leaned on the rail and looked west across the water to the Spanish coast, thought of Charlie and Adele and what might have happened to them if Clontarf and Ebenholz had caught them aboard the Sunseeker.

And now? They'd given their hunters the slip not once, but twice. Was it third time lucky for two men I knew were cold-blooded killers? And if so, who was to blame?

An anonymous tip-off, Rickman had said. Now, who the hell could that be? Who knew where Calum had been taking Charlie and his wife? As far as I could recall, only Eleanor. But that was here, in Gibraltar, and the phone call to Rickman could have come from anywhere. Perhaps someone in Liverpool had seen Calum's black Mercedes draw into the car park, had recognized his passengers as they stepped out into the rain and hurried indoors, and reached for his phone. Or her phone, because Françoise Rickman, I reminded myself, was almost certainly still on the loose in England.

Then I shook my head, because I knew the chances of that happening, of anyone with any connection to Rickman or the murder of Prudence Wise being at that particular address at that precise time were too remote to be considered. No, someone who had it in for Charlie and Adele had learned of our plans, and had informed Rickman. And for the life of me I couldn't think how anyone could have that knowledge unless they had got it from Eleanor, either through her accidentally letting it slip or —

Sian nudged my shoulder. She'd moved along the rail and was standing cosily next to me. She leaned her head on my shoulder. I kissed her hair.

'What's all this?' I said. 'You're acting as if you haven't a care in the world.'

'I haven't, but Rickman will go ballistic when he gets the phone call from Clontarf.'

'Let me guess. When Clontarf and his pal arrived at the flat they were quickly surrounded by armed police making a lot of noise?'

'When those two arrived at the flat, if they ever did,' Sian said, 'it would have been very quiet. Calum and his charges left Eleanor's flat this morning, and a change of circumstances means they cannot go back.'

'Which means Calum fears for their safety.'

'Feared, I think, but not any more,' Sian said. She slipped the phone into her bag, and the warm breeze lifted her golden hair as I followed her towards the steep gangway. 'It sounded as if they were in a bar, enjoying a liquid lunch. I could hear music, glasses clinking, the buzz of conversation. But the person I was talking to was cool, calm and collected — the old, confident Calum Wick. 'Tell Jack to have no fear,' he said. 'Everything's under control and the next move's already worked out.''

'Which is?'

Sian looked back and grinned. 'He's allowing you three guesses. There's twenty quid on it. And that's where the confidence comes in, because he said that as you haven't a hope in hell of getting it right, you can pay him when you see him.'

17

'It hadn't occurred to me,' Calum said, 'that you had sharp underworld ears doing some listening on your behalf.'

'Some working-class people end up sailing expensive yachts on the Med by honest means,' Charlie said with a sly grin, 'others need to cut corners, bend a few rules.'

'And suddenly,' Calum said, 'you are sounding remarkably chipper. I wonder why?'

'Life goes on,' Charlie said, and he leaned across to grasp Adele's hand and give it a squeeze. 'What we both want more than anything in this world is to make that bastard Rickman pay for what he's done. We can't do that if we're crying in our beer while he's a thousand miles away working on his tan.'

'Which suggests you have a plan,' Wick said. 'However, leaving that for the moment, let me get this straight. Certain disreputable but trustworthy contacts in Toxteth warned you that a couple of oddballs were doing the rounds of pubs and clubs, asking questions?'

'Right. As in where we could be found, and it was worth a few bob to whoever came up with an address.'

Wick nodded. 'But so what? Nobody could answer those questions, because nobody knew where you were.'

'Ah, well . . . '

'Charlie, Charlie, what have you done?' Calum said. With a despairing glance towards the stained ceiling, he caught the attention of the girl in a skimpy clown's costume who was loitering nearby and signalled for another round of drinks.

It was a little after midday. They were in Jokers Wild, a club in Catherine Street just about as close as you can get to Paul McCartney's old school without actually sitting at his desk. The main room was small and low-ceilinged, boasting a semi-circular mahogany bar against a lurid matt-crimson wall. Glittering optics were backed by a huge rectangular mirror in a gilt frame. Each of half a dozen wall lights comprised three opaque glass panels bearing the same red-eyed clown, transformed into a dull gnome by the weak glow from dusty forty-watt bulbs. Tall bar stools were of red faux leather. Tables and chairs were positioned in a concentric semi-circle while, along the right hand wall, U-shaped banquettes embraced individual tables and were given some privacy by low partitions of padded red velvet — which was why Wick had ushered the Wises into one of them and sat them in the darkest corner.

Although it was the middle of an autumn day the room was a hot cocoon, trapping heat and the rattle of glasses, bursts of shrill laughter, conversation almost loud enough to drown the unmistakable cadence of the Beatles swinging into the opening bars of Penny Lane. Stan, the barman with a shiny black comb-over and the moustache of a South American gigolo, was keeping the elderly local clients happy by playing music that would bring most of the old softies to the brink of tears. But in amongst those softies, Wick knew well, there were those who would weep crocodile tears from eyes that had long ago lost all traces of humanity and were constantly looking for the main chance.

'The bloke I told,' Charlie said, 'is Adele's brother, Ron, and he's usually . . . trustworthy.'

Calum waited as the dark-haired girl arrived with their drinks, tall glasses awash on a battered tin tray. She placed it on the table with a coy curtsey, slopping more drink in the process, then minced away on her high heels — though not too far, perhaps hoping for a tip.

'I sensed a 'however' in that last remark,' Calum said.

'Yeah, well, Ron might let something slip,

accidentally like. To be honest,' Charlie said, 'Ron never could keep a secret, which is why I told him where we were staying.'

'You wanted him to spread the word?'

'In a nutshell — yes.'

'Well, that's clear enough. We can't stay in Eleanor's flat because 'trustworthy' Ron will by now have sold the required information,' Wick said. 'My flat is clearly out of bounds, because that address must have been known to Rickman's associates for some time. But apparently none of this matters, because if I'm right you have a plan.'

'Absolutely. We've been forced to make a move. And the idea that's been floating around in my mind has now become the only way forward.'

'And that is?'

'We drive to Gibraltar. In your Merc. Or at least as far as La Línea.'

'Bloody hell,' Wick said.

Charlie grinned. 'Right. Well, if a business-man in Liverpool at times needs shady contacts he can call on, the same naturally applies when he moves to sunnier climes.'

'Well I'll be damned,' Wick said. 'You know people there — in La Línea, that is — who are in the know, as it were?'

Charlie grinned, and nodded. 'The thing is, me and Adele, we didn't take those diamonds. But if, in our pursuit of Bernie Rickman, we were to stumble across them, well, that'd be a bonus — wouldn't it?'

'Ignoring the illegality of what you're hinting at, are you saying Rickman himself has those stolen baubles?'

'Why illegal? I'm talking about recovering those diamonds for the reward offered by the Liverpool jewellers: fifty thousand lovely smackers.'

'I do apologize,' Calum said, 'I had no idea.'

'No, and I've no idea if it's Rickman who's got those diamonds, but if they're sitting in a chamois leather bag in someone's bottom drawer they're as worthless as so many pebbles. To be turned into cash they've got to be off-loaded.'

'And trying that in Gibraltar would be too risky. Small town, police on the alert, most of the local villains well known and being watched.'

'Exactly. My idea,' Charlie said, 'is to talk to a scruffy feller I know in La Línea. He walks around in rags, but he's got property. So we move into one of his anonymous apartments we've used before now, get in a stock of beer, frozen paella and chips — for Adele,' he said, grinning, 'then put out feelers.'

Wick nodded slowly, sipped his lukewarm beer, and allowed the noise to wash over him as Charlie watched his reaction then went into a huddle with Adele. Wick, in his turn, wasn't quite sure what he should be feeling, though shell-shocked was probably close to the mark. He was certainly intrigued by Charlie's assertion that the cloud had a silver lining, and not a little awed by what he had done, and what he proposed. Thanks to Adele's brother's flapping tongue they were forced to move out of Eleanor's flat, yes, and so they needed safe, alternative accommodation — but surely driving more than a thousand miles through three countries to rent a scruffy flat in southern Spain was taking precautions a little too far?

Then the wry smile at his own unintentional pun was wiped off Calum's lips as Jokers Wild's door clicked open and evil blew in on the chill autumn breeze.

Wick reached across and touched Charlie's sleeve.

'In your other life in Gibraltar,' he said, 'when you no doubt mixed with various villainous individuals, did you ever come across those two chappies who are over here doing Rickman's dirty work? The ones who were getting drenched on a Welsh mountainside while watching you through binoculars, and have recently — we assume — been talking to Ron?'

'Never saw them, did we?' Charlie said.

'In Wales? No, that's true. All right, then what bothers me is that as they're hunting you there's the possibility they might have photographs. Which would enable them to recognize *you* if they saw you.'

'Doubtful,' Charlie said. 'A bit camera shy, me and Adele, and anyway, at this time tomorrow we'll be racing across Europe in a flash black Merc.'

'Indeed you will,' Wick said, 'and as I'm pretty sure those guys don't know me from Adam, we could get through the immediate crisis without loss of blood. You see, while you and Adele were canoodling away in the corner like a couple of love-sick canaries, two men of menacing demeanour walked in the door. Just now they are at the bar talking earnestly to Stan. One's black and shiny and very well muscled. The other's wearing a hat that's seen a lot of sun, and looks accustomed to wrestling crocodiles with his bare hands.'

Charlie's mouth fell open. Adele gave a little mew of fear.

Wick reached out and touched her hand reassuringly.

'Relax,' he said softly. 'It's going to be okay. Stay in the corner, the two of you. Become as one with the shadows. I'm going over to the bar to give Stan some money. I will casually engage those two beauties in conversation. When you can be sure they're otherwise engaged, slip out of this wee booth and turn yourselves into something resembling that drab wallpaper. It'll make you invisible. Then go confidently but cautiously along the wall to the entrance, and bugger off out of here.' He grinned. 'Okay?'

'Okay,' Charlie said, with an answering grin that looked suspiciously like a grimace. He was holding Adele's hand. He pulled her back even further into the shadows, leaned close and kissed her ear. She squirmed, pulled away and looked at Calum with enormous dark eyes as he left the booth.

The black man had turned and was standing with his back against the bar. He watched Calum's approach without interest and without removing his shades. Black jeans, black shirt, black leather jacket. A suspicious bulge under the left arm. What was it Jack had said, an old Heckler and Koch P7?

Calum nodded to him, got the kind of response he would have expected from a stone wall, and went to lean on the bar alongside the other man. Close up, he was older than he'd appeared. Mid-fifties, Calum estimated, his skin lined by age as much as the searing rays of the Australian sun. The blond hair was coarse, not clean. The eyes, when they slipped sideways at Calum's approach, were the lightest of blue. The Aussies called the interior of their vast country 'the great bugger all', and from what Calum could judge that was what lay behind those eerily pale eyes.

'All right, mate?' the blond man said.

'I'm beginning to think I'll survive,' Calum said, cryptically.

The Aussie nodded, clearly picking up the accent but not the meaning. Stan wandered over, self-consciously smoothing his flap of hair; his upper lip had a tic that made one side of his thin moustache jump. Calum handed him twenty quid in notes, watched him walk over to the till, glanced at the Aussie.

'I haven't seen you or your pal in here before.'

The blond grinned. 'Bloody long way to come for your grog, mate. For both of us.'

'Aye, I know the feeling,' said Calum, suddenly the professional Scot. He paused. 'You know, if you're looking for excitement, maybe a bit of action,' he said, staring directly into the other man's eyes, 'they play cards round the clock in the back room.'

'We've got a couple of very special rooms

all ready and waiting for us,' the Aussie said, 'and other very tasty fish to fry.'

'A saying, I imagine, that can be taken any number of unpleasant ways.' Although his unspoken question had been answered, Calum put on a knowing look and narrowed his eyes confidentially. 'I did notice your friend was rather watchful. You're looking for someone — am I right? Maybe a wee score to settle?'

'You're quite a sticky beak, ain't ya?' the blond man said. Then he shook his head. 'We were, mate, but not any more. The telephone's a wonderful thing. A friend of a friend whispered in my ear from a far distant shore, and as of thirty minutes ago our search is over.'

And then, as if to plant an exclamation mark alongside the Australian's appreciation of modern technology, Calum Wick's mobile phone began trilling and drew just about every eye in the room.

18

Nothing much happened for the next five days.

Sian and I lived like a couple of middle-aged holidaymakers high up on the hill in Eleanor's delightful bungalow, revelling in the bright, clear mornings; in the evenings relaxing in the warm sun with highlights glinting on tall glasses of something ice-cold and mildly alcoholic enhanced by the tartness oozing from thin green slices of citrus fruit.

Sian went back to the gymnasium she'd been using when we were living on the Rock, and got in touch with a businesswoman called Rosa with whom she had liaised and lunched during our twelve months or so working as security consultants. Rosa was delighted to hear from her. She was taking a break from her own PR business, so they met most mornings for coffee at the Copacabana then went café-crawling and window-shopping in the sunlight and shadows of Main Street before taking an alfresco lunch in Casemates Square.

From time to time I got text messages from Calum, from which I was able to track his southerly route across Europe. He'd mentioned Charlie's cunning use of Adele's brother's loose tongue to leak Eleanor's address and get them moving. I'd told Calum that any leak had come not from Adele's brother but from Rickman's anonymous tip off. Quickly realizing that one leak could lead to another, there was, he said, no sign of a Land Rover with a battered bumper hot on their tail. I suggested villains could easily steal a better, faster car and, remembering my own encounter and Clontarf's brutal use of anything on four wheels, warned him to be on the lookout for vehicles rocketing up behind them on hairpin bends through the Pyrenees.

The day after Sian and I spoke to Rickman on board *Sea Wind,* I drove up Europa Road to Reg's house — we'd hired a Fiat Punto — and over morning coffee in the suspended sun room had a word with Eleanor. Tactfully. If she had, in all innocence, casually mentioned to an acquaintance that Charlie and Adele Wise were staying at her flat in Liverpool, she would have been horrified to learn that she might have put lives at risk. So I questioned her without mentioning possible consequences of her actions, but it mattered not anyway because she was quite sure she had told nobody.

'Why would I?' she'd said. 'I told you when you asked could they stay there that I knew what was going on. The jewels, and that. I'm hardly likely to tell every man and his dog, am I now?'

Tough words, spoken in the Liverpool accent that was always thickened by anger, but no more than I'd expected. Tall and white-haired, delightfully elegant in a long shot-silk dress that fell with grace over her lightly-boned frame then tumbled to brush the soft Indian sandals she always wore — or Indian sandal, for one ankle was still encased in plaster liberally scrawled with graffiti — Eleanor Scott had been a widow for twenty-five years and retired for ten. She had lost her younger son Tim to a brutal murder just a few months before, and had borne her grief with fortitude. The flip side of her character would see her moved to tears by the simplest of gifts; on other occasions her brown eyes would laugh at you, dancing with good humour. But she was a strong and independent woman — despite her attachment to Reg — who had never suffered fools gladly, and so my next words were said with some trepidation.

If she'd not said a word to anyone about the use of her flat, I suggested she had told Reg, who was away in Spain, and he might have let the information slip out. I got a similar response, but this time there was a much sharper edge to her tongue.

'Of course I bloody told him. Call it pillow talk or whatever you like, but if you think he blabbed then you've got another think coming. It was the diplomatic service he was in, Jack. And he's an old-timer, isn't he, so he remembers that wartime saying: Be like Dad; keep mum. And he abides by it.'

The plaster was annoying her, and she was noticeably limping when she walked with me up the steps. I asked her why she hadn't cadged a stick from the hospital.

'Didn't want one,' she said.

'Pride,' I said, 'is known to come before a fall.'

'Yeah, well, my fall came first, didn't it, so what's the point in havin' a stick?'

'Steps led to your fall, and the ones we've just climbed are a lot trickier. Anyway, you could borrow Reg's, couldn't you? Hasn't he still got that presentation stick he got when he retired? Malacca cane, a big silver head.'

'No. Soft bugger broke it swiping at some weeds on these very same steps. And steps or no steps, I fell 'cos I was pushed.'

She grinned at the stupidity exhibited by both the men she loved and kissed my cheek, and I knew she'd be watching as I zoomed away down Europa Road in the nippy little Punto. Though I was delighted with the chat and the excellent ground coffee, I'd got no further ahead. Somebody had learned that Charlie and Adele were making for Eleanor's flat in Booker Avenue, and had passed that knowledge on to Bernie Rickman, who in turn had informed his heavies — he said. But had he been lying? Eleanor certainly wasn't to blame. If there had been a tip-off, it had been anonymous. Clontarf and Ebenholz could be anywhere, and as Rickman's was the only name I had to play with in Gibraltar I naturally called on Luis Romero.

★ ★ ★

Romero was one frustrated police inspector, getting nowhere with any of his open cases.

Photographs taken by a young woman, now dead, had linked Bernie Rickman to the suspected jewel thief, Karl Creeny, but Creeny had disappeared and Rickman — as Romero had pointed out at our last meeting — had committed no crime. The murdered man at the airport had walked off his plane and been clubbed to the ground in a narrow passageway. There had been no witnesses. As his wallet and the small holdall he had carried as cabin baggage were missing, it looked like a clumsy mugging gone wrong.

As for his being a courier carrying the stolen diamonds into Gibraltar for Karl Creeny, well, that was wild speculation, but a possibility. Creeny had been in Gibraltar, that was a fact. Charlie and Adele strenuously denied any knowledge of diamonds, but could be lying. Had Charlie murdered the courier? Were they conning Calum Wick, getting him to ferry them across Europe so that they could recover the diamonds they had stashed somewhere in La Línea?

Their daughter, Prudence, was dead, and while Clontarf and Ebenholz were suspected of killing her, any evidence was circumstantial. Hardly that. Chimeric was probably a better description, but even then it was academic because the two men were notable by their absence. We couldn't even be sure that they'd known of, or been anywhere near, Eleanor's flat, because Calum and his charges hadn't stayed long enough to find out.

They were two men clearly working under false names, and as such were virtually untraceable. Françoise Rickman, on the other hand, should have been easy to find — or at least, by keeping a watch on ports, Eurostar and airports, easy to lock into the UK. The trouble was, there was no record of a Françoise Rickman arriving or departing, so the obvious assumption was that she too was sailing under a flag of convenience. Again, this was a likelihood Romero had voiced when last we met.

Short of facts, professional and amateur investigators were falling back on vivid and lively imaginations. It was always interesting to see what popped up when a number of intelligent people put their heads together and concocted elaborate scenarios to explain the unexplainable. What emerged might be wild and wonderful, completely off-the-wall, but such methods had been known to work. It was sometimes called lateral thinking, at other times brainstorming.

Eleanor, in her usual blunt fashion, would have put it another way.

'It might be clever and all that,' she'd have said, 'but really it's all pie in the sky, isn't it?'

★　★　★

On the fifth day, Sian and I had a late dinner in Bianca's.

Bianca's restaurant was popular with holidaymakers and locals, always noisy as evenings wore on, and in a wonderfully picturesque location on the edge of the marina. The windows looked out over a wide front patio with potted plants, and beyond that the concrete walkways stretching out into waters reflecting the bright lights of restaurants, nightclubs and high-rise residences. Alongside those walkways the big yachts were berthed. My brother Tim's yacht, *El Pájaro Negro*, had been there for a long time, rocking and creaking gently at its moorings, and for much of that time ownership had been in dispute. As far as I knew, Tim had bought it from the ex-pat crook Ronnie Skaill — for whom he had once been a part-time smuggler and wannabe buccaneer — but had paid very little of the purchase price. Skaill had been after him for the rest, and that wasn't a good position to be in. My brother had died, shot in the head by Skaill or one of his men, then Skaill himself had died on Gibraltar's rocky heights at the hands of his own son while Sian and I watched, horrified, in the driving rain of that violent summer storm. So now *El Pájaro Negro* was up for sale and, on the opposite side of the concrete strip there was an even bigger yacht owned by yet another crooked ex-pat. *Sea Wind* was a symbol of violence that, from Bianca's, I found it impossible to avoid.

'A penny for them,' Sian said.

'Too noisy to think.'

'Then talk to me.'

'Ah, but in an atmosphere like this that's always risky. For you to hear a word I'd have

207

to be shouting. What if there's a sudden lull, and I'm left bellowing something very rude into the stunned silence?'

'You'd raise a titter, and a grinning barman would probably bring you a free drink. Anyway, you're exaggerating. If you won't talk, I will, because we've some unfinished business.'

'Is this to do with something I said?'

'In the heat of the moment. When you thought I was asleep.' Sian smiled. 'And now, even though you're ex-military, you're scared out of your socks.'

I'd dined on steak with chips, huge onion rings and the usual trimmings, Sian had a calamari salad with some exotic dressing that coated green leaves with a pink slime and tickled my nostrils. But the plates had been taken away, we'd declined afters, and all that stood between us now were tall glasses half full of a rich red Rioja, and cups of steaming liqueur coffee.

'Actually,' I said, 'I'm like that French soldier, Marshal Ney. Napoleon nicknamed him *Le Brave des Braves*. And,' I went on, leaning across the table and so perilously close to cups and glasses they clinked a warning, 'in noise like this the most intimate of conversations can be conducted without fear of being overheard — so fire away.'

'I've been thinking,' Sian said, 'about the big differences in our personalities.'

'Sexes, too. If you've noticed, we're exact opposites.'

'Will you be bloody serious? What we are is a couple of odd characters who are opposites in every respect. We're even quirky in the way we're opposite — arse about face, if you like — and where it stands out a mile is in the way we approach criminal investigation.'

'Our attitude to risk, to danger — is that what you mean?'

'Yes. And I'm sure you know what's coming next.'

'Well, I know I hate violence. The nature of the work we do means I can't always avoid it, but I go after those villains because I want to stop then visiting their nasty forms of violence on any more innocent victims.'

'As do I,' Sian said, 'emphatically. The difference is, I go after them not trying to avoid violence, but looking forward to a good punch-up; I'm never happier than when I'm beating them to a pulp.'

'As in the feller who was left spitting out teeth on board *Sea Wind*. Me sitting down thinking things over; you kicking out like a long-legged chorus girl.'

'Hence arse about face.'

'Yes.' I grinned. 'I should be the one who

inflicts damage, pain, I should be that high-kicking chorus girl.'

Sian rolled her eyes, finished off her wine and started on the coffee. A rim of white froth beaded her upper lip. I reached across and removed it gently with the light brush of a fingertip. And suddenly her eyes softened, the blue became deeper, she lowered her head a fraction causing a lock of blonde hair to slip forward, which she brushed aside absently with a hand that was far from steady.

'Oh no,' she said quietly, 'not the chorus girl. You know, from time to time I've caught myself wondering which is the real you. Is it the man who creates those exquisite miniature figures clothed in gorgeous uniforms, or the other, the man with an army special investigation background who uses those skills to help others? And then one day I realized that there's no difference. Each of those talents — for that's what they are, of course — makes a small part of the world a better place. And you go about both without conceit, without — '

'You make me sound,' I said, 'like some kind of noble savage.'

She giggled. 'Well, if the cap fits — '

'We'll share it,' I said, 'because for all your talk of differences you know damn well that it's the methods we use as individuals that make us an efficient team. With Calum there to exercise a measure of control. And all this talk of you spoiling for a fight is nonsense. What you have is a short fuse. You don't consciously seek a punch-up, you don't go looking for a fight; what you do is explode into action without thinking of the consequences. Usually when someone lies, threatens, or simply rubs you up the wrong way.'

'Which,' Sian said with a sensual pout, 'brings us neatly back to the proposal uttered bashfully when I was half asleep with my red socks up on the dashboard — '

My mobile phone trilled.

I sighed and pressed it to my ear, put a finger in the other to deaden Bianca's din. It was Calum Wick. I listened, nodded, listened some more and said, 'The canoe's closer. You'll find us there,' then switched off.

Sian was staring intently. She said, 'I thought Tim's boat was up for sale.'

'I kept a key. And I'm paying the mooring fees.'

'What did Calum want?'

'He's at the border, about to cross. He's on his own.'

'He's supposed to be. Isn't Charlie Wise arranging some accommodation over there for him and Adele?'

'Yes.'

'So?'

19

'This wee nutter, Charlie Wise,' Calum said, 'has an image of himself which, frankly, is complete and utter balls. He's got this crazy idea that he can rub shoulders with the worst kinds of European underworld riff raff and they'll scamper to do his bidding at a mere snap of his podgy fingers. And this, as those guys well know, is a man who made his living manufacturing pink bloody bog paper.'

'One of life's necessities,' Sian said primly. 'I take it everything that could go wrong has gone wrong?'

'Disastrously so. This contact Charlie was relying on to come up with some safe accommodation across the border, Mario some-thing-or-other, is operating on home territory, his nose sniffing the air for the smell of ready money. And he'd just heard of cash being offered by a man in Gibraltar for information relating to a couple of names. Christ! Out of a clear blue sky, those names dropped in his bloody lap.'

I grimaced. 'Charlie phoned him from the UK, digging for a different kind of information?'

'Exactly. Charlie heard about this other

reward, fifty thousand quid being offered by the Liverpool firm for the safe return of their stolen goods. He at once thought of his Spanish contacts, thought there must be someone there who could provide information about the diamonds: who's holding them, what's their next move — the wheres, the whys and the hows of any sale.'

'But, after that phone call, he was as good as dead.'

'Mario was probably already fantasizing about how he was going to spend the reward he'd get for shopping Charlie when he picked up the phone and called Bernie Rickman.' Calum scowled at me. 'I drove Christ knows how many miles across Europe and ended up delivering the poor bastards to the enemy.'

His words were irate, but there was a gleam in his dark eyes and Calum Wick, I realized, was thoroughly enjoying himself. He was his old, relaxed self, sprawled full length with his ankles crossed on the only long and comfortable seat in the canoe's saloon. A Schimmelpenninck cigar smouldered between his paint-stained fingers; from time to time he reached up to stroke his salt-and-pepper beard and even by the saloon's subdued lighting I could see that he'd managed to drive all those miles without once cleaning his John Lennon glasses.

Sian, as always, had her legs drawn up on one of the seats, and looked as soft and as drowsy as a kitten. But she was listening intently to Calum, toying idly with her loose blonde hair, occasionally sipping from a glass of water.

I was Captain Bligh, pacing the deck in torment. There was a slight movement beneath my sandals as the dying fringes of a heavy swell rolling down the straits reached the marina and stirred the sleeping yachts at their moorings. Ropes creaked in protest. Somewhere, metal tinkled. And in my pacing past the canoe's neat oval portholes I was always conscious of a gleaming white shape and aware that, on the other side of the concrete walkway, Bernie Rickman's *Sea Wind* was still sneering down at us — and with justification.

I flopped into the remaining chair, groaned, and ran fingers though my hair.

'So you arrived at the address Charlie had been given, expecting to be met by this Mario — and then what?'

'We came in on the A383, hit La Línea early in the evening. Charlie was navigating. He directed me through classy suburbs, houses in groves of palms, festooned with bougainvillea, with long drives barred by locked gates. Stockbroker belt. Where we finished up it was a lot less salubrious: littered streets gradually narrowing to become little more than a maze of back alleys, walls of flaking stucco, rusting iron balconies, threadbare nightdresses and underwear hanging limply from drooping overhead clotheslines.' Calum paused. 'And would you believe when I pulled in alongside one of those crappy buildings at the end of a lofty terrace, there was another black Mercedes sitting in front of mine, with two grinning men in suits leaning against the boot watching our arrival.'

'Clontarf and Ebenholz,' I said. 'But how the hell — '

'If you say so. I didn't ask. I know they were the same two blokes I saw walking into Jokers Wild. They were careless enough with the way their jackets hung for me to know they were armed; one was black and the one who told me cheerfully that it was much quicker by plane had an accent you'd have got used to if you were painting outback fences.'

I nodded. 'Suits, you say. A clever move. They flew in from Manchester, changed their image so they became just two more of Gibraltar's lawyers and financiers drinking lattes in the coffee shops and bars. We don't know their real names, but clearly those names don't ring police alarm bells. Then

Rickman got word from meretricious Mario, they crossed the border and waited for you to hit town.'

'They acted like gentlemen. Charlie was impressed. The Aussie told him the place where they were parked was a tip, that Mario had got them classier digs for the same price. Charlie beamed. Adele looked wary, but was left with little choice when the two suits ushered them into the Merc. Charlie waved his thanks, shouted something about seeing me, and they drove away in a cloud of gritty dust with me standing there like a leftover haggis. It took me all of thirty fucking minutes to find my way through that maze of streets to the border.'

'And you wouldn't be able to find your way back to that block?'

'Waste of time because they're not there, Jack,' Sian said, 'and I'm at a loss to know what we can do next. We're back in that same situation where no crime has been committed. Charlie and Adele are two adults who arrived where they were supposed to, were met by two respectable men in a respectable car, and were whisked away.'

'Could be a waste of time for Rickman, too,' Calum said. 'If Charlie's been telling the truth, he knows nothing about those diamonds.'

'That's what bothers me,' I said, 'because who's going to believe him? I can see Charlie and Adele in some dank cellar, duct-taped to chairs, and in such a situation Karl Creeny's methods of persuasion don't bear thinking about. My guess is he'll start on Adele with the pliers and the blow torch, seeing her as Charlie's soft spot.'

'Christ, Jack,' Sian said, 'will you shut up.'

'I know, it's hard to stomach.'

'So we stop it.'

'Just like that?'

'Yes. Somehow. You told Romero you don't like being used. Well, it's gone way beyond your hurt pride. We've been inextricably linked to the Wise family ever since Prudence talked to us in the Eliott Hotel. She's dead; Charlie and Adele are in deep trouble. We've got to find them, and save them from those two thugs. If we succeed, we'll also find the diamonds, and the airport killer. We can wrap this up, but we've got to move, and fast. There's no time to lose.'

'What if I'm wrong?' Calum cut in. 'What if Wise had been lying from the start? If he has, then he's no better than Creeny and we leave him to his fate because he's a thief and a killer.'

'Jack,' Sian said curtly, 'what's your impression?'

'Of Charlie?'

'Has Calum got a point? Or what? Come on, let's have your thoughts.'

I frowned, remembered the two of them in North Wales, Charlie and Adele, looking sad and forlorn in their Mediterranean togs while their daughter lay cold and still in a mortuary and outside Bryn Aur the wind and rain lashed the bleak mountain slopes.

'I think Charlie has been out of his depth from the moment he retired and moved to Gib,' I said. 'Well, he told us all about it, didn't he? Set off south with high hopes, and, keen to make an impression, he eventually got in with the wrong crowd and found himself swimming with sharks. Cunning bastards, crooked bastards, well able to manipulate him, to use him. Bernie Rickman polished his ego, told him what a clever lad he was and Charlie suddenly found himself skipper of a bloody big yacht, cruising the Med with Adele — only, after a while, he was shocked to discover that there was a price to pay. But by then, of course, he was in too deep. I don't know what he was involved in, probably small-time drug smuggling, almost certainly people smuggling — taking half a dozen illegal immigrants at a time from Africa across to Italy or France.'

'So in that respect, at least,' Calum said, 'he

became no better than Rickman,'

'In the eyes of the law, that's true, but to Charlie's credit the luxury lifestyle palled and he became sickened by the illegal activities. He couldn't take any more, so he began working on a plan, a way of escape.'

'I think that's a reasonable assessment,' Sian said. 'We know what he did, trumpeting that trip to Tangier when he had no intention of going all the way. And if you're right, and he'd been working on that idea for some time, then he's telling the truth, isn't he? He has to be. He was far too involved in a very risky venture of his own — engineering his and Adele's escape to a cleaner life — to pay any attention to newspaper reports of a robbery in Liverpool. He knew nothing about the diamonds.'

Was she right? Could I trust her judgement? I was pretty sure I could, because she was at the very least echoing my own feelings.

Yet even as Sian's closing words told us emphatically that we were committed to saving Charlie and Adele, beneath us the deck tilted, rocked, settled.

We had been boarded.

I looked at Sian. She'd slopped water from her glass, not from the canoe's gentle movement, but from her start of alarm. We had, after all, been discussing the worst kinds of thugs and now a stranger had come calling.

I was out of my seat. Calum remained horizontal, but was no longer relaxed. I looked questioningly at Sian. Still curled up, and with a damp patch on her thigh, she spread her hands in a 'search me' gesture.

'Whoever has just stepped on board,' Calum said helpfully, 'is not acting furtively.'

'Difficult to do with success,' I said, 'when the floor you're walking on is floating on water.'

And then the saloon door clicked open, swung wide, and Reg Fitz-Norton strolled in with worn brogues poking from beneath cavalry twill trousers, a paisley cravat tucked carelessly into the fraying collar of his white shirt and a nervous smile on his face.

20

'I've got myself in a spot of bother,' Reg said, 'and, frankly, you're making things a hell of a sight worse.'

Sian, deciding that as her leg was damp she might as well be wet all over, had kissed Reg, twiddled his ponytail and gone for a shower. Calum had yet to move. I was trying to look intelligent.

'You've lost me, Reg,' I said. 'It was easy to work out that you'd trodden on a few toes, but are you saying the push on Eleanor that led to her fall and a painful broken ankle was a warning of more to come unless you . . . ?'

'Unless I hand something over, old boy. At a financial loss, which I'm supposed to bear. Trouble is, I no longer have it.'

'Explain. No, I'll do it for you. You've been dabbling in dodgy art again.'

'Yes.'

'At Bernie Rickman's expense, which is what he hinted at. Fingers burnt, and so on. I gather he had a deal going and you snuck in and snaffled the goods. Sold them on, at a profit.'

'Eloquent, accurate, but unhelpful. What I

want to know is what you're going to do.'

'Nothing, yet, because I can't see how I wouldn't be making that situation a hell of a sight worse. Or worse in any respect. I'm not involved, Reg.'

'You don't go poking an already angry bear with a sharp stick, Jack.'

Calum stirred. I'd feared he was dead.

He said, 'You know, I do believe Reg is asking us to lay off Rickman.'

'I am,' Reg said. 'Rickman when angry is dangerous. Anyone in the firing line is at risk. So I want you to forget all about those diamonds. If you back off, Rickman will go off the boil.'

'But Rickman,' I said, 'wants us to find them.'

'Not any more he doesn't, old boy. I told you he's fuming, and I must say he has good reason. If you remember, the last time you were on *Sea Wind* you accused *him* of stealing those diamonds.'

'Indeed I did. But during that talk his frightening description of what was about to happen in Liverpool pretty well ruled that out; his men were still over there, and they were furiously following up an anonymous tip-off. It was a good one. And if he no longer needs my help, it's because Rickman believes he's found the diamonds.'

Reg's eyes narrowed. He looked puzzled. 'If he has,' he said, 'it'll be a miracle that could well save my bacon.'

'Why a miracle?'

Reg hesitated. 'Well, because I thought Charlie Wise had those diamonds — and hasn't he gone missing again?'

'That was very short-lived.'

'Oh dear,' Reg said absently, and I could see his mind working furiously.

'Reg, Reg, come on now, you said it yourself, this could work in your favour,' Calum said. 'If Rickman's got his hands on the diamonds, surely your troubles are over? Hell, he might be overcome with emotion, become tearfully philanthropic and give you a hefty cut.'

'Why?'

'Let bygones be bygones. Honour among thieves and all that rot.'

Reg rose to his feet.

'A deal done honourably is not theft,' he said stiffly, 'even if the goods in question are — '

'Questionable?'

'Have a dodgy provenance,' Reg said, and was unable to suppress a grin.

'Heaven forbid that should be said about your artistic fiddles,' I said, also getting to my feet. 'Anyway, Reg, if Rickman has found those diamonds then it's over, isn't it?'

'Not quite,' he said, 'because unfortunately his making a profit from stolen jewels won't get him off my back. However, it does change everything. I asked you to forget those diamonds, but if Rickman has them then it's your duty to report the matter to the police.'

'What a brilliant idea. With Rickman safe behind bars, that transaction you finagled — '

'Handled with honour — '

' — remains a done deal and you and Eleanor can ride off into a Mediterranean sunset.'

'Do your best, old boy. Talk to Romero. Eleanor does quite often; they're close friends.'

There was a heavy silence when Reg had gone. The canoe rocked gently when he stepped down onto the concrete, just as it had when he'd come aboard. Again it settled. There was the faintest lapping of ripples against stone, against fibreglass hulls, then all was still. I looked at Calum.

'What the hell was all that about?'

'If it's any consolation, I don't think it means she's having an affair.'

I grinned. 'Might not be that bad an idea, though,' I said. 'No, I don't know if he's realized he let it slip, but Reg Fitz-Norton must have been on board Sea Wind when

Sian and I were talking to Rickman.'

'We didn't see him, so how do you know?'

Sian had come back in time to catch what I'd said, smelling of steamy soap, swathed in a cuddly towelling robe and rubbing her blonde hair into tumbling disarray with a big fluffy towel.

'He knew we'd accused Rickman of stealing the famous stones. And I remember, when I walked out while you were by the rail phoning Calum, I heard him calling to someone. There was an answering voice, male, by the sound of it. Reg's mistake tells me it was him.'

'That's like someone saying, when they hear a man talking in darkest Africa, oh, gosh, that must be Desmond Tutu.' She draped the towel over her folded arms, shook her head so that her golden hair fluffed out damply, and perched on the edge of a chair. 'If Reg is in deep schtook with Rickman, why wouldn't he be in there grovelling?'

'Aha, so that's what that wee diplomat's been doing all his working life,' Calum said.

'Well, politicians and the like call it by another name,' I said, 'but favours are always bought in one way or another so there must be a lot of crawling. The only person who knew Charlie was going to be using that flat in Booker Avenue was the owner, Eleanor, my dearest mother. She told Reg, of course, and now I know he was on *Sea Wind* I'm wondering if he thought of his own troubles and saw an opportunity to buy off Rickman.'

'If it occurred to him, I'm sure he'd do it,' Sian said, curling up and tucking her bare feet under her robe. 'Look at it this way: what does Reg owe Charlie Wise? I mean, Reg sees Charlie as at least half-crooked anyway, doesn't he? So why not throw him to the wolves he's been running with? Or what was it you called them? The sharks he's been swimming with.'

'I tend to agree,' Calum said. 'Reg being a good guy would salve his conscience by convincing himself that handing the name over wouldn't automatically seal Charlie's fate.'

'Mm, probably rolled some mental dice,' Sian said, 'which came up in Charlie's favour, because he got away. From what was going to be a Liverpool trap, anyway, although after that he didn't, did he, not in the end?'

'About which, incidentally, we must do something — and bloody soon,' Calum said.

I nodded, agreeing wholeheartedly but thinking along different lines.

'What I can't get my head around,' I said, 'is why Reg came steaming in here telling us to forget all about the diamonds. Rickman, he suggested, was still angry with him. But if we've got this right, then selling Charlie down the river should have put him in the clear, all debts paid.'

'Then forget it, because we've got it wrong,' Calum said flatly. 'Reg was on board *Sea Wind* grovelling but getting nowhere.'

'Right, and brain working overtime he thought another way round Rickman was to get us to drop the search for the diamonds, and he could take the credit?'

'Yes, only that wasn't going to work for him either,' Sian said, 'because then you told him he was too late 'cos Rickman had found the diamonds. Thanks to that anonymous tip-off.'

'Which takes us back to square one. The anonymous tip-off's impossible.'

'Ah, but now I've thought of something else. Remember you phoned Calum when he was en-route to Liverpool? Okay, so the mobile phones must have been hacked. That Aussie bum was listening and taking notes.'

'Him or his pal Ebenholz.' I thought about it and nodded. 'I don't see how they managed it, but rule out Eleanor and Reg and there's no other way.'

'You're talking piffle,' Calum said, and he rolled his lanky frame from the horizontal to the vertical and made for the drinks cabinet. 'In that mobile phone conversation, Booker Avenue was never mentioned.'

He splashed whisky into a glass, cast a questioning glance in our direction. We both shook our heads. He shook his, with obvious impatience.

'For God's sake, I can't believe three people with our experience are spending so much time going round in bloody circles,' he said. 'Look, it no longer matters who leaked the Booker Avenue address, because that was five days ago and we've moved on — and not very successfully, I might add. Also, while my heart bleeds for poor, confused old Reg, his troubles with Rickman have got nothing at all to do with stolen diamonds.'

'And us wasting time with them isn't helping Charlie and Adele,' Sian pointed out.

'Exactly,' Calum said. 'Charlie and Adele are getting no help whatsoever, and how long is it now since I watched them driven away by two grinning hyenas in suits?'

'Too long.' I nodded. 'Logic tells me to go to Luis Romero. He can call on more men, and more facilities.'

'And almost certainly waste yet more time cutting through red tape. No, we've been through that, Jack. No offence has been committed, remember? And in any case it's all happening in Spain.'

'Last suggestion: Romero has contacts over the border.'

Calum's grin was savage, dismissive. 'Aye, and so did Charlie, and look what happened there.'

I took a deep breath, reached across for Calum's drink, finished it off for him and slammed down the empty glass.

'Okay, we let diplomatic Reg sort out his own troubles. Starting now, we put our heads together, work out an acceptable plan. Then we cross the border into La Línea de la Concepción and we go hunting for a couple of old-age pensioners. I've grown to know them, and like them, and up against hoodlums like Clontarf and Ebenholz they haven't a hope in hell of helping themselves.'

21

There was a soft, warm breeze wafting in from the bay. It carried with it the clean salt taste of the sea. Somehow it found its way across the promenade and the wide highways where night traffic flowed, curling its way into the narrower side streets and then to others even more constricting that were still named *Calle this* and *Calle that* yet were little more than gloomy alleyways cutting between the crumbling walls of tall buildings. The breeze whispered across squalid dwellings where lights gleamed a dull yellow, televisions cast a blue sheen, music blared and people conversed, argued, screamed and wept in half a dozen different languages. Litter rustled at its passing. And when the breeze grew capricious, plucked a torn, stained copy of *The Olive Press* from a cracked pavement and carried it high to wrap itself pennant-like around a lamp post, the woman flattened against the filthiest of walls in the deepest shadows was shocked by the sudden overhead flapping, and gasped in terror.

'It's all right, Addy,' Charlie said. 'Just the wind, just an old newspaper.'

'Yeah, this time,' Adele said. 'Next time it could be them pouncing, grabbin' me by the throat, and I'm shaking at the thought.'

'No need. They're fools. They locked the door, forgot about the window and the fire escape, and didn't factor in Mario's duplicity. He gave us away and pocketed the money being offered, then hung around and let us out when their backs were turned.' He chuckled. 'Men that stupid need a map to find their flies, a video explaining how to lift the tab, lower the zip. And so on.'

'But when they get back from wherever it was they went and find us gone they'll go berserk, leave no stone unturned.'

'For worms and woodlice,' Charlie said, grinning at her in the gloom, 'under stones is a good place to look.'

'I feel like a bloody woodlouse, standing here,' Adele said, shivering. 'Somebody's been peeing against this wall, you know that?'

'Come on.'

Charlie took her hand, pulled her out of the shadows.

They'd clattered down the iron fire escape after Mario, exchanged high-fives and watched him race away into the darkness, then legged it up the street in the opposite direction until their chests were raw and they were sagging at the knees. The stinking wall had kept them upright. They had waited for their breathing to calm, listened fearfully for the sound of a Mercedes returning; forced themselves to take the time Charlie needed to marshal his thoughts, get his bearings.

'We head into the breeze, keep it on our faces. It's coming off the sea and Tony's got an apartment overlooking the bay.'

'In streets like these, wind swirls all over the place.'

'Then we make for the light, but stay in the dark.'

Adele started to laugh, but Charlie was tugging her along and she picked up her long skirts and concentrated on staying upright on high heels, on getting enough air into her lungs to stay alive. At that thought she did laugh, and then Charlie was laughing with her and they were wobbling dangerously when the walls ahead of them were suddenly painted with bright light and a black car heeled over as it swung into the street behind them.

'Shit,' Charlie said.

He flung himself sideways, used his shoulder to drive Adele off her feet. She crashed awkwardly down on a pile of wet, foetid rubbish behind a cluster of foul plastic bins. A bony cat hissed from under her, spat, its green eyes luminous. Charlie swung a kick at it, then overbalanced and fell on top of

Adele. She squealed. He clamped his hand over her mouth. She bit it, then gagged, and his nose was assailed with the smell of rotten wet bread, fish, bad eggs and whatever the cat had been depositing.

The car was moving slowly down the centre of the narrow street.

'They're lookin' for us, must have been to the flat, know we've scarpered,' Charlie whispered.

Adele mumbled a muffled reply. She was lying on her side in filth, holding a handkerchief to her face.

'But they're flash bastards, full of themselves,' he muttered, 'they'll not get out of the car unless there's a good reason.'

He wriggled further into the space between bins and flaking wall, realized he could go no further and would be forced to back out. They couldn't do that in a hurry so they'd painted themselves into a corner, into a fucking no-way-out trap . . .

The powerful engine was a gentle purr. Stones popped from beneath the wide tyres. A wheel dropped into a pothole, sprayed filthy water. It splashed against the bins; would, Charlie feared, draw the eyes of the watcher on that side.

He screwed up his face, shut his eyes.

From the open window of the car an

American voice like gravel falling on a coffin said, 'Something moved over there.'

'It wasn't me, sir,' Charlie whispered, and had to bite back a giggle. Adele elbowed him in the ribs. She had her mouth covered and was trying to breathe through her ears. Charlie heard the slow-moving car draw to a halt. The door clicked open. Footsteps crunched, stopped.

'Forget it,' another voice drawled from the car. 'There's a skinny cat slinking away, that's what you saw. Get back in, mate, we'll never find 'em. There's more people here than we've got rabbits in Oz.'

The door slammed. The engine roared. Wheels spun, spraying gravel, and the Mercedes sped away. From behind the reeking bins Charlie sneaked a look and saw the gleaming black shape, its tail lights glowing red as it slowed for the next junction, turned, and was gone.

He climbed to his feet, using one hand on an overloaded teetering plastic bin to drag himself upright. He reached back and extended his hand. Adele took it with a wet slap. She almost pulled him off his feet as she struggled up out of the refuse. One foot slipped. A high-heeled shoe made a soggy, sucking sound. She left it, hopped after him as he moved out of the stinking shadows.

'I thought you were going to leave me there,' she said. 'Rush off and give chase, all macho, shout expletives, throw stones.'

'As if. It was just, that new perfume you're wearing had me confused, it really is a knockout.'

'It had me close to spewing me ring up,' Adele said. 'So, what now, Chas?'

'They went that way, and probably stopped just round the corner, so — '

'Not being born yesterday, we tiptoe in the opposite direction, then leg it.'

'Absolutely. And when we get to Tony Ramirez's' — he pulled her to him and planted a wet kiss on her forehead — 'you spend some time under a hot shower with lots of smelly gel, dump your clothes in the bin and borrow some from his girlfriend.'

'Second time in a week. It's getting to be a habit.'

'Could be called cross-dressing, couldn't it? Or not. Anyway, when that's done we settle down for a long talk with Tony. A good friend, and one hell of a fixer. Got us off that boat and safe into Spain without asking awkward questions.'

'But in addition to that — '

'Yes, he rubs shoulders with shady characters on both sides of the border. Arranges dodgy deals, but he won't have a clue where those diamonds are' — he grinned, and winked at Adele — 'and he'll never in a month of Sundays know *exactly* what's going on.'

'Or who he's working for.'

'You've got it. Tony doesn't know the guy's name — nobody'll ever know that — and he doesn't know where he is, but he'll have been approached by phone and now Tony'll be getting in touch with wealthy Arabs or Russians with loads of dosh, and dreaming of his cut. He'll know when an offer has been made, and accepted. And, when the time's right, he'll know the location where the diamonds are going to change hands.'

Charlie was still watching the end of the road, eyes alert for movement, for the return of the men in suits, the glitter of steel in the crap street lighting.

'And he'll tell us because?'

'Even the best of fixers has to have something to fix,' Charlie said, 'and without me, Tony Ramirez had zilch.'

Still holding his wife's hand, Charlie moved out from the shelter of the bins and walked quickly away from the corner around which, he believed, the two men in the Mercedes were patiently waiting with their cocked pistols.

Adele, grimacing, minus one shoe, hopped valiantly as she was tugged along in his wake.

22

Talking and drinking into the early hours — and getting nowhere — makes the next morning something to be missed, even cancelled. I crawled out of bed just after nine and left Sian face down in the rumpled bed with her blonde hair decorating the pillow with filigrees of gold. When I'd thrown on jeans and T-shirt, downed a couple of glasses of cold water and made it out on deck, Calum was already there. He was leaning on the rail smoking a Schimmelpenninck and gazing out across a bay bathed in misty sunlight where cargo vessels of all shapes and sizes floated like abandoned iron hulks on glass-like seawater.

'To the bungalow,' I said. 'We'll grab some breakfast while working out what to do about Charlie and Adele.'

'Time's running out.'

'Hence the rush.'

'And Sian?'

'Still asleep.' I held up my car keys, jingled them. 'Come on, let's go.'

The Rock's steep upper slopes were like a warm middle ground between the thin mist veiling the town and harbour and the familiar levanter cloud that streamed away to the west from the Rock's summit. That put Eleanor's bungalow in shade. I parked, climbed the steps and opened up, and while Calum boiled the kettle for coffee I split and buttered rolls, put them on plates and took them through to the living room.

We were still eating them, in a thoughtful but mostly unproductive silence broken only by the slurping of hot coffee, when the door banged open and Bernie Rickman walked in followed by the American, Ebenholz.

★   ★   ★

'Where are they?'

'The stolen diamonds? Or should that be twice-stolen diamonds?' I managed to look confused. 'Well, as already pointed out, you snaffled them for yourself and sent Mutt and Jeff chasing across Europe to disguise the fact.'

'I'm talking about Charlie and Adele Wise.'

'Last seen entering a car with two men in suits,' Calum said. He put down his empty mug, sat back and tossed a chilling smile at Ebenholz that left the muscular heavy unmoved.

'They made a pig's ear of it. Wise and his

wife slipped away while their backs were turned and crossed the border into Gibraltar some time last night,' Rickman said. 'You lot befriended them in Wales, arranged a safe house in Liverpool — '

'Flat, actually, and safe is hardly — '

' — then planned their escape in the Flying Scotsman's car. That suggests that when they crossed over last night they'd have come straight to you.'

'Ah, well, that cross-Europe jaunt was Charlie's idea,' Calum said, 'and as I was unable to save them yesterday I imagine my manly charm has lost its attraction.'

Ebenholz took one stride forward and hit him across the face, a backhand blow with a full arm swing and lots of knuckle. Calum rocked sideways. Blood trickled, seeped into his beard. He straightened, licked his split lip experimentally, looked thoughtfully at Ebenholz.

'I know Ebenholz is German, and a nick-name,' he said, 'and I'm sure you put a great deal of thought into the choice, but I'm afraid you got it wrong. Means ebony, doesn't it, so let's say a charitable five out of ten. Now, if you'd chosen *Kartoffel* I'd have taken one look at your head and nose and given you eight out of ten, while the choice of *Scheisse* — which, as you probably know, means . . . er

. . . excrement, would have guaranteed full — '

The second blow from Ebenholz came from the other side, a closed fist this time, the vicious crack as knuckles hit cheekbone rocking Calum the other way. This time his eyes darkened. He shook his head, partly to clear it, partly out of disbelief.

'You really have no idea what you're letting yourself in for, pal,' he said softly, and came out of the chair in one smooth reptilian movement.

Ebenholz was faster. He stepped back. The Heckler and Koch P7 came out of his under-arm holster in a blur. The slide had been pulled back. He held the pistol in two hands, picked a spot between Calum's eyes, curled a finger around the trigger — and grinned. The tall Scot stopped. There was a long moment while they stood eyeball to eyeball — or as near as dammit, given the intrusion of the pistol. Then Calum brushed contemptuously past the stocky man as if he didn't exist and stood with his back to us, gazing out at the sunlit vista falling steeply away on the other side of the wide windows.

I sighed. 'You've probably noticed we do a lot of talking,' I said. 'It's always proved useful; tends to confuse those not capable of putting more than two or three words together in a way that makes sense. And you're not making any sense at all. We don't know where Charlie and his wife are, and they did not steal those diamonds.'

'When Charlie told you that,' Rickman said, 'he was lying through his teeth. Maybe you should cut back on the talking and do some listening.'

'He wanted out. He'd had enough.'

'Bollocks. Thanks to me he had a fucking big yacht, and that and the money I was paying him for services rendered gave him entry to those exclusive ports all along the French Riviera. He rubbed shoulders and clinked glasses of champers with heads of state, Hollywood producers, Russian oligarchs; rubbed up against young women sexy enough to give old men strokes.' Rickman grinned. 'The kind I mean used to be called apoplexy. And the point I'm making is Charlie was living life to the full. Then he got wind of a diamond robbery and, being a simple lad, he got greedy.'

'Charlie knew nothing about the diamonds.'

'Me and him were like that,' Rickman said, crossing middle and index fingers firmly and flopping down in Calum's vacated chair. 'He knew about the Liverpool robbery long before it took place. Knew Creeny planned it, knew when and how the gems were being brought into Gib. So he made his own plans — and they were good ones. Cast ground bait by talking about a Tangier trip, which really had me fooled. Then he whacked the courier over the head, took the diamonds and sailed away into the sunset. But only so far. Spanish pals took them off the *Alcheringa* before my boys could get to them, landed them on the coast. And that would have been it, never would've found them if, by a stroke of luck, poor old Pru hadn't popped up dead.'

'With a koala stuffed in her mouth. You have an Australian working for you. He was in Wales at the right time. What does that suggest?'

'I'm not responsible for his movements, but I'd say that makes him a typical Aussie. Most of 'em like to spend a couple of years in The Old Dart getting a taste of civilization.'

'And your wife?'

'What about her?'

'The Astra carrying Pru's body into Wales was picked up on CCTV being driven by a woman, blonde hair.'

'Lots of them about.' Rickman shrugged. 'At the time you're talking about Françoise was on holiday in Spain. Go down to the border and check. Or send your pal, Romero. Her car will have been booked in and out.'

I couldn't think of anything to say. It was

stalemate, an impasse or, in a term more familiar to Ebenholz — who had moved to stand watchfully near the door from where he had a clear view of the whole room and everyone in it — a Mexican stand-off. My reading of the situation was that Rickman had called on us out of desperation, not really expecting any joy. Calum had apparently come to the same conclusion.

He'd turned his back to the window and had been leaning against the sill and listening without expression.

'What a complete and utter waste of fucking time,' he said.

'I have to admit I agree with you there,' Rickman said.

He began moving towards the door. Ebenholz beat him to it and was out and down the steps, either treating Rickman with deliberate contempt or unaware that the man existed. It crossed my mind that of the two villains I preferred the Australian — probably because I'd spent several years Down Under and had grown used to their dry humour and laconic way of talking. And, aware that Rickman seemed to be hanging back expectantly, and vaguely wondering why, I conformed to the description of my own loquacity and filled the space with talk.

'By the way,' I said, 'I thought those two

clowns were inseparable. Where's Clontarf?'

'Wondered when you were going to get round to noticing,' Rickman said, his hand on the door, his eyes ablaze with fiendish delight. 'You took your time, finally made it, then asked the wrong bloody question.'

'Really?'

'Yeah, really,' he mocked. 'The question you really need to ask is, where is Sian Laidlaw?'

And when he went out and clattered down the steps, he thoughtfully left the door wide open for me.

★   ★   ★

I took the Punto down through the Rock's hairpin bends at a speed that always kept two wheels on the road, cut through town without any recollection of doing so and at Marina Bay left the car parked at an angle that suggested I was either drunk, incapable or both. When I slammed the door, tumbled out and sprinted, my trainers slapped the concrete strip and echoed flatly from the hulls of yachts where rich owners were enjoying morning cocktails while working on their tans; and when I hit the deck of Tim's canoe with both feet, rocking the boat as big as it was, the wave generated was a mini-tsunami that lapped against adjoining vessels and set green olives shivering in dry martinis battling with mind-splitting hangovers.

I walked into the warm, airless saloon cringing, expecting the worst. Well, expecting emptiness at the very least, expecting that particular muffled silence denoting the absence of human life, which would leave me wondering if Sian had gone downtown with her PR friend Rosa, or was now being held in a rat-infested cellar near the commercial waterfront with the door guarded by the manic Glock-toting Australian, Clontarf. I'd forgotten to mention to Rickman that not only did I talk too much but that I frequently let my imagination run riot. I was doing that now, and knew it, but it didn't stop me squeezing my eyes shut and remembering another time and a similar entrance that had revealed my brother lying dead on the settee. This time . . . ?

The door banged behind me. The echo faded into the expected silence. I opened my eyes.

Sian was standing at a mirror, arms up as she fiddled with the band that she uses to restrain her thick blonde hair. She spun in alarm. I reached her in three long strides, pulled her into my arms and buried my face in the hollow of her neck. Her hair was soap and scent and softness, her skin silk, her body the enveloping warmth of the womb.

After a long moment she gripped my arms and held me away. She looked into my face, put the tip of a finger to each of my eyes in turn, her mouth a small O of concern.

'Jack,' she said tenderly, 'your cheeks are wet.'

'Your hair, Soldier Blue,' I said huskily. 'Often does that; golden strands get caught in my long eyelashes, draw tears of pain.'

'But if I didn't know you better, I'd have sworn you were crying.'

'How much better *can* you know me? What's the phrase, joined at the hip?'

'Mmm,' she murmured softly, pulling me close and thrusting gently, 'though hip's a bit wide of the mark, wouldn't you say?'

'Close,' I whispered, 'but no cigar.'

'Goodness, not a panatela, that's for sure.' She leaned back from the waist, her eyes dancing, did a little lower-body squirm. 'I'm no expert but there's a really big cigar Reg smokes, it's called a Cuaba Salomones — '

'And just moments ago,' I said, 'I was musing on how often I let *my* imagination run riot.'

'Ah, yes.' Brought back to earth with a bang, Sian pushed me firmly away, looked hard at me. 'You charged in here like a one-man SWAT team, Jack. What the hell's happened?'

'Rickman's idea of a cruel joke. He came barging into the bungalow with Ebenholz. Last night Charlie and Adele managed to break away from the two men in suits and crossed into Gib. Rickman was convinced they'd come to us. We talked, got absolutely nowhere, and before leaving he suggested that you had been taken by Clontarf.'

'Nobody's been here. I breakfasted, showered yet again, guessed you'd gone to the bungalow and was on my way up.' She plonked herself down on a chair. 'Besides,' she said, 'you put the canoe up for sale and forgot all about Tim's shotgun, the expensive Verney-Carron over-and-under. I admit I was nervous here on my own with *Sea Wind* just across the way, so I went looking and found it in a locker. It's loaded. I'd've cut Clontarf in half.'

'It would have come in handy at the bungalow. Because you weren't there, Ebenholz took his frustration out on Calum and drew blood.'

'Bugger.'

I grinned. 'Anyway, although Rickman was insisting the Wises must have come to us, his heart wasn't in it. And now this threat to you has been shown to be without substance, I'm sure he's going to leave us alone.'

'Mm. The bit about Charlie and Adele's interesting though, isn't it? They got away from those two nutters — which must have taken guts and a lot of luck — but why Gib? I know they got shafted by their Spanish so-called friend, but if they still want to get close to the diamonds and claim the reward, what's this latest move of theirs telling us? That the diamonds are here, have been here all along?'

'Rickman planted some worrying thoughts,' I said. 'I've sort of grown to like Charlie, and would love to think he's been telling the truth. But the story Rickman gave me was all too plausible. He and Charlie Wise were as thick as thieves — '

'Actually they *are* thieves.'

'Yes, I know, which thought makes the rest much worse. If Rickman is to be believed, Charlie loved the life he was leading, swanning about the Med in a big yacht, mixing with the super rich. He was in Rickman's confidence all along so knew about the diamond robbery in advance. And the way Rickman sees it, Charlie had developed a taste for the high life; opportunity presented itself, and he got greedy.'

'Which takes us back to that long-ago talk

in Reg's house, and the follow-up conversation in Luis Romero's office. That was the way we had it worked out: Charlie stole the diamonds, devised a cunning plan that saw them sailing halfway to Tangier before being plucked from the Sunseeker by their Spanish pals.'

'With the diamonds.'

'Yes. Taken off the Sunseeker in a holdall or something. But in that case the diamonds are still in Spain. Pru was murdered, which yanked Charlie and Adele out of hiding. With security the way it is they can't possibly have carted them all the way from Spain to the UK, then back again by car across Europe. Then across the border last night . . . ' She trailed off, frowning. 'Hang on, why did I say that, I'm missing something here — aren't I?'

'He could have taken the diamonds with him, all too easily. Have you ever been stopped at an airport, walking past those green signs put up by customs with nothing to declare?'

Sian grimaced and shook her head. 'You're not getting it. If he took them with him rather than leave them buried somewhere in Spain, and got away with it,' she said, 'then the final stage of the round trip was by car and they were in the boot of Calum's Mercedes for all of five days.'

I was speechless. Had we been that close to the diamonds? Had they been there, practically in Calum's paint-stained hands, all the way to La Línea?

In something of a daze I wandered through to the tiny galley and spent a few thoughtful minutes making coffee. I carried the two steaming mugs through with an open packet of butter shortbreads, and by the time I sat down I'd had another thought that made my hair stand on end.

'What happened last night when Calum drove through suburbs decked with a riot of blossom and into the shadowy and far less salubrious areas of La Línea?'

Sian sipped coffee, snapped a shortbread biscuit, stared at me.

'Charlie and Adele found two armed nutters in suits waiting for them, and were left with no choice.'

'Indeed. They went with them. As anyone would. But did our Wise friends go toddling off empty-handed, perhaps with a couple of toothbrushes sticking out of Charlie's shirt pocket, or did they stall long enough to drag their luggage out of Calum's boot?'

'Christ on a donkey,' Sian said. 'That must have been at the back of my mind. If they left their luggage with Calum, and he came over last night — '

And then, having the same effect you might get by inserting a finger in an electric socket, my mobile phone trilled.

★ ★ ★

'Hello?'

'It's Charlie.'

'Good-time Charlie, Champagne Charlie — '

'Charlie fuckin' Wise.'

'Oh, *that* Charlie. Well, hang on a minute and I'll pass the phone to Bernie — '

'Bloody hell, no, don't do that — '

'Relax.' I grinned at Sian. 'I'm winding you up, Charlie. Rickman's not here, More to the point, where are you?'

'Out of sight. And with no time to waste. Did Calum tell you about the reward?'

'Offered by the Liverpool firm for recovery of their diamonds? Yes, he did.'

'Well according to a friend of mine, Tony Ramirez, we're entering the end game.'

'Is that some kind of spy jargon? The only end game I know has something to do with chess.'

There was the sound of a harsh, indrawn breath of exasperation.

'The man who's got the diamonds has now arranged a sale. To an Arab, to a Russian — I don't know, and I don't care, and nobody's ever going to know his name. But it'll happen in the next few days. So someone's got to be there, right, to jump in, like, all guns blazing, put a stop to it and recover those diamonds for the rightful owners. And whoever it is doin' that has to know that it's me who's done all the hard work, and then make sure it's my name goes to those Liverpool jewellers.'

I was looking at Sian. She raised her eyebrows. I slowly shook my head.

'If it's going to take place over here,' I said, 'the Gib police need to know. If it's across the border, then it's the *Guardia Civil*, the Spanish cops. So why are you phoning me?'

'Come on! Me and Adele are not exactly on the run, but you know I can't go strolling into a police station. I stay undercover, or I can kiss goodbye to the reward. And that's where you come in.' There was a pause. 'Also, there's something else.'

'Go on.'

'Tony didn't come up with this; it's something I worked out. I'm pretty sure I know the name of the man who's got the diamonds, but that's not something I can discuss over the phone. We need to meet.'

'Okay. Give me an address, and the best time.'

There was silence. I knew he was wondering if he could trust me.

'If I don't know where you are,' I said, 'there's not much chance of us meeting.'

He grunted, then gave me the information. I had nothing to write on so closed my eyes and relied on memory — it was a simple address in Catalan Bay, on the other side of the Rock. When I switched off the phone, Sian was on her third biscuit, and had refilled her coffee mug. I sipped mine. It was lukewarm. I brought her up to date, told her Charlie wanted to see me at ten that night.

'Jack, we're going to Reg's. Dinner, remember, seven-thirty for eight?'

'Stacks of time. Nothing on the Rock's more than fifteen minutes away.'

'You thinking of taking Reg?'

'Why would I do that?'

'Well, I'm not thinking of his diplomatic skills. But this thing with the diamonds is the darker side of high finance, or sort of, and isn't that his line?'

I grinned. 'Are you saying he's a crook?'

'I'm suggesting he knows the crooked ways of a particular class of rich people.'

'And I'm sure you're right. Anyway, going alone might be a mistake, so I'll give it some thought.'

Sian nodded. She was watching me closely.

'It sounds straightforward. So why do you look mystified?'

I held up the phone, waggled it.

'It's like that anonymous phone call that leaked Eleanor's address to Rickman. I still can't understand how that happened, and neither can Eleanor — and now there's this. Tell me, Sian: where and how did Charlie Wise get my mobile phone number?'

23

Dinner was over, a piquant Spanish paella cooked using the menu from a book Eleanor had picked up in a Liverpool charity shop, served in deep Chinese dishes hand-painted in red and gold, washed down with a chilled Italian Soave and followed by baked Alaska, Moroccan coffee and Abernethy biscuits. Calum the Scot would have recognized those — he'd graciously declined the invitation to join what he said was a family gathering — and would certainly have smoked a Schimmelpenninck in their honour.

It was a quarter past nine. Sian and Eleanor were relaxing in the living room on pale ivory leather as soft as chamois, bare toes curling in the thick pile of Persian rugs, gin and tonics in delicate glasses turning their fingers blue as they chatted idly to a background of soft music played by flamenco guitarist Paco Peña.

Reg hadn't allowed the Bose stereo's speakers into the suspended sun room so that's where he and I were sitting, the wrap-around windows giving the effect of being surrounded by the night's velvet blackness, the distant town's lights everywhere reflected. I was nursing my usual Aran single malt, served in a heavy cut-crystal glass. Reg was drinking an ice-cold Heineken straight out of the can. He said he'd heard that was the lager Daniel Craig would be supping in his next movie, and what was good enough for James Bond, Reg said, was certainly good enough for him.

'According to Adele,' I said absently, 'Charlie insists on Laphroaig Quarter Cask single malt Islay Scotch whisky.'

'Typical,' Reg said. 'Her, I mean, not him. Dammit, you won't find me putting on airs and graces,' he said, and he lifted his green can with a grin.

'Charlie told me that things are hotting up,' I said. 'That's why he wants to see me.'

Reg grunted. 'Wondered about that, old boy. Seem to remember we had him down as the jewel thief. Came to that conclusion the first day, didn't we, and when we spoke on poor old Tim's yacht you reckoned Rickman had found him and that was the end of it. Obviously not the case. Or did he?'

'Oh yes. But since we last spoke I've had a visit from Rickman. He came to the bungalow. Charlie and Adele got away, and made it back to Gib.'

'But this business of Charlie and the jewels?'

'Over in the UK he pleaded his innocence very convincingly. I'd just about got around to believing his story when Bernie Rickman came bouncing into Eleanor's, raging at their escape, and with a scenario almost identical to the one we'd pictured: Charlie planning and executing a daring robbery, complete with exit strategy.'

Reg pinged his can with a fingernail, his brow furrowed. 'Rickman's theory may have matched ours, but you do realize that if it points to Charlie having the diamonds, then he's miles out, just as we were?'

'Do I? I know I discussed this at length with Sian and Calum. We came to the conclusion Charlie could have been carrying the diamonds from the time they jumped ship in the straits. All the way to the UK, and back again. We even thought for a while that Calum might have unwittingly carried the diamonds to Gib in the boot of his car. No such luck, of course.'

'It's all nonsense anyway, old boy.' Reg shook his head. 'Charlie hasn't got 'em, never had 'em — and that's a gnarled old diplomat giving you the benefit of his vast experience. I mean, he wouldn't phone you if he was trying to sell them himself, now would he?' He thought for a moment. 'So this 'hotting up' business. What d'you think Charlie means by that? And where's he getting his information? D'you know?'

'I've absolutely no idea. But another thing I learnt from Charlie in the UK is that there's a reward for the recovery of the diamonds, and Charlie's got his eyes on it.'

'Well, there you are. Sort of proves his innocence as far as the theft goes, and me a clever clogs for guessing right.'

I grinned. 'A guess? I thought it was your vast experience. Anyway, Calum ferried the two of them overland from the UK to La Línea. It was when they got to the address they'd been given by a man called Mario that they were taken by Rickman's two heavies and, as you rightly said, that would have been that. But a short while ago I got a phone call from Charlie. He *did make* it back to Gibraltar. I'm seeing him at ten o'clock tonight, so if he *has* got information he must have been working his socks off between their being taken by Clontarf and Ebenholz, and making it across the border.'

Reg nodded. 'If he knows the name of the man who has the diamonds, that means he can identify the airport killer.'

'Yes. And as Charlie mentioned an end game, 'hotting up' must mean a deal has or is being arranged.'

'As in the diamonds are about to change

hands for a king's ransom. And Charlie, being after the reward, intends to scupper the deal.'

'Mm. Which brings me to the reason this dinner was an excellent idea: I wanted to talk to you. I've no idea what Charlie's going to say to me, but if there is a deal, and he wants me involved — then I'd like you to be there with me.'

Reg was silent for some time. Silent, and very still. Then he looked down at the can he was holding, took a deep breath and shook his head. When he spoke, his voice was gruff.

'I'm overwhelmed, old boy. Baffled, I must admit. Honoured, too — definitely. Disbelieving — well, that's understandable because of my age, yet a look at your face is enough to tell me you're serious, and I . . . '

He shook his head again.

'Come on, let's join the ladies.'

With a slap on my knee as he passed he was up out of his chair and trotting off down the carpeted steps into the living room, an elderly man with a pony tail, a can of Heineken and a definite spring in his step.

'You will never in a month of bloody Sundays,' he said to Eleanor, 'guess what Jack wants to do.'

'God, don't tell me *he's* takin' up fishing?'

That got a roar of laughter from Reg, and an arched eyebrow and an offended glance in his direction from Sian.

'You may think that's a big joke,' she protested, 'but we did daydream about doing something just like that when we retired, didn't we, Jack? A boat out in the bay, a couple of rods, a six-pack dangling in the water.'

'The only fishing Jack's doing, my dear,' Reg said, plonking himself down on the arm of Eleanor's chair, 'is for villains with a haul of stolen diamonds they're offering to the highest bidder — and he wants me to join in the hunt.'

'Make up your mind,' Eleanor said, winking at me, 'is it hunting or fishing? And what does he want you to do, hold his hand? That's all you're good for, and you know it, but the job's already taken. Sian does that when you're both in a tight spot, don't you love?'

'No, it's the other way round; I hold hers to restrain her,' I said. 'She's got a short fuse, quickly loses patience. If I don't hold her back, she's eyeball to eyeball with men twice her size, then flooring them with what I think's called a *yoko geri keage*. Often fatal. Or was it a *yoko geri kekomi* you used on Ebenholz?'

'Neither. Not the first, anyway. That was a *ushiro mawashi geri*.'

261

'A wha'?' Eleanor said, finishing open-mouthed after deliberately exaggerating her accent.

'If my memory serves me correctly,' Reg said smugly, 'it's Japanese for the reverse roundhouse heel kick. Attackers usually aim to strike below the waist to maintain their balance.'

There was complete silence.

'Bloody hell,' Eleanor said, absently fiddling with his pony tail, 'I hope you're not thinking of emulating her, not with your blood pressure and dicky back.'

'Actually,' I said, 'if you can switch the context a little that's just why I do need Reg. You're a high flier, aren't you, Reg? Not in a kicking sense — '

'Oh, I wouldn't be too sure, old boy — '

' — but in the way you cosy up to big-time wheelers and dealers. Those up in the financial stratosphere. And while we can be pretty sure the person peddling the diamonds is nothing more than a petty thief and a vicious killer, the person who puts in the winning bid will almost certainly be a man of substance.'

'But not averse to buying stolen goods,' Sian said.

'Probably gives him a buzz. So he's amoral, but with millions stashed in banks from

Gibraltar to the Caymans. I'm not thinking too far ahead because I don't know what Charlie's going to tell me, but it's possible we won't catch the thief until the moment the jewels are being handed over: cheap crook with stolen diamonds; amoral billionaire with a suitcase full of banknotes. So you can see my reasoning. If the situation gets sticky, it'll be an advantage to have along a man who speaks that kind of language.'

'Then if I really am going to be of use to you,' Reg said, 'I'll start by cautioning you against thinking in stereotypes. A thief this chap with the diamonds may be, must be, but I'm not so sure about vicious, petty or cheap. The killing at the airport could have been an accident. And it took brains, wouldn't you say, to outwit the likes of Rickman and that feller Creeny? A clever man, in my opinion, and if I'm right then you must take great care.'

'You too, I'd say, because Bernie Rickman's almost certain to be involved, and aren't you two still at loggerheads?'

'Indeed we are,' Reg said, 'and that's one reason I'm jumping at the opportunity of becoming a soldier of fortune on your team. I'm itching to get back at that blighter.'

'Then you'd better get dressed into something suitable.'

It was Reg's turn to stare. As the silence lengthened, Eleanor tugged at his sleeve.

'Wakey wakey, sunshine, you're off on a mission so go'n get your loins girded.'

Sian yawned, stretched, then snuggled deeper into the corner of the enormous leather sofa.

'If I'm asleep when you get back, carry me out to the car. Or are you going to drop me off at the bungalow on the way?'

'If it *was* on the way I would, but it's not, so I won't.'

Eleanor chuckled throatily. 'Double Dutch, as usual. Anyway, she's staying here to keep me company.'

'On which note,' I said, 'we'll say adieu.'

And I bent to kiss Sian on the top of her blonde head, waited until Reg had thrown on a jacket, then followed him to the door and the steep steps up to Europa Road.

* * *

It was twenty to ten. As I was going the long way around — through town, Winston Churchill Avenue, Devil's Tower Road — I estimated that the drive would take a little over fifteen minutes. There was a car park at Catalan Bay, just off Catalan Bay Road. From there we could walk to the address Charlie had given me in less than a minute, so I intended to go all the way around to the eastern side of the Rock as slowly as I could, short of switching off the engine and applying the handbrake. Or driving all the way in reverse Reg said, with a fierce grin.

I took the Punto tootling down past the brightly-lit Rock Hotel with Reg a diminutive figure in the passenger seat, radiating enthusiasm. He looked for all the world like a frail old man, but under the jeans, pink shirt and teal cord jacket he was built like a whippet. What do they say about sprinters, they get their burst of speed from fast-twitch fibres? Well, that's what Reg must have been using when he came down the bungalow steps the time he thought I was one of Ronnie Skaill's thugs. In a fierce fight he'd tire quickly, because that's what fast-twitch fibres do, but by then the fool who'd mistakenly judged him a pushover would be flat on his back, out for the count.

I couldn't have chosen a more worthy colleague.

★ ★ ★

The address was a block of flats I knew of in Catalan Bay, and Charlie and Adele were ensconced in the top apartment. I thought that strange, because in the event of an assault by enemy troops there'd be no way of escape. Maybe Charlie saw it from the other viewpoint: if an assault was launched, there would be no way in for the attackers without their suffering casualties.

Reg used language that was much less gung-ho and tempered with common sense when we discussed the situation on the way in. Maybe, he said, it was the only apartment vacant.

There was no lift, and a lot of stairs to climb. When we got there, Charlie opened the door and let us in without even checking who had his finger on the bell. So much for my anticipated siege mentality. Adele, wearing a shapeless coral dress, was sitting curled up and slumped sideways on a shabby sofa in a posture reminiscent of Sian but without the charm or the style. An equally shabby standard lamp with a frayed shade shone weak light on the glass in her hand, the cigarette smouldering between her fingers, and emphasized the deep purple shadows beneath her eyes.

Charlie, sweating profusely, flopped down beside her without the usual offer of drinks, and dragged a weary hand across thinning hair that looked like a spider's web on a rainy day.

'What's he doing here?' he said. He jerked his chin at Reg. 'Isn't he one of Rickman's pals?'

'Rickman hates my guts, old boy,' Reg said, and he sat down on an overstuffed easy chair and beamed at Charlie.

'He's here for backup.' Reg preened. I ignored Charlie's snort of derision. 'More to the point, how'd you get away from Rickman's boys?'

'Loyalty. The guy who gave us away came back to let us out.'

'If he got paid twice, where did the loyalty lie — or your perceptions of it?' I smiled. 'So what then?'

'We worked our way through the back-streets — '

'Through the rubbish tips,' Adele said. 'Through the cat crap, the slimy food — '

'Shut up you, silly old bat — '

' — last month's paella, every month's sanitary — '

'Christ, you're pissed,' he said, spinning away from her and standing up.

At that she collapsed into giggles.

'Of course I am, I'm thinking about all that lovely lolly,' she gasped when she was able to speak, 'loads and loads, put us back where we belong — '

'I told you to shut up.'

He was almost shouting, bent over with his face close to hers. She pouted, subsided, and he stood back up again and thrust his hands into his pockets.

'One way or another,' he said, breathing hard, keeping his eye on her, 'we made it to Tony Ramirez's waterfront penthouse.'

'You mentioned his name on the phone. You also mentioned a deal had been arranged.'

'That's what I've been saying, if anyone cared to listen,' Adele said, sulkily. 'There's this scary bloke, Creeny — '

This time a savage glare from Charlie was enough to cut her short.

'That was the other thing I mentioned on the phone,' he said, and he crossed to a stained sideboard and poured half a tumbler of whisky from an open bottle.

'Laphroaig Quarter Cask single malt Islay?' I said.

'I wish,' he said, and there was wistfulness there, but also a light shining in his eyes. 'Maybe when we get that reward. And we will,' he said, 'because that's what I was on about on the phone, but wouldn't say. You've been wondering who the guy is holding the diamonds. Well, I can tell you now it's Karl Creeny.'

'Is that something you dreamt up while

lying awake at night?'

'Absolutely not, it's straight from the horse's mouth. Tony's talking to him as the man with goods to sell, and then there's these other parties — '

'Yes, yes, anonymous Arabs, Russians, whatever,' I said impatiently.

I frowned, found a chair and sat down, thinking it through. Charlie rejoined Adele. Calmer now, he rubbed her arm, his face softening. She smiled weakly, whispered something that could have been an apology.

'But Creeny and Bernie Rickman were in this together,' I said. 'Then Creeny blamed Rickman for losing the diamonds. Rickman's desperate to get hold of you, because he believes you stole them. And if you didn't, well it's pretty clear someone else snatched them from under Creeny's nose.'

'No.' Charlie shook his head. 'What Karl Creeny did is he saw the writing on the wall when my girl Pru accidentally took his picture. He knew after that there was a good chance everything would go pear-shaped.'

'What, he expected Pru to go rushing to you, you'd inform the police and there'd be a raid?'

'Not that, no, because as far as Creeny knew I was on their side; I worked for Rickman, didn't I? It was Rickman — I don't think Creeny trusted him. His nerve, you know? If Rickman panicked, *he* could go rushing to the police to shop Creeny and save his own skin. Creeny saw that straight off, an' he didn't hang about. The courier couldn't be talked round; he was what you might call 'programmed' to hand those diamonds to Rickman. So Creeny didn't bother talking; he simply whacked him over the head when he was taking a short cut away from the airport, took his holdall with the diamonds in it, and crossed into Spain.'

'But Creeny wouldn't get through customs, not if he had to show his passport.'

'Depends which one of several he had with him, wouldn't it?'

That stopped me. I looked at Reg, my oracle. He shrugged.

'It makes sense, old boy. Creeny masterminded the Liverpool end of the jewel robbery, and lots more before this one. He'd be used to thinking on his feet, making split-second decisions.'

'I find it hard to believe.'

'Who then? We both thought it was Charlie. Then you got the idea it was Rickman who'd stolen them for himself and was weaving a web of deception to cover his tracks. Never likely, that one; Rickman hasn't got the brains. But Creeny? Well, now that it's been put to us, I really can't imagine why we didn't reach that conclusion ourselves.'

I sighed deeply.

'So, this deal, Charlie?'

Again he glanced at Reg. Though the naked suspicion had gone from his eyes, he was clearly wary of saying too much in the ex-diplomat's presence.

'I could always leave the room,' Reg said helpfully. 'But then, if you give Jack vital information in my absence, you'll have to kill him so he can't tell me later.'

Adele giggled.

'Yeah, well, there's no need for any of that because Tony hasn't finalized the negotiations; hasn't worked out time or place yet.' He looked at me apologetically. 'Forty-eight hours should see it settled, but all I can do is promise I'll phone you soon as I get the news.'

'And what form will this handover take?' Reg said. 'I assume it will be in a place not overlooked, a place where there's also no chance of anyone approaching the scene unobserved.'

'A deserted airfield, big flash black car with tinted windows parked right in the middle, headlights full on.' Charlie grinned, enjoying himself now. 'Another car rolls up, this one old, scratched, parks so it's like two dogs snarling. Couple of guys in black suits climb out of the big car, one carrying a suitcase stuffed with money. Then the passenger door opens and out slides this little feller, wearing shades — '

'Oh do give it a rest, Charlie,' Reg said, 'you really have been watching too many movies.

'But if we ignore the airfield bit,' I said, 'I bet he's got the scene just about right. Trouble is, I can't think of anywhere here in Gib that fits, other than Casemates Square — which is overlooked — or Europa Point, the former sports field.'

'Forget Europa,' Reg said firmly. 'That open ground's overlooked from high viewpoints on two sides. If the balloon goes up, the roads back to town are too easily blocked, and this rich buyer will have minders alert for any sniff of a trap.'

'Right, so all we can do is wait for Ramirez to wrap this deal up,' I said, and I rose to my feet with Reg catching my eye and following suit.

We departed with a wink from me for Adele and from both of us a quick shake of Charlie's hand. It was cool but clammy, I noticed. He'd lightened up towards the end, but for most of the time we were there he must have been a bag of nerves. Hence his erratic behaviour towards his wife. I wondered about those nerves as we made our way back to the car park at the north end of the little bay, because he'd told us very little and would deny all of it if pressed. So why was he frightened? And if not frightened, what? Acting a part, and feeling the strain? Continuing to pull the wool over my eyes, as Rickman had insisted?

'He's not the most confident of men,' Reg said, catching my mood, reading my mind. 'I think you'll find poor old Charlie would be a pool of sweat when doing something simple like talking to a bank manager — in those long-ago days when such a meeting was possible, of course.'

And on the drive back to his house on Europa Road, despite a lingering sense of unease, I couldn't think of anything to suggest he was wrong.

24

The next day, Calum and I had an interesting talk with DI Luis Romero. It was disturbing because, in closing, the Gibraltarian police inspector dropped a bombshell: it appeared that I was not the only person certain individuals involved in the diamond theft were talking to. And it was also exciting, because the discussion and what emerged from it brought home to me the truth in what Charlie Wise had said: we *were* approaching the end game, and that realization certainly got the adrenalin flowing.

Or the sap rising, as Calum would put it, and I was never quite sure what he meant.

After the anti-climax of the late-night meeting at Catalan Bay I'd taken Reg home to Eleanor and, under a brilliant, star-studded sky, Sian and I had driven up to Eleanor's bungalow where Calum was already asleep in his room.

At breakfast we all agreed that there was nothing more we could do until Charlie heard something concrete from Tony Ramirez and came through with time, date and location for the big sale. Then, dishes washed and house all tidy, we trotted down the wooden steps and enjoyed a long, sunny walk down the steep slopes from the bungalow into town.

We left Sian at the Copacabana where her friend, dark-haired Rosa, was sitting smiling a welcome at an outside table. From there we continued on down Main Street with no particular destination in mind, and encountered Romero outside the bank. After handshakes all round and a brief moment of indecision, we cut through Tuckey's Lane to Irish town and Sacarello's coffee shop, found a vacant table on the lower floor and ordered coffee and rolls.

'So,' Romero said, eyeing me critically as we all sat back, rolls finished and our second cups of coffee in front of us, 'what did Charlie Wise have to say to you?'

I looked at Calum, No help there. He'd breathed into his coffee cup when drinking, and was fully occupied wiping his misted glasses.

'Go on, Luis, how did you find out?' I said. 'Was it yet another anonymous phone call?'

'Much simpler than that, Charlie and Adele were logged crossing over from Spain. It was quite easy to discover that they had rented an apartment in Catalan Bay, and one of my men was watching the house.'

'Expecting what?'

'Not your arrival, that's for sure,' Romero said. 'And you haven't answered my question.'

'According to Charlie, it was Karl Creeny who killed the man at the airport and has the diamonds. Over in La Línea a man called Tony Ramirez is arranging their sale. Charlie will inform me when he knows more.'

'It was Creeny who planned the theft of the diamonds in the first place, so it was quite clear he would not let them go without one hell of a fight,' Romero said bluntly. 'But Ramirez introduces a new twist, and is certainly a name to conjure with.'

'Conjure with . . . ' Calum rolled the words, nodded approval. 'Such words from an officer of the law warn me that this Ramirez is a character always up to tricks, most of them dirty, and a very slippery customer well able to wriggle his way out of trouble.'

'If he was in America,' Romero said, 'they'd say he was 'lawyered up'.'

'Not helpful.'

'All it takes when Ramirez is pulled in is one phone call to the *abogado* he retains, and we're stymied.'

'So *are* you going to approach him?' I said. 'Bring him in for questioning?'

'He's on Spanish soil, so out of my reach.

276

Besides, it would be stupid. All I have are vague suspicions based on the word of a man like Charlie Wise.'

'Right, so all we can do is wait for Charlie to phone?'

'We have no choice.' Romero shrugged. 'And then we must trust Ramirez to give Charlie the right information, and Charlie to pass it to you without altering it to his advantage.'

Romero smiled, and pushed his empty cup away while watching my consternation as that statement sank in. 'And there is another possibility,' he said, 'which you may not have considered: is Charlie perhaps a clever little Scouse double agent, also communicating with other people, giving them information relating to the movement of those diamonds that is very similar to what he has told you, but different in its essentials?'

'Other people?' I stared. 'Are you telling me your man watched us leave the apartment then walked in on Charlie, and Charlie's been talking to you? You knew about Creeny, and Ramirez?'

But Romero was away from the table and already leaving. A smile still lurked on his lean features, but there was no humour in his hard blue eyes when he stopped at the foot of the steps and looked back.

'I recall that when you left my office at the beginning of this affair, I suggested that when you returned to your farmhouse in Wales you would be well out of it. Nothing has changed the feeling I had then. So if you are staying to see this through to the end, then I advise you to take great care.'

★ ★ ★

Ten o'clock that night. Twenty-four hours after the Catalan Bay meeting with Charlie Wise. Warm. Humid. The sun's passing had left the sky an angry red away to the west. We were dim figures in its lingering afterglow, for we had not bothered switching on lights. In the bungalow's gloom there was an air of . . . oppression, foreboding? — or was that just my state of mind, which left me describing the sunset as angry when on any other night it would have inspired poetry and turned my thoughts to romance?

Perhaps it was, though nothing had happened after the surprise that came with early-morning coffee to further darken my mood.

From Sacarello's the day before, we'd made our way back to Main Street and so down to Casemates Square where we joined Sian and Rosa for a lunch that stretched well into that sunny afternoon and eliminated all thought of what had been discussed with Romero.

With Rosa heading for home and husband — they lived very close to town — we gazed up at the Rock, soaring above us in brilliant late-afternoon sunshine, thought about the long steep walk back to the bungalow and at once headed for the taxis lined up on the down slope from Linewall Road.

Once back home, the rest of the afternoon was passed in sleep. We were woken by Eleanor, who called in to check that we weren't destroying her home. She stayed to cook dinner with Sian while I let Calum beat me at chess, then departed after a cosy time chatting with a warning to me that I mustn't forget Reg when Charlie's call came through.

That casual reminder of the task we had set ourselves was an unwelcome jerk back to reality, because I'd spent the day blithely ignoring the fact that Luis Romero had knocked me sideways.

Put at its simplest, the dapper DI had given us food for thought. Taken to extremes, he'd made us — me — feel like a uniformed constable plodding a foggy Victorian beat in heavy leather shoes while believing himself to be Sherlock Holmes. It took Sian to put into words what tactful Calum had taken as read but not cared to point out.

'You either forget the whole idea of clearing up this affair and we go back to Wales, or you ignore everything said by Romero and wait for Charlie to phone.'

'Yes, but I wonder what Charlie's been saying to him?'

Sian flashed a glance at Calum, and rolled her eyes.

'Jack, that meeting this morning didn't happen, okay?'

Calum, sprawled at full length as always, seemed totally unconcerned.

'Similar to what he's told you, but different in its essentials, according to Romero,' Calum said. 'So, if it were me in Charlie's position I'd be stating my terms, demanding guarantees from the local police that if the diamonds are recovered the whole of that reward's going to end up in my pocket.'

'You think that's all it is? He hasn't been passing on additional information?'

'I have no bloody idea. In just the same way, I wasn't present at the Catalan Bay meeting last night so I'm forced to take your word for what went on there, and — '

'Now hang on a minute — '

' — if I was beset by the same nagging doubts that have begun eating away at you I might well be imagining a poisonous alliance between you and that diplomatic dipstick — '

'Oh for God's sake.'

'Exactly. Pure bloody nonsense. As is tormented conjecture about what one man might have said to another — '

And then, of course, my mobile rang.

★   ★   ★

'What time is it now?'

I hung up the phone. They were watching me, indistinct shapes in the shadows draping the unlighted living room, listened to the dying echoes of a one-sided conversation that had told them nothing.

Sian leaned sideways from her chair and switched on Eleanor's red-shaded table lamp. We all blinked in the sudden glare. The clock on the wall by the oak bookcase answered my question: it was 10.30.

'The sale,' I said, 'will take place at Eastern Beach. The south end.'

'Close to Devil's Tower Road,' Sian said, nodding quickly, frowning. 'Certainly not overlooked, and it's a fast road in and out, though it can be blocked. Strange choice.' She looked at the clock, back at my face. 'What time?'

'Eleven. Half an hour. We're cutting it fine,'

'You mean Charlie's *cut* it fine,' Calum

said, already on his feet.

'Phone Reg,' Sian said.

'There's no time — '

'Jack, you promised.'

'All right, yes.' I spun away, walked to the window, already keying my mother's speed dial number. 'You two, get . . . I don't know, suitably dressed, find some lethal weapons — Yes, Eleanor, is Reg there?'

'Oh, God, Jack, no, is it happening tonight?'

''Fraid so. Can you give him a shout?'

'It'll have to be a loud one; he's fishing at Europa Point, he says night time's the best — '

'But he has got his mobile with him?'

'I suppose — '

'Okay, sorry for cutting you short but we need him now.'

I clicked off, pressed the key for Reg, aware that the red table lamp was illuminating an empty room, my ears picking up the sound of hurried movements in distant rooms.

'Reg,' I said as the phone was answered, 'we need you now, pronto, so if you can you get to the bungalow in, say, five minutes?'

'Sorry, old boy, but that's an impossibility. I climbed down the rocks near the lighthouse, walked a good way over pretty rough terrain to my favourite position, a ledge over the water. Getting back in a hurry would be a scramble, and we don't want two broken legs.'

'Then I'm afraid we'll have to leave without you.'

'Oh, sod, I thought you had me down as a vital addition to the team? Surely you can hang on for half an hour?'

'Reg, I can't even offer to pick you up at Europa, because isn't there a road block there?'

'Yes, road works of some kind, has been for days, but does that matter?'

'Time matters. I'd need to come all the way back again because this is happening at Eastern Beach on the other side of the Rock.'

'Nevertheless you need my professional expertise. Without that you could be in deep trouble.'

'We're in trouble anyway if we don't get a move on; to be at the location in time we should have been on our way fifteen minutes ago.'

I broke off as Sian and Calum emerged from the bedrooms, looking like members of an SAS team dressed for night action.

'Reg, I'll come and talk to you later, give you a blow-by-blow account.'

I clicked off, silencing his loud protests, pocketed the phone.

'Black T-shirts, black jeans, black trainers . . . won't that make you two a mite conspicuous on a moonlit Mediterranean beach?'

'I was yearning to wear that short yellow frock,' Sian said, 'but then I thought of launching into a *ushiro mawashi geri* and my modesty overcame my flair for fashion.'

'I dumped the kilt and sporran idea for the same reason,' Calum said.

'And lethal weapons?'

Sian grinned, showed me her hands, like hard blades, stretched out a foot. 'Armed and dangerous. So come on, Jack, make it a fashion threesome. And on the drive down to Eastern Beach we can work out how black garb and our close-combat skills can help us overcome men carrying Glocks and Hecklers — and that's just Clontarf and his buddy.'

As I ran for the bedroom, Calum was raising the bar.

'If it is a Russian oligarch doing the buying,' I heard him say, 'you can forget Rickman's boys because at the very least we'll be up against a couple of — '

I shut the door, and my ears.

25

The tension in the car was palpable. We were raring to go, eager for confrontation, for seeing — if there is such a thing — the end of the end game.

Calum was sitting in the back, and through the mirror I could see his glasses glinting as he turned his head this way and that, ever watchful. Sian was beside me in the passenger seat. She'd brought a bottle of water with her, from which she took the occasional delicate sip. She offered it to me. I shook my head, and as we scooted along and I caught a glimpse of the car's reflection in a shop window, I couldn't resist a smile.

We looked like three wannabe terrorists who'd searched high and low for a fast car to steal and made do with their granny's Punto. One thing that could be said for it was that it wouldn't attract attention. It was getting late on a warm evening; teenagers in cars better than ours cruised by with windows down and music blaring, and if those suntanned youngsters were looking forward to some action at Eastern Beach, it was the kind involving frothing cans of alcohol and some intimate contact with the opposite sex.

As usual, Sian was reading my mind.

'At this time of night there'll be plenty of cars parked there,' she said. 'Doesn't the choice of location strike you as odd?'

'I've been thinking about that,' Calum said, leaning forward with his hand on my shoulder. 'This is Gibraltar, for God's sake, and all that's happening is one man is passing a small package to another guy. Hell, it could be done in broad daylight, on Main Street, and nobody would be any the wiser.'

'Then choosing a beach location where the car they arrive in will be just one of many is good thinking,' I said. 'If they dress like tourists, or locals, they'll be invisible.'

Sian was nodding. 'If you're right, that creates another problem: they'll be difficult to spot. Two blokes leaning against a car enjoying a smoke, eyeing the passing talent, and while doing that there's a casual exchange of goods that goes unnoticed. And it's not as if we'll recognize them, because we won't: we don't know who's buying or who's selling. If Creeny really has got the diamonds and he's going to be here, all we've got to go by is that picture Pru took, death warmed up on board *Sea Wind*; sitting down, so we've no idea how tall he is. And if it's a Russian coughing up the cash, well, there was a time when they all looked like Khrushchev . . . '

While she was talking I'd approached the roundabout by Victoria Stadium and turned right into Devil's Tower Road, which was a long straight run through a scattering of industrial buildings standing under the towering north face of the Rock. Once they thinned there was nothing but open ground, car parks, and the long stretch of Eastern Beach that ran north before being stopped dead by the eastern end of Gibraltar airport's runway.

'Charlie didn't give us enough time to think this through,' Calum said as I slowed. 'Certainly not enough to come up with anything close to a Plan A.'

'Too bloody true,' I said. 'We got the phone call, looked at the clock and the adrenaline rush blew us out the door. Now, common sense says this'll be like looking for one particular strand of hay in a bloody big stack; tells me we should call it a night, go straight back and get out of these silly clothes.'

I'd turned onto the beach road. A line of parked cars stretched away in the bright moonlight. Couples were strolling up and down the long road. Gaggles of youngsters in shorts were down on the wet sand, drinking from cans or splashing through the shallows with wild shrieks.

'If we open the doors and get out looking like this,' I said, 'we'll be mistaken for armed police on a drugs raid.'

'If that means we need a Plan B,' Sian said, 'I suggest we phone Luis Romero, tell him what's going on and leave him holding the ball. Then we can do what you suggest and toddle off home to bed.'

'Mm, I don't think even that's necessary. Luis hinting that he was talking to Charlie means he may know more than us. It also removed any obligation on my part to keep him informed.'

'Then the least we can do is cruise the length of the beach, very slowly, and see if we spot anything unusual. Nobody'll take much notice of us if we stay in the car.'

I'd drawn to a halt while Sian was talking. Now I pulled away again, and headed slowly down the straight stretch of beach road. I accelerated up to a reckless ten miles an hour, flicking sideways glances at the cars parked on the left of the road.

'What time is it?'

'Gone eleven,' Calum said. 'Almost ten past.'

'Well, as no suspicious cars were leaving when we got here — '

'Suspicious?' Sian giggled. 'How can you tell a suspicious car from the ordinary kind?'

'By its occupants.'

'What, all dressed in black?'

'We know what you're getting at,' Calum said, 'and you're absolutely right. No cars of any kind were on the way out, so I don't think we got here too late.'

'If they're already here,' Sian said, 'they're either sitting in one of these cars, or down by the water.'

'Most, if not all of the cars, are empty,' I pointed out.

'Yes, and that's a hell of a long beach; half a mile, more than that? Dammit, they could be anywhere, Jack.'

I'd reached the airport runway end of the road. There was a turning area. I made use of it, began cruising back the way we'd come.

'There's nobody standing by any of these cars — '

'Looking suspicious,' Sian said, gurgling.

I glanced to my left, across the wide, sandy beach. 'If they're down there by the water and I park and we get out, in this moonlight they'll see us coming a mile off.'

'Give it up, Jack,' Calum said suddenly, and he slumped back in his seat. 'You told Reg you'd talk to him later. Let's do that. Give the cocky little feller a good laugh at our expense, and while we're there we can console ourselves with a wee dram.'

I had no argument to offer. It had been a wasted trip, and that surely wasn't the end of the world. Yet as I took a last look at the beach, put my foot down and headed back towards Devil's Tower Road and the looming Rock face, I couldn't get rid of the feeling that Charlie Wise had been playing us the way Reg Fitz-Norton, down on the rocks at Europa point, was learning to play fish.

26

There was a car parked outside Reg's house when we got there, leaving me just enough room to pull in off Europa Road, my hired Punto, nose-to-nose with Reg's Nissan Micra. Fishing rods were draped across the Micra's roof rack, lead shot hanging from a line glinting wetly in the moonlight.

Reg must have just arrived. We climbed out of our cars as one. He was wearing stained jeans, a faded denim shirt, a fisherman's waistcoat with its pockets weighted down with . . . I don't know, weights, floats, worms and maggots? There was a guarded look on his thin face. He didn't know whether to be angry, or offer his congratulations. What he was doing, I think, was studying our faces for some clue about how to proceed. In the end, of course, he settled for diplomacy.

'No signs of injury, old boy, so it must have gone extremely well.'

'It didn't go at all, Reg.'

The tenseness left him, and a huge grin spread across his face.

'Well there you are, you see. I did warn you that leaving me behind was a big mistake.'

I shook my head. 'We were sent to the wrong location. Charlie led us up the garden path.'

'Ah.' He nodded sagely, and gestured with a sweep of his arm for us to go ahead of him down the steps to the house. Sian and Calum started down as Reg put a hand on my shoulder as I went past and said, 'What d'you think Charlie's deception signifies? That we were right all along, and he's the feller flogging those jewels?'

'Actually, Reg, I'm getting weary of the whole bloody farce.'

Reg chuckled. We'd reached the bottom of the steps. Sian and Calum were waiting politely by the door. There was a jingle as Reg reached into his pocket for his keys.

'The old dear might be dozing,' he said, 'and the last thing we want to do is disturb — '

He stopped, frozen in the act of poking the key at the lock. Metal had barely touched metal when the door swung away from him, pulled open by the man standing in the hallway. Ebenholz was a silhouette framed in the unusually bright light from the living room. It glinted on the weapon he held casually in his right hand. Reg took half a step backwards. He looked sideways at me, a stunned expression on his face. Then, behind us, there was the hard, oily metallic clack that anyone who has served in the army will have heard a thousand times and will instantly recognize.

I swung around. The Australian, Clontarf, was at the foot of the steps, broad and sinewy in jeans, sandals and a T-shirt with cut-off sleeves. He was holding the black Glock in both hands. Rock steady, it was aimed at a point midway between my waist and my knees.

'All you've got to do to avoid a future singing like Kylie Minogue's canary,' he said, 'is go on into the house as if nothing has happened.'

'Nothing has — not yet,' Sian said sweetly.

She'd stepped sideways, away from Calum. He had hold of her wrist; an iron grip restraining a middle-aged blonde tornado.

Clontarf grinned appreciatively at her. 'Sorry to disappoint you, darl, but you're caught in a crossfire and there's a sweet old lady in the house at the mercy of a man not known for his patience.'

Reg growled something unintelligible, then pushed his way scornfully past the impassive Ebenholz. I heard Reg call out something as he entered the living room, heard Eleanor answer, her voice clear and untroubled, and over it all the hard laugh that I knew must have come from Bernie Rickman.

I looked at Sian, tilted my head towards the house. 'Come on, Soldier Blue. This is about Reg, not us. He needs help.'

'Sounds like a good old Aussie nickname,' Clontarf said approvingly, and as we trooped into the hallway he was close behind us. I heard the door bang shut, the soft whisper of his trainers. If Ebenholz was following him, the muscular man was as silent as a kitten on a carpet.

The living room's gold-shaded table lamps were switched off, the ceiling's central light fitting delivering a harsh glare which banished the usual warm shadows from the room's corners. I guessed Eleanor had been relaxing cosily with a book and a tipple while waiting for the intrepid fisherman's return, when Rickman and his merry men came hammering on the door and turned the place into a lighthouse. I didn't know what had been done or said by any of her visitors in the interim, but she seemed entirely unfazed. She was curled up on the white sofa looking as relaxed as I'd ever seen Sian in that same position. Reg, on the other hand, was sitting beside her, clasping her hand tightly. He looked like a convicted prisoner watching the judge don his black cap.

Clontarf and Ebenholz had drifted to

positions on either side of the living room door. All weapons had been tucked out of sight: Ebenholz's under his short jacket; Clontarf's down the waistband of his jeans in the small of his back. Calum circled around behind the sofa, rested his hand on Eleanor's shoulder. Sian dropped into one of the big chairs; if Ebenholz was a kitten padding across a carpet, Sian was a stalking cat now stilled and awaiting the opportunity to pounce.

'Who are those two?' Eleanor said, jerking her head at the two men by the door, her voice dripping with scorn. 'Your two goons?'

She was looking straight at Rickman, her gaze contemptuous. Rickman was standing over by the suspended sun room with the star-spangled night skies at his back, drinking some of Reg's whisky and looking smug.

'They're highly respected employees of mine,' he said, and Clontarf was forced to cough into his hand.

'Yes, well, I don't know what you think you're doing breaking into my home,' Reg said, 'but if it's about the money I owe you I'm flat broke so you're wasting your time.'

Rickman grinned. 'This is a bit like that caper where I say you show me yours and I'll show you mine.'

He was ignoring Reg completely, watching

me, waiting for a reaction.

I moved to a space away from obstacles. 'What the hell are you talking about?'

'It's like this. Before I tell Reg if my time's being wasted, why don't you tell us all how you've been wasting yours?'

'What, and waste even more? You've been in this with Creeny from day one so you know that tonight he was selling those diamonds. We were all set to scupper his deal. The location we were given was Eastern Beach. We were misinformed.'

'By a long way. Karl's been in Tangier ever since he had his picture taken. And he hasn't got any diamonds to sell.' Rickman took a sip of whisky, looked at me with amusement. 'Who was it misinformed you? Charlie? Well, he would, wouldn't he? Sent you on a wild goose chase.'

'Are you still insisting he planned this?'

'Absolutely.'

'And he's got the diamonds?'

Rickman shook his head. 'He planned the lot, the theft, his escape — which I freely admit showed a lot of flair, and only went wrong because he hadn't anticipated the violence his scheming would provoke. His *treachery*, if you like. But the crucial point here is that what happened to poor old Pru didn't put the kybosh on Charlie's plans; it only delayed them. And in answer to your last question, no, Charlie didn't steal the diamonds. In fact, he's never had a sniff of them.'

'You just said — '

'What I said was, Charlie *planned* the theft.'

The room fell silent. Rickman looked around brightly, waiting for a response. None came.

Rickman shrugged, said, 'Reg, old Ebenholz there, he likes the look of that little Micra of yours, fancies a drive in it, so if you'd let him have your keys — '

'I don't see why — '

'It's not a request.'

'If taking my new car is some bizarre way of recouping your losses — '

'Come on, Dad,' Clontarf said, grinning, 'give us the flamin' keys.'

'If that car has one scratch on it when it's returned,' Eleanor said, fixing Rickman with a gaze cold enough to freeze blood, 'you'll have me to deal with. D'you think you're up for that?'

Given the armed reception waiting for us when we arrived, that might have sounded like a reckless question. But the weapons that had threatened us had been tucked away before she could see them; there was no obvious threat and I found myself wondering if Reg had ever told Eleanor how much trouble he was in with Rickman. If he hadn't, then there was no reason for her to link her broken ankle to Rickman's wife, Françoise, no reason to believe she was in any danger. All talk so far had been about stolen diamonds, and I'm sure she felt safe in the knowledge that a robbery in Liverpool city centre and all that followed had nothing to do with her and Reg.

Rickman met Eleanor's challenge with a roguish wink that brought a flush to her cheeks and tightened her lips, and for the second time that night there was a jingle of car keys as Reg tossed them to Clontarf and he sent them looping across the room to Ebenholz.

'Why does he need Reg's car?' I said as the door closed behind the big man.

'The short answer is I left mine down on South Barrack Road so we could storm the hill.' Again the grin. 'This way's quicker.'

'And the long answer?'

'Difficult. So why don't you ask me something simple, like what Charlie was playing at tonight?'

'Go on then. What was he doing?'

There was a sudden thump followed by an angry exclamation. Clontarf had moved over to sit on the arm of Sian's chair. With one thrust of a stiff arm, she'd dumped him on the floor. He rolled over and stood up, his blue eyes ugly. Rickman lifted a warning hand. Sian smiled sweetly.

'Jack, if Charlie gave us the wrong location,' she said, 'then he did it so that he could go to the right one.'

'Why would he do that?' Calum said, leaning nonchalantly with his hands now resting on the back of the sofa, his glasses halfway down his nose. 'He's been protesting his innocence all along, and if we can believe Rickman then it seems that the wee man really didn't have the diamonds.'

'All right, then let's look at the only other way it could have been worked,' Sian said. 'If Charlie didn't have them, he sent us chasing shadows to leave the way clear for his mate. He had a partner in crime.'

'Fair enough, but the way clear . . . to where?'

'Somewhere else.'

'Dear oh dear,' Rickman said, 'how on earth did you lot get such a hot reputation?'

'The answer to that question is down to qualities beyond the wildest imaginings of a greasy crook like yourself,' Reg said. He was up on his feet. His rigid stance would have brought a gleam of approval to a sergeant major's eyes. 'It's quite clear this visit is not about me at all, but about those confounded diamonds,' he went on. 'All right, so if that's the case then why the hell don't you get to the bloody point, and then get out?'

'Cut to the chase?' Rickman nodded. He was now sitting on the upper of the two carpeted steps leading to the suspended sun room, the empty glass by his side. 'Well, it is getting late, so why not?' He looked at me. 'I'll simply mention one name: Tony Ramirez.'

'Ah,' I said, feeling all at sea but nodding wisely.

'And ah ha,' Calum said, and as he poked his glasses up with a forefinger he actually looked as if a penny had dropped. 'Like a Spanish chappie called Mario, who sold Charlie down the river, Ramirez indulges in double- or even triple-dealing.'

'Don't we all?' Rickman said.

'How much are you paying him for information?'

Rickman shrugged.

'So why are you here? If Ramirez told you where it was happening, why aren't you there?'

'Be like shutting the stable door,' Rickman said, 'when the jolly old horse has bolted.'

And then he looked quickly across to the door as it opened with a bang to admit Ebenholz. The big man came in carrying a

300

rectangular basket. It was damp, dirty, fastened with a leather strap. It brought to that elegant room a strong smell of fish. He sent Reg's keys clattering onto the coffee table, dropped the basket onto the Persian rug. It landed with a solid thump.

'In the trunk,' he said.

'Oh dear,' Reg said, his voice tight with fury. 'Here's me been down at the point fishing, and what did you find in the boot of my car? A fishing basket.'

Ebenholz had moved around the table. Clontarf was already down on one knee. Strong fingers drew wet leather from a brass buckle. He flipped the lid open, sat back on his heels.

The basket was packed with banknotes.

Into the stunned silence, Eleanor said softly, 'Well I'll go to the foot of our stairs.'

27

'What the hell is going on?' Reg said. 'Look, that can't be my basket, someone's done a switch.' He glared at Ebenholz. 'You, of course, that's why you took my keys and went out there with some cock and bull story.'

Already on his feet, staring at the neat bundles of banknotes, he tried to dart past the big man. Ebenholz stepped across to block him. Clumsily, Reg barged him with his shoulder and started for the basket. Ebenholz moved just enough to give himself room. His muscular arm swung lazily. The side of his clenched fist hit Reg's forehead with an audible thwack. The old diplomat seemed to take off. He hit the sofa and bounced, then flopped sideways with his head in Eleanor's lap. His eyes were glazed. He grunted, twitched, struggled to rise.

I looked at Calum, standing behind the sofa. He gave a slight shake of his head. Sian hadn't stirred from her chair, but she'd changed her position and her eyes were moving constantly from Ebenholz to the Australian.

Still sitting on the step by his empty glass,

Rickman said, 'Have we quite finished?'

'Could go on all night for all I care,' Eleanor said, 'but I'll never in a month of Sundays believe this old sweetie stole that money.'

'You're absolutely right,' Rickman said. 'He didn't.'

'So I'll say it again, then: why don't you bugger off?'

'Ah, would that it were that simple,' Rickman said, and looked around happily. 'Got a Shakespearean sound that, hasn't it? And so it should have, because this is either a tragedy or a bloody farce. Or both.'

'Get on with it,' I said softly.

'Yeah, back to the chase.' Suddenly, Rickman changed. His eyes narrowed. Something evil swirled in their depths, and I heard Eleanor draw a sharp breath.

'This is how the plan — Charlie's excellent get-rich-quick scheme — was to be wrapped up,' Rickman said. 'After that unexpected delay, Charlie made it back to Spain and got Tony Ramirez to locate a buyer and arrange the sale of some stolen diamonds — '

'Charlie didn't have 'em — '

' — and come up with a time, and a place,' Rickman went on, ignoring Reg's dazed protest. 'The agreed place was Europa Point. The buyer would bring the money in by boat.

303

The seller — Charlie told Ramirez — would be Charlie's partner. This guy had listened to Charlie's idea for stealing stolen diamonds, and thought the plan brilliant because it would make this feller rich and enable him to get back at another guy who was giving him aggro. The partner snatched the jewels at the airport — '

'Christ, no, you're wrong,' Reg said weakly.

' — and he's had them ever since. And Charlie told Ramirez the seller would know his partner — waiting down there at Europa — because he'd be an old guy fishing off the rocks, a little runt with grey hair snatched back in a pony tail. The diamonds would be in a leather pouch, inside a fishing basket.'

Reg said something that went unnoticed, because it seemed everybody was now ignoring the little man. I was leaving Clontarf and the American to Calum and Sian, who were watching them intently. It was Rickman who interested me, because I sensed this story would have a twist in the tail.

'So once Ramirez had arranged the deal,' I said, knowing how this had to end, 'he informed you.'

'Not directly, no,' Rickman said. 'What Ramirez did was go to Karl Creeny. In Morocco, remember? Only not exactly Morocco, but Ceuta, which, of course, is a Spanish enclave over there and much closer to Gib than good old Tangier. It was Karl who kept me up to date. Karl who sailed across the straits earlier today. And it was Karl who did a midnight deal with diplomatic Reg Fitz-whatever.'

'You're talking nonsense,' Calum said. 'Why would that bloody crook spend a fortune buying back stolen diamonds?'

'Well, the answer to that is, he didn't.'

Grinning, Clontarf again went down on one knee. He reached into the basket, peeled a banknote off the top of one of the piles. Beneath it there was blank paper. He did the same with each of the piles in turn. He was left clutching a handful of genuine banknotes, and we all stared, mesmerized by the sight of a basket full of plain copier paper neatly cut to the shape and size of banknotes.

'Without violence, and for little more than the cash he carries in his back pocket,' Rickman said, 'Karl's got his diamonds back.'

'Then why are you here?' Calum said. 'None of this is necessary. Creeny sails away with his diamonds; Reg would have come home and had fun counting his piles of waste paper — a win-win situation for you and Creeny, so why this palaver?'

'Because as of now, we've got Reg,' Rickman said, and he lifted a hand, pointed his forefinger like the barrel of a pistol at the white-faced diplomat, and cocked his thumb. 'And for dear old Reg it's payback time. Too bloody right it is, because he did something much worse than cost me a small bloody fortune. See, Reg, the man who brought in the diamonds, the man you conked on the head at the airport, well, he was Karl Creeny's younger brother.'

28

The was a moment of complete silence.

Eleanor's face had turned chalk white. She looked up at Reg, who had struggled to his feet and was standing as if turned to stone. Then she shook her head in despair and slowly leaned forward to rest her face in her cupped hands. I think Reg saw the movement out of the corner of his eye. Either that, or a storm of hair-prickling thoughts galvanized him: the realization that if he didn't act fast he was going to be taken to one of the Rock's most desolate spots and made to suffer before he died.

With the rasp metal makes when dragged across a coarse zip he pulled out the heavy service revolver that had been weighing down his fishing waistcoat and stepped back to face the world. He cocked the gun as he moved, swung it wildly, desperate to shoot somebody but torn between three targets.

The couple of paces he'd taken backwards took him within Sian's reach. She placed both hands on the arms of her chair, used them as fulcrums and executed a modified scissor kick. The precise attacking manoeuvre was a blur. Her instep snapped crisply against Reg's wrist. The crack had the sickening sound of breaking bone. The pistol flew from Reg's hand and demolished the ceiling light fitting. Crystal shattered. There was a fierce blue flash. Instantly, all light was extinguished and we were transformed into indistinct shadows lit by starlight twinkling through the suspended sun room's windows.

Sian's foot was still in the air when I leaped fishing basket and coffee table and drove Reg bodily backwards onto the sofa. Groaning, clutching his wrist, he went down, narrowly avoiding a collision with Calum, who at that moment was using one hand to vault lightly over the sofa's high back. The lean Scot landed on both feet and launched himself at Ebenholz. He took the muscular man around the thighs in a crunching rugby tackle and drove him backwards off his feet. Arms flailing, Ebenholz landed on his shoulders on the coffee table. The wooden legs splintered; the table collapsed, its top split. Without pause, Calum pulled back, sliding his hands down the dazed man's legs. When he reached his ankles Calum took them in an iron grip and stood up. He stepped back, dragging Ebenholz off the table's wreckage.

Then, like a hammer thrower bringing the first slow movement to his sixteen-pound weight, Calum leaned back and began to pull Ebenholz around in a circle. The heavy body dragged a colourful Persian rug into a crumpled rag. The coffee table's sharp splinters clung to Ebenholz's clothing, his skin. Then the big man's shoulders left the floor. Airborne, he was being whirled through a full 360 degrees. Calum leaned back, moved even faster. With a hammer-thrower's balletic footwork he rotated to the edge of what might have been a throwing circle, but for Calum the edge of that circle was the two steps leading to the sun room — and there, a man sat.

Ebenholz's body hissed across the steps, waist high. Rickman had been watching the action while rooted to the spot, but now he was panicking, scrambling out of the way but far too late. Ebenholz's shiny skull hit him above the left ear with the sound of a cleaver biting into beef. Eleanor gave a tiny shriek of horror. Rickman was knocked sideways; a man hit by a train would have been no worse off. He rolled down the two low steps, his weight dead.

And suddenly, as Calum spun, a warm liquid sprayed through the starlit gloom. I felt it across my throat, heard Sian say a disgusted, 'Ugh', heard Eleanor retch; despite the gloom I saw a clear dark line being painted around the room's walls. It was

Ebenholz's blood, the blood of a man as good as dead.

Then Calum let go of Ebenholz's ankles.

The big man was limp, knocked unconscious by the clash of heads. As his ankles were released his shape seemed to collapse in upon itself. Like a heap of crumpled clothing of an impossible weight he smashed through the suspended sun room's wide window, carrying away the glass and frame with the sound of a Savoy waiter dropping a tray of drinks on a marble floor. His violent exit was followed by a long moment of suspended silence in which nobody breathed. Then I heard a distant splash.

'A long way down,' Calum said, dusting his hands, 'and that sounded like a direct hit on a swimming pool.'

'Jack!' Sian cried, 'The Aussie's gone; he's taken Reg's car keys.'

'Oh, let him — '

'No, he murdered Pru, he's the one we want.'

She was gone, rushing for the open door, trainers slapping the parquet along the hallway.

'Calum, stay here. Watch Reg and anyone left alive,' I said, and ran for the door.

Sian almost caught Clontarf. As she reached it, the front door banged back against the wall. The Australian was already halfway up the steps when she ran out. I left the house in a rush, saw Sian make a desperate upward leap, fall flat on the steps' hard concrete edges, hook a hand for his ankles — and miss.

The slide back down was painful.

I grabbed her around the warmth of her waist, hoisted her to her feet.

'Let him go,' I said softly, 'they're finished, done for — '

'I want him.'

Up above, a car's engine burst into life.

She wriggled out of my grasp and started up the steps.

'Wait, I've got the keys — '

'Then come on, move yourself.'

There was the high whine of a tortured engine and repeated crashing as we climbed. When we reached the top, I saw the cause. The way I'd parked, Reg's Micra was boxed in. Clontarf was in the driving seat and using the car as a battering ram, rocking back, then forward, smashing into my hired Punto. His teeth were bared in a fierce grin, his lean hands claws on the wheel. There was the stink of rubber, of hot oil, but he'd succeeded in driving the Punto backwards in juddering, jolting jerks on wheels locked by the handbrake.

Clontarf glanced back and, seeing there was now room, ripped the lever into reverse. The two cars' bumpers were locked. The Micra's tore off with a screech of shearing metal. Clontarf took the car all the way back, slammed against the low stone wall then engaged first. Sian ran forward. Part of the wall had collapsed. She grabbed a stone block in both hands, used it to shatter the Micra's driver's window. Glass showered over Clontarf. Sian followed it with the heavy block of stone, slamming it down with all her strength. It smashed Clontarf's left hand against the steering wheel. He snatched it away, roaring with anger. I saw the shine of blood as he took a swing at Sian's face and let the clutch out with a jerk.

The Micra's sudden violent motion was too much for Sian. She was thrown off, staggered back against the wall close to the steps, then recovered and ran for the Punto. I was already wrenching open the driver's door, my eyes on Clontarf, expecting him to head straight down Europa Road towards town. But to achieve that he would have to swing right to get around the Punto, then execute a sharp turn to the left — and there appeared to be something wrong with his steering.

Sian threw herself breathlessly into the

passenger seat, slammed the door. I started the engine, switched on the headlights — well, one headlight, the other was a scattering of broken glass on the concrete. In the glare I saw what was wrong with the Micra. Clontarf's harsh treatment had crumpled the car's left front wing back against the tyre, preventing the wheel from turning far in that direction. Clontarf was unaware. He swung the car right, away from the Punto and out into the road, then tried to turn left. There was the sound of tearing rubber. The car stayed straight, slowly headed for the opposite wall. Again he tried that left turn, then again — and gave up. I saw him slap the steering wheel in frustration. Then with a howl of tortured rubber he swung the Micra in a tight right turn and accelerated along the flat road that would lead through a succession of slopes and bends to the winding hill down to Europa Point.

'Got him,' I said, teeth clenched as I accelerated and took the one-eyed Punto up through the gears, my eyes on the two receding tail lights.

'How? He gets to Europa ahead of us he can go all the way around the Rock anti-clockwise, and that Micra's a newer, more modern car so he could be across the border — '

'No. To go anti-clockwise he needs to have

a working left-hand lock — which he hasn't
— and that's if the road in that direction was
open — which it isn't.'

'How d'you know?'

'Heard it somewhere. Reg confirmed it on
the phone when this long night was getting
under way; road works, a barrier, or some
such.'

I was passing the old naval hospital on the
brow of the final hill, the old Buena Vista
barracks visible against the night sky to my
right as I began the descent. Driving too fast.
Clontarf's tail lights were gone, out of sight,
but only because of the tight blind bends.

I risked a sideways glance. Sian was hanging on to the grab handle. She had the window
down. We could both hear the scream of Reg's
Micra, not too far ahead.

'How are you feeling? You slid backwards
down concrete steps on your squashy bits.'

'A tame trick, compared to Ebenholz. He
dived a hundred feet into someone's swimming pool. Christ, did you see that, Jack?
Calum threw him straight through Reg's
picture window.'

'Mm, and prior to that I think he used the
big man as a club to crack Rickman's skull
like a ripe coconut.'

'So he's dead, or a vegetable.'

'Him and Ebenholz. Two down, one to go.'

'And then there's poor old Reg.'

I swung round a bend with a squeal of rubber, dropped sickeningly down a steep slope and saw the sea ahead of us, the twinkling lights of cargo vessels. And the fierce glow of brake lights. A few hundred yards ahead, Clontarf had come across a red and white barrier blocking the road to his left and discovered his mistake.

'Reg,' I said tightly, 'has turned out to be a twisting, lying, murdering bastard.'

'Yes, granted, but he must have some bad points.'

I chuckled, tension leaking away as I snatched another sideways glance and saw my Soldier Blue looking at me with wide, innocent blue eyes.

'What he's got,' I said, 'is a broken wrist — '

'Jack, watch it, there's a fork ahead, I think Clontarf will have taken the high road — '

'And I'll take the low,' I said, nodding quickly and suiting action to words.

'Yes,' Sian said, 'and what Clontarf can do when he spots that barrier is simply turn hard right and come back up this way.'

'If he does,' I said, 'he'll meet us, at speed, so brace yourself.'

But he didn't.

The road ahead stayed empty. Then it twisted and turned through a residential area

315

where lights glowing behind the occasional window marked the home of insomniacs or mothers with teething babies and then we were out in the open again and on the plateau of flat land lying between the tall white mosque and the lighthouse. A hundred yards away the Micra was drawing to a halt and, before it did, Clontarf was out and running.

'Jack!'

I nodded, banged my foot down and tore across that open space with gravel rattling like buckshot under the wheel arches. I slid to a stop alongside the Micra, used momentum to throw me out of the car and saw at once that Sian was even faster.

'He's heading for the rocks, down by the sea,' she cried, running away from me in the moonlight. 'Why?'

'D'you want to go after him?' I shouted, 'or hold a conversation?'

I heard her laugh breathlessly. Then I'd caught up with her, and together we raced across the rise where tourists gather to gaze at a map etched in bronze and across the sea to darkest Africa, then down again through the gap in the wall and the clamber down several flights of steep wooden steps that took us to the soft cool whisper of the sea, lapping glistening black rocks, and the sight of

Clontarf less than fifty yards away to our right, and struggling.

'Where the hell does he think he's going?'

'He's an Aussie,' I said, 'a beach bum, a surfie. He's at home in rough seas and tonight's calm anyway. Once he saw that road block, I think he got the idea of diving in and swimming around to Camp Bay, or Little Bay.'

'Damn, that's spur of the moment but an excellent idea,' Sian said as we started after him, 'because I don't fancy a race in open water and it's a hell of a long way round if we're forced to go by car.'

'Yes, well . . . '

Already I was breathing hard and, like Clontarf, finding the rocky terrain rough going. Sian was lighter on her feet, but the black trainers weren't the best footwear for slippery rock. And just as she slipped for the third time and said something unladylike, I dropped a foot into a hole and felt an ankle twist.

Clontarf had remembered his Glock.

I saw him dip his hand to his waistband. He turned to face us. I heard the crack of the shot. The muzzle flash winked brightly. It left a black spot in my vision. The bullet whined somewhere overhead. A second followed, much closer. I heard the crack as it hit rocks behind me, the whine of the ricochet, and the desire to stay alive saw me duck far too late, put too much weight on my ankle and drop a knee heavily on jagged rock.

I gasped, rolled away from the pain and braced myself for the next shot then saw that Clontarf had been buying time. He'd turned away when his two fast shots had sent me diving for cover and was making his way across the rocks, angling towards the sea. His objective was now clear. Along the stretch of shore he had been traversing, the shallow waters rolled in and lapped and foamed at a minefield of black boulders with razor-sharp edges. If he'd tried to enter the sea there, he'd have been cut to ribbons. Looking ahead, he'd seen how the hard ground gradually flattened and sloped upwards towards the sea, where it finished in a ledge. No sharp rocks. A clear plunge into deep water.

'Jack, this way!'

Sian. Even before Clontarf had started shooting she'd realized that away from the rocky shore and closer to the high sea wall there was a rough track. She'd been making for it when the shots rang out and I was doing my best to be invisible. Now she'd reached it, and she was racing along in the lee of the wall, eating up the space between her and the Australian.

Clontarf heard her shout. He looked back, saw her, snapped a desperate shot that chipped stone from the wall above her head. Then he turned and renewed his frantic scramble across the rocks.

Limping, swearing, I hopped and jumped and scrambled until I reached the track in deep shadow along the wall. Then I started after Sian with the lolloping gait of a three-legged camel. Her blonde hair was a beacon, drawing me on. She was now level with Clontarf but, dammit, she would have to cut back across the rocks to reach him. He was closer to the ledge, but moving painfully slowly. I calculated that he'd get there just ahead of her. If he did, one long flat dive into calm seas would carry him to freedom.

Sian saw the danger. She left the wall, the track, and began picking her way nimbly from rock to rock like a sure-footed goat. I grinned admiringly from the shadows, urged her on mentally as I ran, then saw that though I was closing and she was now but ten short feet away from Clontarf, she was going to lose the race.

In desperation, I shouted.

'Sian, you'll lose him, throw something, brain the bugger.'

Then Clontarf's feet shot from under him and he fell flat on his back.

Sian was on him like a big cat.

Away from the track and halfway across the rocks, floundering, I could only watch in horror.

Sian threw a leg across Clontarf in an attempt to straddle him then went for an arm lock that would flip him over onto his face. He bucked her off, spun from the prone and chopped at her neck with one hand while using the other to pivot and sweep his legs at her body. She blocked both tries, went for his throat with a half fist. His chin was tucked into his chest. He got a foot under him, a hand on the ground, and regained his feet. As her fingers clawed for his eyes he went in low under her arms and grabbed her around the waist. She tried a side fist at his temple, but his shoulder was against her belly, his head buried under her arm and hard against her breast. Sian wrapped her arms around his neck. She hugged his face hard against the softness of her body. He'd been gasping for air. Now he was suffocating. He twisted, jerked — then lifted her off her feet and stepped towards the edge of the rocky ledge.

And again his foot slipped.

He was thrown off balance. Sian's weight pulled him down. He released her. She fell away from him with her shoulders over the very edge, twisted her head to stare down at the drop to the sea. When she looked up again I saw her blue eyes widen, her hands scrabbling either side of her for a hold.

Clontarf laughed, and draw back a foot to kick her into space.

So I followed the advice I'd called out to Sian. With my final stride I scooped up a rock, smashed it across Clontarf's skull, and as he went down I stepped across him, grabbed Sian's hand and pulled her upright.

'Olé,' I said, raising her hand high. 'If this was a bullfight, I'd present you with an ear.'

'Oh, bollocks, Jack,' she said breathlessly. 'If he hadn't been slipping and sliding . . . what was that, what was doing it?'

'The old man and the sea saved our bacon,' I said, gazing down at a mess of bones and flesh and silvery scales. 'While Reg was waiting to swap diamonds for cash he really did do some fishing. The fish he gutted but left here because his basket was full were Clontarf's undoing.'

29

Three o'clock in the morning. The coolness that always comes at that time; the sensation that time itself is standing still. A stillness in the air that could presage a storm, or a death, or a bright new dawn. And always the feeling weighing down those who are aching for sleep that everything is too heavy, too much trouble, requires too much effort; when every effort is needed just to keep leaden eyelids from drooping over eyes clogged with grit.

Or perhaps that's just the perception of what we're supposed to experience at that unearthly hour, for Lord knows enough had happened that night to keep each one of us awake for a week.

We were in the bungalow, high up the Rock. Sian was curled up, blonde hair wild and free, glowing with good health. Calum was stretched out, legs crossed at the ankles, the lenses of his paint-smeared John Lennons almost opaque in the pre-dawn light. Eleanor was in her favourite chair, white hair touched by the faint light from the window, looking as bright as a sparrow about to begin a chirpy dawn chorus. I was in another chair by the bookshelves, resting my ankle on a padded footstool, stifling a yawn.

Luis Romero was standing looking out of the window.

I'd just asked him a question.

'So tell me, Luis,' I'd said, 'where are we up to? Who's living, who's dead, who's under arrest, who's going to get off scot free?'

Eleanor provided one answer.

'Reg confessed. The idea for it all came from that Charlie Wise, but Reg murdered that bloke at the airport, took the diamonds, and tonight he sold them.' Her smile was ice. 'For a basket of plain paper — typical of him, and serve him bloody well right.'

Romero was coming away from the window, highlights glinting in his polished black shoes.

'He was . . . shamefaced,' he said. 'Freely admitted his crime, though stressing that he hadn't intended to kill the man. He spent most of the time looking at your mother.'

'Because I knew he was up to something, didn't I? That woman attacked me, pushed me down those steps, and that was it for Reg: I knew the little bugger'd go after them like a terrier. He had a double incentive, because he was already being harassed by Rickman — but I knew he'd done something really awful when that silver-topped cane turned up broken.'

'He told you he'd done it swiping at some weeds,' I said.

'Reg,' Eleanor said sweetly, 'wouldn't know a weed from soddin' watercress.'

'No, but he was devious enough to pass my mobile number to Charlie. And he must have been the anonymous caller, giving Charlie's Liverpool hidey-hole away to Rickman, and I can't understand why he'd do that. There was always the risk that Charlie, under duress, would give Reg up to save his own miserable life.'

'But all Reg could see, perhaps hope for,' Romero said, 'was Charlie dying, leaving Reg to search for a buyer but pocket all the proceeds.'

'Mm. Greed again.'

Romero smiled. 'As for the others, the man we know as Clontarf will be held on suspicion,' he said, and to my faint surprise the detective sat on the arm of Eleanor's chair and rested his hand on her shoulder. Faint surprise turned to genuine amazement when my mother winked at me.

'Suspicion of murdering Prudence Wise?'

Romero nodded. 'Pending forensic details from the UK — DNA and so on. The other man, Ebenholz, was dead when he was pulled from the swimming pool behind a house on South Barrack Road.' He looked steadily at me. 'It seems that by some misfortune, during the disturbance that occurred in Fitz-Norton's house, Ebenholz fell through the sun room window.'

'Glory be,' Eleanor said, and she looked at me wide-eyed.

'Rickman is severely concussed,' Romero went on. 'It's possible he tripped and banged his head on the coffee table, leaving it badly damaged.'

'The table?' Sian said, 'or his head?'

Romero smiled, shrugged. 'It matters not. I'm quite sure we'll find something to charge him with if he wakes up.'

'Which leaves Karl Creeny and the diamonds,' I said.

'And the fact that he got away with them,' Sian said, 'will forever go down as one of our failures.'

'Our first.'

'Our only.'

'Aren't you forgetting Charlie Wise?' Romero said.

'Indeed I am,' I said, 'and he's a crafty little crook, but I'm sure he's disappeared to dream about what might have been.'

'That's not exactly what I meant.' Romero paused, looked around the room, let the tension build.

Calum stirred, stretched.

'I think I can see where this is going,' he said, 'because I got to know that wee chappie quite well when he craftily finagled a drive across Europe.'

'He's crafty all right,' Romero said. 'It was Charlie's scheme, but like the best masterminds he let someone else do the dirty work while he stayed in the background and kept his nose clean. What I don't think Reg realized was that Charlie would have made a good hedge-fund manager.'

'Ah,' I nodded, beginning to see the light. 'Sort of like backing a horse each way instead of to win?'

Romero nodded. 'While you three were cruising up and down Eastern Beach, Charlie was on the phone to me telling me what was about to happen out at sea, but deliberately not giving away Reg's position at Europa. Suffice it to say that soon after his call two police launches took up station out in the bay, and they were able to intercept a tender heading out from the Rock to a fishing boat, which earlier that day had sailed across from Ceuta.'

'So the diamonds,' I said, 'have been recovered? And there's nothing to stop Charlie claiming the reward?'

Romero nodded.

'And Karl Creeny?'

'Lying on a cot in a cell, watching dawn break through a barred window.'

I took a deep breath.

'So all's well that ends well,' I said — then looked at Eleanor. 'But what about you and Reg? Your beau's looking at, what, a life sentence? How d'you feel?

'Blasé, if that's the right word; not all that bothered. Which may sound cold, cruel even, but he's asked for it and anyway, it wasn't as if everything was going all that smoothly. Relationships cool, don't they? Maybe things had run their course, you know? I mean, I wasn't brought up with that toffee-nosed talk, and while it was a novelty at first, after that it became . . . oh — '

'A drone?' Calum said.

Eleanor brightened. 'Exactly. D'you know what I mean?'

'Absolutely. Bagpipes have a drone, but it's not too noticeable because there's a tune being played at the same time. Whereas Reg — '

'Was all bloody drone.'

'You never mentioned this,' I said.

'You're my son. D'you think I discuss my intimate affairs with you?'

I grinned. 'Eleanor, a drone's not intimate.'

'It is when you're in bed tryin' to read.'

'And is this something I should take note

of?' Sian said, 'seeing as your son and I are soon to be wed?'

Eleanor beamed. 'I've got an even better idea, love,' she said. 'Why don't we discuss wedding plans together?'

And with a sharp elbow she emulated her future daughter-in-law and dumped a surprised but delighted DI Luis Romero onto the bungalow's hard wooden floor.